RISKY GAME

NASHVILLE STEEL BOOK FOUR

STACEY LYNN

Risky Game

Nashville Steel Series

Book Four

Stacey Lynn

Copyright © 2023 Stacey Lynn

Content Editing: Emily Lawrence Editing

Proofreading: Virginia Tesi Carey

Cover Design: Shanoff Designs

Risky Game is a work of fiction. Names, characters, places, trademarks, and incidents are used fictitiously or are the product of the author's imagination.

All rights reserved. No part of this work may be reprinted, reproduced, or transmitted in any form without written permission of the author, except by a reviewer who may quote brief passages for review passages only.

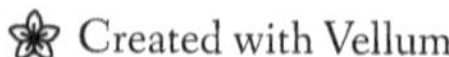 Created with Vellum

CHAPTER 1

LOGAN

"VANESSA, you can't do this right now." I paced back and forth in the hall. One hand held my phone while my other made a mess of my hair. My wife—no.

My ex-wife was a master professional at giving me horrific headaches at the absolute worst time.

"I know, Logan, but this is a trip of a lifetime. How am I supposed to say no?"

"You're supposed to say no because you're in charge of our *child*. Not sure why that's so hard for you to understand."

She scoffed.

My damn wife. *Ex.* My damn ex-wife. We had this all worked out. She had full custody of Amelia during the season. I saw her on holidays and my bye week. The occasional home game weekend, which was going to be hard enough. Hell, it was hard enough not knowing when I was going to see her again, but this?

"It's only for three months!"

"That's half of my damn season!"

I shouted back at her. Clenched my jaw. Inhaled a breath that did very little to settle my anger and frustration. She planned on leaving the country for three months so she could travel across the Mediterranean with her new boyfriend. Her new boyfriend she moved in almost as soon as I moved out.

Okay, so it was two months later. Whatever. The point was, this was my first season head coaching. I left everything in California, fought a decent if not still completely sucky custody plan with Vanessa over Amelia, but it was what was best for our daughter. I barely had the time to brush my teeth these days, much less become a full-time single parent.

"You just don't understand. You never did. Anything I ever wanted—"

Not this again. "Enough. You can't guilt me on this, and we're both already clear on my failings. I don't need to rehash them." I hadn't been a good husband. Not in the last few years. I completely acknowledged it and took full responsibility for my part in my marriage failing. I couldn't even deny it, so when I got this coaching job—the dream of a lifetime for me—I hadn't hesitated to accept. I'd just been overly confident in the idea Vanessa would come with me.

"My first game is next week, Ness. Can't you guys push this off? Until January?"

"Italy in January and February? Come on, Logan. It'll be freezing and miserable then."

My eye twitched. Of course. The weather was more important than her daughter. She hadn't always been this selfish or thoughtless. Apparently, a lot had changed for both of us in the last seven months.

"What am I supposed to do with Amelia? I'm working all day and now traveling."

"Hire a nanny."

"Right." I scrubbed my hand through my hair again and scoffed. "Because I can go hire a fucking nanny so easily and quickly."

"I can have her go to your parents then."

They'd love that. But they weren't Amelia's parents. They were mine.

Why was I even arguing about this? I hated only getting to see Amelia on FaceTime. Since that was the only contact I had with her until she was able to fly out here during our bye week in October, I was dying for one of her ultra-healing and extra-calming hugs. I'd figure this out. Just like I'd always had to figure things out.

I spun on my heels, intent on taking another lap back and forth across the hall, and came to a stop.

Our kicker, Jassen Moore, stood there, glancing at me, then in the other direction he must have come from like he should probably hightail it out of here. His discomfort couldn't be more obvious.

I sighed and held up a finger for Jassen to wait a second. He wouldn't have come searching for me if he didn't need something. As far as players went, he was pretty chill and didn't require a lot. "When do you leave?"

"Monday." She had to be smiling. She sounded way too peppy. I wanted to throttle her through the phone.

Monday was five days away. Four days to figure out how to win our last preseason game. Five days to find a nanny and get a room ready for my daughter.

"Send her out here. I'll figure things out." I'd do anything for Amelia, even if it meant she needed to spend the days with me on the field for a while. Hell, she was four. She wouldn't mind. She'd probably have a blast.

"Her plane lands at six."

"You've already scheduled her flight." I shouldn't have been surprised. Of course she did. She knew I wouldn't say no.

"I'll text you her flight information, and don't worry, her flight leaves before ours, so we'll be with her until she boards the plane. A flight attendant is supposed to sit next to her on the trip and then wait for you to come and get her at the gate. I already bought your ticket to get there, too."

How very thoughtful of her.

"Bye, Vanessa."

I hung up before I could do more screaming. It wouldn't help anything. She'd had this all planned and scheduled before she called to ask, "Hey... would you be mad if..." which was exactly how she started that conversation.

"I can come back," Jassen said as soon as I dropped my phone to my side. "Sounds like now isn't a good time."

Now was the worst time to be a country away from my daughter and my ex-wife, and it wasn't the first time I'd wondered if I'd done the right thing in taking this job.

A team on the heels of winning the Super Bowl, veteran players who were more like brothers and some excellent rookies and trade deals over the summer, I thought we'd show up for our first preseason game looking like the champions they were.

That hadn't happened and now the final preseason game was this coming weekend, and they still weren't playing like champions.

Everyone was frustrated. Me most of all. As much as I loved Amelia and missed her and wanted her in my arms every single day, her coming right now was the worst possible time.

Hell, I hadn't even had time to decorate a room for her in the house I'd bought.

"It's fine. What's up?"

"Cole's sprained his ankle. Trainer sent me to get you."

"Shit. PT room?" I was already headed in that direction.

"Yeah." Jassen hurried next to me, gave me a quick look, and cringed. Looked away. "I couldn't help but overhear your conversation, which I'm not seeking details about, but it sounds like you need a nanny?"

"Quickly. Yeah." I gave him the brief rundown. He had two

small kids and a pregnant wife, so we'd spent some time talking about our kids this summer and early fall.

"I, um...I have a sister."

My feet froze to the cement. "She's a nanny?"

"No. Art history major in college, but she's just moved in with me and Molly to help with the kids. She's taking some time off school to pay off her loans before going to grad school. But Molly will be feeling better in a couple of weeks, and she's great with them... if you need some help..."

It couldn't be this easy. There was no way. The opportunity to have someone I trusted—well, a family member of someone I trusted—be there to help me? Way too coincidental or simple.

"Give me the day to think about it. And thanks."

"No problem. Just let me know."

"Why don't you just pay off her loans?"

Jassen rolled his eyes. Chuckled. "You meet Ruby and you'll understand. She'd be living in a box on the street before she took my help like that. Letting her live in my guest house to save her rent money was as much as she was willing to take."

"Stubborn then."

"Independent, but yeah. But she loves Luke and Brittney, and they love her, so..."

"Right. I'll let you know."

We reached the PT room, and I shoved the door open.

My worst fear hit me straight in the solar plexus when I caught sight of Cole. Up until that moment, I'd hoped Jassen was wrong. Once again, that was me.

Cole's dark hair was a sweaty mess from practice, and his scowl had to be as large as mine when I was talking to Vanessa.

"Tell me how bad it is," I barked, making both him and our trainer jump.

This season was starting off as a shitshow and if our quarterback, one of the best in the league, was out?

We were fucked.

Everything in my life was suddenly becoming absolutely fucked.

———

"Go home. Rest and ice and do everything Morgan and you discussed. We'll figure this out."

"Eden's going to kick my ass. She made me swear not to get injured, and here I am… fucking hobbling around like a toddler."

"Yeah, because Eden's the concern here."

Shit. I wasn't this big of a jerk. Rarely anyway.

Cole flinched. "Yeah. Shit, sorry. I'm as pissed as you are, I swear. But it's only a couple of weeks. I'll be okay by game one."

Three to six weeks' maximum rest according to the physical therapist, and Cole was already knocking it down to two. I didn't blame him. As far as injuries went, he got lucky, and if he weren't so thick-headed and if I weren't so distracted earlier at practice, I would have seen the way he was limping. As it was, I'd put him back on the field after he got hurt, a complete fluke when he rolled his ankle trying to escape the pocket and our defensive pressure. Which was about the only thing the team was doing right these days.

God. Was all this upheaval my fault? I'd shown up, respected the veterans, let them know I was there to work with them. I'd barely made adjustments to the plays they were used to. Nothing was *new* on the team except for me, a new kicking coach, and a handful of new players.

This last month should have been a cakewalk. Instead, we were all floundering. Cole Buchanan getting hurt was the absolute last thing this team needed.

"I'll talk to Damien. See if I can watch some film with him over the next few days, point out where he's been less than stellar."

We'd lost Sam Crawford in the off-season, the former backup

QB, but who could blame the guy? He'd gone to Detroit and was getting his chance at being a starter. That meant we'd drafted a rookie quarterback in the first round, and since I'd banked on Cole's health, possibly the dumbest thing I could do, I'd spent most of our cap on defense.

Damien Hopper was good. But his nerves were getting the best of him, and the speed of the pro versus college was something he simply wasn't adjusting to. He needed to get faster. Fast.

"That sounds good. And rest, Cole. Even if it kills you."

We said our goodbyes and I headed to my office. I didn't have time to spend watching more film, nor go over my notes of what we needed to work on tomorrow. I didn't have time to meet with the other coaches to rant, again, at how we looked like a bunch of rusty rec league players trying to play a pick-up game twenty years past high school.

I needed to get a plan in place for Amelia.

She'd always come first, even before football.

RUBY

"AUNNY RUBY! Aunny Ruby! I a pirate! Grrr!"

A pint-sized, bubbly-legged pirate attacked me as soon as I stepped out of my Civic. Luke ran at me, foam sword in one hand, eye patch covering one eye. His platinum head of hair shone in the sunshine and his pirate growl made me bite my tongue to stop laughing.

"You certainly are!" I crouched down and swept him into my arms. I waited to stand until I was steady in my heels.

I'd had a hell of a day job hunting. Who knew interviews for cocktail waitressing positions in Nashville, where there were bars on every corner, would be so depressing and difficult. Fortunately, my nephew Luke could wipe it all away with his bare belly and sticky fingers. I lifted him above my head and blew a raspberry as he squealed.

"Stop! Stop!" A foam sword smacked my temple and I feigned a cry of pain.

"Oh. You got me." I set him on the ground and rubbed my head. "I thought we were friends, Lukey."

"We're not friends."

"We're not?" My hand went to my chest. *Ouch.* "I thought we were besties."

"I only friends if you have a sword." His dusty blue eyes narrowed on me, daring me.

Dare accepted. "All right, pirate. How about you give Aunt Ruby a few minutes to get into proper pirate gear and you go hunt me down a sword so we can steal some jewels?"

"Jewels?"

I ruffled the mop of hair on his head he got from his mom. "You got it. I'll be back, okay?"

"'Kay. Mommy says sissy is sleepin', though, so we hafta be quiet."

"I can be quiet. Can you?"

"Sure!" he shouted.

I pressed my lips together to keep from laughing. Luke was never quiet.

"Sneak into that castle right there." I pointed to his house. "Hunt me down a sword, and if you can find one, meet me back by the front door in a few minutes. But you need to listen to your mommy, okay? And be super quiet. Like a ninja."

"But I a pirate."

"Pirates are sneaky and silent, too. Can you do that?"

His lips pushed out, and he nodded. Then, in the loudest whisper, declared with confidence, "I can do that."

I waited while he snuck toward the house, tiptoeing on his sneaker-clad feet, and when he was at the front door, I headed toward my brother and wife's guest apartment above the garage.

There, I dropped my purse on the couch, grabbed a bottle of water from the fridge, and in less than the five minutes I'd promised, I slipped out of my heels and Kelly green summer dress I'd worn to interviews and was back into my preferred summer attire of black athletic Lululemon shorts and a racerback tank to beat the wretched Nashville heat.

By the time I came back outside, pulling my dark hair into a ponytail to keep it off my neck and shoulders and turning into a sweat pile in forty seconds flat, Luke was waiting for me on the front porch. No swords. No eye patch, and he'd changed out of his khaki shorts and sneakers to now wearing only swim trunks.

"Will you swim with me, Aunny Ruby?"

Considering Luke changed his activities and desires with the snap of his fingers, I'd planned ahead and already had my bikini on beneath my outfit. "What happened to the pirate gear?"

"Sword is in sissy's room."

Ah. "Sure thing. Let me check with your mom first, okay?"

"She said yes if you said yes."

Of course she did. Molly was the sweetest, most wholesome and gentle woman I could have ever envisioned waltzing into my brother's life. They'd met when he was a kicker at Oregon State. Not the most glamorous of football positions, but he was also the first one to take a beating if his team lost the game and he'd missed a kick. That hadn't changed since he'd gone pro and now played for the Nashville Steel, but I'd long since stopped following every single game of my brother's career. Not because I didn't love him, but because for him, it was a job he loved, not something that defined him.

His family, both me and the one he created with Molly, defined him.

"All right. Let's go find her then." I held out my hand and he plopped his sticky fingers, probably from a peanut butter and jelly sandwich from lunch, into mine. And we headed into their home.

Molly was in the kitchen, hair pulled up. She probably hadn't yet showered. Purple half-moons rimmed her lower eyes, and she was wearing cut-off flannel shorts and an oversized T-shirt. Probably a shirt that was Jassen's back in college due to how faded it was.

"Still not feeling well?" I asked as she munched on a Saltine cracker with a can of ginger ale in front of her.

"Are you suggesting I look like I'm half dead?"

"Kinda?" She was too sweet to lie to.

Molly laughed and chucked the cracker at me. "I don't get it. I never got sick with Luke and only had an aversion to chicken when I was pregnant with Brittney, but this little one is sucking the life right out of me." Her hand went to her small, barely distended bump, and she rubbed it as if she felt the need to apologize for saying something unkind about the baby inside of her.

"What do you need help with?"

With a three-year-old, a one-year-old, and Molly being ten weeks pregnant and my brother's season starting soon, my life had hit rock bottom at the exact perfect time for my brother and sister-in-law. They'd all but *begged* me to move in with them while I worked on getting my finances back together. Since they were the only family I had, I'd agreed, but taking their guest apartment above the garage was the only help I'd been willing to take.

Jassen and I fought about it for weeks. The envelopes of cash shoved beneath my door finally stopped when I stomped into his house one night, stack of hundreds in one hand and a lighter in the other. I held them both above the kitchen sink and threatened to light them all on fire if he gave me any more money.

"Fine." He'd thrown his hands up in exasperation and Molly had hidden her laugh behind her slim fingers. "Have it your way, but you're the most stubborn, stupid person I've ever met in my life."

"Yeah, well, you've known me my *whole* life, so it's not a surprise, is it?"

He'd scowled at me, kissed my cheek, and whispered, "I'm worried about you," before leaving the room.

Molly's gaze had followed his departure with a worried look she didn't wipe away nearly fast enough for me to see. "You can tell us what happened, you know."

"Nothing happened. I want to pay off my loans and save some money before starting grad school so I don't live in debt forever. It's as simple as that."

It wasn't the first lie I'd ever told my brother, but if he found out what really happened, he wouldn't think I was stupid and stubborn. He'd hand me the Biggest Idiot Ever Award.

"It's all right if Luke and I go swim?" I asked her.

"Please. And thank you." She sipped her ginger ale. "I swear, once I'm feeling better, we really won't rely on you so much."

"It's no problem." I gave her a quick hug. "Truly. You've all given me everything I already need. And I'm happy to be here helping, especially with Jassen busier now."

"You know we love you, right?"

"I love you all too."

She gave me that same worried look Jassen wore in my presence these days. I kicked the guilt of everything I was hiding to the back of my mind.

I had a swim date in my near future. The rest of my future could wait a while.

———

Jassen came home while I was feeding Brittney and Luke hot dogs and macaroni and cheese. They might have had a shit ton of money these days but were still the simplest people on the planet. You could take the kids out of the run-down apartment in the poorest neighborhood in Omaha, but you could never take away their love of cheap hot dogs and box mac'n'cheese.

Molly, now feeling better, had gotten in a shower and was able to eat her own small bowl of mac'n'cheese. Color was back on her face and it only brightened further when the door to the garage opened.

Brittney woke up cranky from her nap and the only way to keep her quiet was to hold her. *Not* a sacrifice, but after hours of hearing her whimpering, I was ready to head to a quiet home, spend the night with a glass of wine, and trying—again—to stop thinking about how much I'd screwed myself over in the last couple of years.

"Daddy!" Luke jumped down from his chair and raced toward his dad.

As soon as Jassen came around the corner, Luke was draped over his back. Arms practically strangling my brother, feet tucked in tight around his stomach.

Molly's face lit up, and that pinch of regret and pain at how naïve I'd been to think my ex actually loved me hit me hard and fast. He couldn't have, when it was so obvious the way these two stared at each other was real love. Paulie never came close to looking at me the way my brother smiled at his wife.

I buried my face in Brittney's shoulder, blowing a raspberry against her to hide the emotions. Over my dead body would Jassen ever find out what Paulie did to me.

"Hey there, sweetie." Jassen walked straight to Molly, almost like he didn't even see me, and kissed his wife. "How are you feeling?"

"Better. Thank you. How was your day?"

"Mine was great. The team..." He made a face and shrugged it off before turning to me. "Are you going to let me hold my daughter, or are you taking her home with you?"

After the day I'd had with her? He didn't have to ask. I handed her over. She smiled and squealed—happily, not grumpily—as soon as Daddy had her in his arms. "Just wanted to wait so she didn't get covered in all that kissy slobbery stuff you and Molly do."

"Ruby!" Molly slapped my shoulder.

Jassen rolled his eyes. "I might have found a job for you today. If you're interested."

"Waitressing? How'd that happen?"

"Not waitressing. But my coach might be in need of a new nanny."

"A nanny?" My lip curled. It couldn't be helped. Yeah, I

liked Luke and Brittney, but they were blood. My niece and nephew. The laws of nature demanded I think they were the cutest souls to walk the planet.

Jassen chuckled. "Think about it tonight. He called me in after practice was over and asked." He scratched his jaw and kissed Brittney's forehead. "He's recently divorced, and Amelia was supposed to stay with her mom during the year, but something changed, and now she's coming in a few days. He's stressed, and now his daughter..."

He gave me a pleading look. One I hated because my heart was weakest toward my brother. It couldn't be helped. He'd protected me and taken care of me my entire life. Outside of him offering to hand me however much money I needed, I wasn't sure I'd ever said no to him.

"I'll think about it," I muttered.

"That's all I ask. Thanks, Rubes."

"Yeah. Yeah. I'm going to head back to my place. You all enjoy your night."

I gave them all cheek kisses and laughed as Luke followed me to the front door. He did it every night I left. Said he stayed on the stoop to make sure I was safe.

"Night, Aunny Ruby!"

"Night, buddy!" I waved back at him once I hit the top of my stairs and waited at the doorway until he went back inside.

Cute damn kid. And my brother was raising him well. It wasn't a huge surprise because Jassen was incredible, but considering we had never had a decent man in our lives growing up, well... I was damn proud to call him my brother.

It was later, after I'd taken a quick shower to wash off the chlorine, after I'd started a load of laundry, and after I'd poured myself a drink when I finally considered the potential job.

A nanny. Jassen had only mentioned one girl, a daughter.

One kid. Maybe I could bring her here so I could keep helping Molly.

Well, damn.

I could probably do that. Wasn't like I had other job offers blowing up my phone.

Nannying for one little girl.

How hard could it be?

CHAPTER 3

RUBY

HARD.

Nannying for the new coach of the Nashville Steel was going to be hard, and Amelia wasn't even in the same time zone yet. But *hard* was all I thought as soon as Logan Caldwell appeared in his doorway after I rang his doorbell, showing up three days after my brother floated this idea to me. After getting three more rejections at bars I'd interviewed for as a cocktail waitress, it'd taken me a full twenty-four hours to agree to meet with Logan. I had questions. I had a full list of them to ask to make sure this would work, but right then, staring up at him from two steps down on his front porch, I couldn't remember a single one of them. Thank God I'd remembered to type them up on my phone.

Logan's face was granite. His eyes were iron. His entire body was *hard* from all those muscles he couldn't hide beneath his T-shirt and athletic shorts.

"Ruby, I take it?"

"Uh. Um. Yeah." My head was a bobblehead on someone's car dashboard but *damn...* At least a decade older than me, this man was *fine*. His wavy, thick hair was tousled on top, short on the sides, and I couldn't quite tell if he was trying to grow a beard, liked to keep it cut short, or just didn't give a damn about shaving. Regardless, Jassen had in no way prepared me for who I was about to meet. "That's me. Mr. Caldwell?"

A deep furrow dipped between his thick brows before he stepped backward. "Please. Logan will work. Come in. Thanks for agreeing to meet with me today. I know it was short notice."

"No problem." I tore my eyes off his face. It was too stunning. Unfortunately, my gaze just fell to the rest of his body as he led me toward his living room. Shoulder muscles. A trim waist, that ass... those calves. What was it about a guy with sexy calves that did something to me? I wiped away drool forming at the corner of my lips and focused.

This was a job. One I might need if I ever wanted to get back on the path I'd dreamed of since fourth grade.

No eye-fucking the boss allowed, even if he was the most delicious piece of man candy I'd ever seen.

"Would you like something to drink?"

It was nine in the morning. A mimosa had never sounded like a better idea.

Probably not the best thing to request during an interview. "I'll take a water. Thank you."

Maybe some hydration would cool me down.

Logan stared at me. One beat. Then two. A third to make it extra awkward between us before he finally nodded. "Right. Have a seat, or look around, or whatever..." He swung out an arm. Whatever what? I could see most of his main floor from where we were standing, awkwardly staring at each other. "Sorry. I wasn't expecting all this, and it came so quick. I'm making this weird."

"Better you than me." I grinned, shrugging my shoulders.

"Right." That earned me a smile, a breathtaking, knock-me-off-my-ass kind of smile I'd think about for days, and he walked away, taking it with him.

I hadn't decided if I even wanted to do this, but I had to be blowing it already.

"Your home is nice and your backyard is gorgeous."

"Thanks," he called out. The fridge opened and slammed shut, but I was stuck on that backyard view. Beyond the infinity pool, the backyard sloped down and, in the distance, past rows of what probably used to be raised garden beds but were now only filled with dirt, was a small lake. It was private, had to be considering I'd pulled into a gated neighborhood complete with a security guard. But the view... I loved water. Freshwater. The ocean was angry. Loud. It was exciting and enticing.

But freshwater?

Calm. Peace. Even now, the water was practically glass it was so calm. I could have a cup of coffee every morning in one of those black metal chairs facing the water, watch the sunrise and the day awaken, and be satisfied with anything I was doing.

"You like the water."

He'd walked up next to me, visible in the window's reflections, and handed me my water.

I twisted the top off. "That obvious?"

He was standing next to me, and he suddenly reminded me of campfires and s'mores and burning oak and cedar. Damn... he smelled like the perfect fall night with leaves changing colors, crunching beneath my feet.

I stepped away and caught the way his jaw tensed as he looked down at me before he went back to the backyard. "I need to baby-proof the pool for Amelia. I thought I'd have more time."

He was right. There was a fence around the perimeter of his yard, but nothing between the sliding glass door and the pool. One misstep, one moment of distraction, and that could end badly for a little girl.

I doubted he was even talking to me like a potential employee, just rattling off a list of things he needed to do.

"Jassen and Molly have one. I'm used to keeping an eye on Luke and Brittney. How old is Amelia?"

He grinned down at me this time. His sparkling white teeth were visible in the window's reflection, and I chugged my water.

It might be impossible to work for this man if I wanted to see that smile on his face all the time.

It made my knees weak and my belly flop.

"She's four," he said, with all the love only a father had for his daughter. Jassen used that voice a lot. "Come on. Let's go sit and talk."

Where I'd have to actually look at that face.

Damn. I might have just walked into a whole pile of trouble, but whatever. I needed the money.

———

We took seats in his massive living room. Two full-sized couches made an L-shape and on the opposite side from where I was sitting were two chairs. A large, square coffee table filled the space between all the furniture. It was all warm, creams and pale blues, and nothing at all what I figured a *guy* like Logan would have in his house.

He'd gotten his own water from the kitchen and after he swallowed a large gulp, set it down on the side table between the two chairs.

"How much did Jassen tell you about what I'm looking for?"

"He said you're recently divorced, and your daughter has to come stay with you earlier than expected."

"That's it?" His brows tugged in again, and I wasn't sure if he didn't believe me or if he was surprised. But there was definitely more to the story.

"Should there be more?"

He huffed. Not quite amused, more irritated. It was defi-nitely not humor that made him reach up and scrub a hand through his hair. One chunk of wavy hair made the perfect curl at the center of his forehead.

"My wife and I got divorced last spring. She decided not to follow me out here when I was offered the coaching job."

"Oh... well, that's..." Rude? Horrible? I wasn't sure how to respond.

"Not all her fault. To be honest, I wasn't a great husband the last couple of years, but I guess I'd figured since we had Amelia, that she wouldn't want the family to be separated. That was my bad."

A man who took responsibility was weird. A man who knew he didn't have a good marriage but assumed the woman would always stay with him? I couldn't say that was all too surprising. My thoughts must have been printed across my face in bold, large font because Logan smirked.

"Yeah, trust me. That was a pretty dumbass thing to think. Anyway, Vanessa and I had a custody agreement, a plan. She got Amelia during the season, I got her on holidays and, in the off-season, I'll move back to California to be closer so we can share as much equal time as possible. Last week, she decided to change that."

"She doesn't want her daughter?" I couldn't help the judgment that seeped through my tone. It was too close to home, a dagger to the heart.

Logan scowled. "She's decided to go on an extended European vacation. Last-minute offer she can't refuse."

"Oh." I sat back on the couch, trying to wipe away the *total* judgmental thoughts I was having. What kind of mother *left* her children for months on end... I mean, outside my own.

"Obviously, it's a surprise to me. She'll be here Monday, and I'm starting the season. With coaching and it being my first year, I'm under a ton of stress. But I love Amelia, so obviously I'll do whatever I can, but, well, you know how hectic our schedules can be during the season."

He said it like I should. And yeah, obviously I knew they traveled and were busy. But hectic? Molly had always seemed to take it in stride, and Jassen never complained. "Sure."

"You don't know?"

"Um... Jassen doesn't really talk about work when he's at home." It was probably the worst thing to say, and Logan's brows rose. "I mean, it's just... he likes to come home and be with his family, and I've only recently moved in with him, so I guess I don't know... we don't talk about games and stuff."

That time, it was definitely amusement that made Logan chuckle. "You don't pay much attention to his games, do you?"

"Honestly?"

The humor in his eyes returned to the original iron when he opened the door. "Always."

Damn. Okay. Despite the swirling in my stomach that looked incited, I could be honest. "Not really. I love my brother, and he loves what he does, but I guess to him, it's never been the only thing that was important to him, or even the most important thing, so it never really became mine."

"Huh." He leaned back in his chair, scrubbing his hand against that stupid curl that did its little floppity-flop thing again, and my stomach copied it.

Goddamn. There was no way I could nanny for this man. I'd have to spend time with him. Talk to him.

And every time I looked at him, my mouth watered and my fingers wanted to fix that little curl. Maybe play with those waves.

Trouble. This was trouble and I'd recently resolved to stay far away from it.

"I know you just moved in with your brother to save some money and stuff, but with all the travel I'll be doing, would you be willing to move in here instead?"

Oh... What a cruel freaking joke this life was turning out to be.

MY WEEK HAD BEEN ENTIRELY UPENDED. For the last two days, when I wasn't running plays, watching practice film, or chewing out the guys on the field for the constant, ridiculous, and rookie mistakes, I was glued to my phone, scouring online shopping sites and forking out an arm and a leg for Amelia's new bedroom furniture. Hell if she'd get here on Monday and not have a room that felt like hers. Lucky for me, she had no hesitation in talking about all the things she loved the most, which was why her bedroom would soon be decorated with gerbera daisy bedding and curtains and unicorn pillows and rugs. Shopping for it all made my head spin, but while I might have been a great football coach, I was an even better dad.

I was dying to get my arms around her, and up until I answered the door earlier, I was so damn thankful for Jassen for talking to his sister and getting her to agree to at least meet with me.

But now? Goddamn, she was beautiful. Young. So damn young for me I shouldn't have been thinking about her that way at all, but her beauty was undeniable. Long, tan legs that rose to thick hips, a trim waist, and gorgeous breasts. She was wearing leggings and a simple T-shirt, and I didn't mind at all the casualness of her clothing. This wasn't a professional job interview. It was for a full-time babysitter.

Bonus, the T-shirt clung to her breasts, more than a handful, and her ebony hair had waves and a shine to it that only made me crave the beach more.

And I'd just invited this young woman to move in with me.

"Will that be a problem? I know you moved down here to help Jassen and Molly, but they're only ten minutes away."

Fifteen with traffic, but close enough she could still help her niece and nephew if that wasn't too much for her.

"I didn't actually."

As she spoke, my eyes were drawn to the elegant cross of her legs, one thrown over the other. Her slip-on Converse dangled from her toes as she swung her foot back and forth.

She was dressed like a high schooler. Maybe a college student. I shouldn't be thinking about how she was dressed at all.

"Jassen said—"

"I know. The timing worked out at a time when I needed to take a step back, reevaluate what I want." As she spoke, her lips pursed together. They formed the perfect pout, but there was something to the look on her face. Something sad.

It was none of my damn business.

"Anyway, yeah, I guess, sure. If you need me here, that makes total sense. Molly's ten weeks pregnant and should be feeling more like herself soon, or at least that's what she keeps hoping and telling me. But being here, especially when you're out of town or working late, makes the most sense."

Late nights. Coming home to a house that had life and noise in it instead of what I'd endured the last six months since moving. Quiet drove me insane, and now I could envision it.

Amelia's laughter. Her hugs when I walked into the door and the way she used to crawl into our bed when she had a bad dream.

Yeah, I was no longer all that mad at Vanessa for her trip. She handed me everything I was missing.

"Are there expectations or duties you have for me, specifically?"

Right. She was here for a job, not for me to leer at her like some creep who was way too damn old for her.

"Amelia's four. I haven't been able to find a preschool for her to go to yet, so if you could help with that, that'd be great. She was set to go back in California and was looking forward to it, and that'll give you a couple hours to yourself. Mostly, though, I need someone to take care of her. Hang out with her during the day. Take her to the park, swim with her. If there's a way she can meet kids that you know of, that'd be great too."

"What about if I take her to Jassen's? Would that be okay? Luke is three. They might get along."

"Yeah, of course. I don't know if I want you driving all over Nashville or anything yet with her, but if there are places nearby you two can go, that's great."

"What about chores? Laundry? Cooking? That kind of thing."

I shook my head. "You're not my housekeeper. I don't expect that. Clean up after Amelia during the day and you might have to give her simple meals and stuff. I usually leave here at eight-thirty, and I can have her up and ready for the day by then and stuff, but lunches. Some dinners. And then, well, the weekends when I'm gone, obviously, might require more work."

Ruby rubbed her lips together, thinking. Her lips were full, a light pink, and plump when she pushed them out and to the side.

I couldn't have her say no to this. I needed this possibly way more than she needed it. "I'll pay you eighty grand, through Christmas. Even if Amelia leaves earlier." But I was already planning on talking to my lawyer.

If Vanessa was so willing to leave Amelia for three months

shortly after our custody agreement was set, what would she do in the future?

"What? Why? That's... that's twice as much as the average salary and you're not hiring me for a year..."

Her stammer was adorable. So was her indignation, the shaking of her head.

My hands curled into fists. I wanted to run my fingers through those long locks of hers, inhale the coconut and beachy air perfume or shampoo she used...

I choked down the thought, thinking of my ninety-year-old grandmother in her kaftan dress instead. I brought up every image of the wrinkled, leather-skinned woman who was not at all conducive to the hard-on I was definitely not going to be sporting right then.

Do not fuck the nanny. Do not flirt with the nanny. Do not lust after the nanny. Hell, never be attracted to a teammate's sister, and if you were, never *ever* act on it. Cardinal rules every man and player knew. And I wasn't just a player—I was their coach. Their leader.

I'd stop being attracted to Ruby as soon as I took care of my needs.

I gathered my self-control and reminded her. "This is totally last minute. I'm desperate for the help, and I have no idea when Vanessa will actually be home again. I need to secure help at least through Christmas."

"And if she leaves earlier?"

"I'm agreeing to pay you eighty grand through December. Regardless."

"That's a lot of money, Logan, and I'm not sure—"

"And for the next twelve to fourteen weeks, you'll be doing half of the weekends alone. You said you moved to Nashville to get your finances in order, right? Won't this help?"

I wasn't above manipulating her. Jassen had told me the same thing and she had too. I prepared to see what Jassen called her independence rise to the surface as she inhaled deeply, but my gaze was drawn to her breasts as they rose and fell.

My hands were itching to squeeze them, and my mouth watered at wondering how she'd taste.

Shit. It'd been way too long since I had sex. That was the problem.

She was going to be my daughter's nanny—hopefully.

"It would help, for sure," she muttered, looking uncertain. Unwilling.

"It's what I would offer anyone in this scenario, but you'd really be helping me out. I don't like the idea of leaving Amelia with a stranger when I'm going to be gone so much."

"I *am* a stranger."

"You're Jassen's sister. That tells me all I need to know."

He was straitlaced, solid, and loyal. He loved his wife and his kids and was always an encouragement on the field. His position kept him separated from the majority of the fold, and it could have made him isolated, but he wasn't. When our team was on the sidelines, he was always walking up and down, encouraging everyone. Constantly praising them and getting them fired up.

"Yeah, well, Jassen's a saint," she huffed again. Chuckled a little bit. "Perfect, really."

She seemed pretty damn perfect to me. I kept my mouth shut. Gave her time to think, but with every passing second, fear swirled.

If she said no, I had no idea what I'd do. I'd called a nanny service, but I was hesitant to hire any of them. All the older women wore pinched expressions like they'd be irritated too easily and the thought of a younger woman in my home, someone I didn't know at all, was an immediate no. I didn't care if the person the service management found for me to call was used to catering to wealthy people or celebrities, or if some traveled with music stars while on tour with their families.

The thought of leaving Amelia in this home? In a new state I was barely getting comfortable in and then leaving her with a stranger… someone who could do anything with her… hard pass. Which reminded me I needed to get security cameras set up.

I couldn't be too cautious, even if Ruby agreed.

I leaned forward and settled my forearms on my thighs. Attraction to this young woman aside—I could avoid that—I needed her too much in other ways.

Ruby glanced around the house. I'd had a designer order basic furniture, enough to get me started. I told her I wanted it warm and comfortable, so everything was a shade of cream or other neutrals. Personally, it was boring as hell and bland, but I didn't really care what I sat my ass on to watch television alone, late at night.

I'd put up pictures of Amelia, though, and even a couple with her and Vanessa so she could see her mom when she came to visit. There were photos of her with my parents too, who were *itching* to get their claws in Vanessa for doing this to me.

My parents already had a vacation planned to check in on me next month, make sure I was doing okay with Amelia. They would have rushed right out if I'd asked. It didn't matter I was thirty-six. My mom was always there if I needed her.

It'd taken me hours to convince them it'd be fine, that I had things handled. I was a grown man capable of taking care of my own kid and life, but I was still looking forward to their visit.

And it'd give Ruby some time off if she wanted it.

I had no idea what Ruby saw when she kept looking around, sucking her bottom lip into her teeth and nibbling on it before she refocused on me.

"What do you think?" I asked. My palms were sweaty. My heart was racing.

If she said no….

She grinned, and goddamn, it was a beautiful smile. "I think you should give me a tour so I can start getting comfortable here."

———

"Yes! That is how we do this!" I was flapping my arms, throwing fist pumps into the air while I practically jumped onto every offensive player jogging off the field.

We were winning, and it was an incredible feeling.

"Whatever you did with Damien this week worked a miracle," I said to Cole. He was standing next to me, ankle booted, but he was still positive he'd be back by week one.

"He's a quick learner and intent on being the best he can be. He'll be great once the rest of his jitters wear off, that's all. He needs the confidence."

He was certainly getting it now, with a twenty-yard pass under heavy coverage that fell perfectly into Dawson Butler's hands in the end zone.

The team looked almost entirely like a different team when I arrived at the stadium last Thursday. I was hours late, after giving the tour to Ruby that took three times longer than it should have. It hadn't been her fault. It'd been all mine. The more questions she asked about Amelia, the more she laughed and talked to me about what she did with Luke and Brittney... I'd been having so much fun *talking* with her, I'd almost forgotten I had practice at all until she'd gotten a notification on her Apple watch and asked me, "Don't you need to get going?"

And then I'd arrived at the practice facility. The team was running plays, practicing, like they didn't miss me for a second, and they'd looked *perfect*.

Not great for my ego. Because maybe the problem *was* me. But our early morning practice was the same, and we were winning this afternoon's game easily. It was the last preseason game, and after struggling to win one and lost two others, *this* was what was going to have people thinking we could take another Super Bowl.

It was also the first time most of our starters were playing the majority of the game instead of the backups and the guys who'd still been competing for a roster spot. That only made it more impressive, though, because that meant Damien had thrown that pass against a D-line full of starters, and he wasn't croaking like he'd done last week.

"Looking good, Butler." I slapped his helmet as he jogged off the field, yanking off his chin straps. "Great catch."

"Thanks. Team's looking good today."

I crossed my arms over my chest and readjusted the mouthpiece of my headset. "I suspect that has something to do with you?"

He wasn't sure of me when I got the job. Hell, he was only a few years younger than me, and he'd had a lot of respect for the coach who retired. This past summer, when I laid out my vision for what I felt my role was and what I believed him to be, I'd hoped had changed that. I hadn't been entirely sure until yesterday, and that was mostly because Dawson kept his mouth shut a lot. Didn't speak up. Showed up, put in the work, talked to the few guys he was close with, and then left.

But the team talked, and I'd overheard more than one murmuring variations of, *"Yo, Daws is right. This shit matters and we're fucking it up..."* or *"I want Coach to be proud of us..."*

Dawson, eagle-eye focused on the defense taking the field and lining up, shrugged. "You told me I was a leader. Figured there was no better time than to begin being one."

"I appreciate it."

He was a hard nut to crack. The guys who goofed off and acted like clowns and like this was all fun and games were easier to relate to. They were playing a game they loved, and it showed. Dawson played football like he was out for revenge. It made it harder to know where his head was, what his goals and motivations were, other than winning.

He smirked. "Don't get a big head over it, Coach. I just didn't want to look like a fool out there in a few weeks."

"Rest assured, no big heads here yet."

"Yeah, wait until the end of the season when everyone sees how miraculous we all are thanks to you." He punched my shoulder and headed to the bench.

From Dawson, it was the biggest compliment I could get.

I refocused on the game and was thrilled when the rest of the game went smoothly. A couple dropped passes but no interceptions for Damien. No sacks. He finished the game looking like the rookie quarterback we'd need him to be if Cole's ankle didn't heal quickly, and by the time we got to the locker room, there were finally cheers and whoops and hollers full of praise instead of moaning.

"All right, all right. Listen up!" I took my place in the center of the locker room and surveyed the team.

My team.

"Yo, yo, yo! Coach is talking!" That came from behind me, and soon the room quieted, all eyes on me, fifty-three men in all manner of undressing.

"You all know the stress I feel this season, being one of the youngest coaches in the league and it being my first year head coaching. Gotta say, when I took this job, I thought the preseason would be a lot smoother than it has been. Maybe that's my own cockiness and ignorance, but I think we can all agree it's been a struggle, not what any of us have wanted to see or feel."

There were murmurs of agreement, some shoulder slaps, and encouragements thrown out, but I wasn't done.

"Until today. Today, every single one of you showed up, showed off the work you've been putting in, and I'm damn proud of you all. Damn proud not only to be your coach, but to be a part of this team."

"That's right! Coach! You're one of us now!" Mason Yeets was in the background, fist-pumping the air, bringing his usual excitement to the team.

"Thanks, Yeets." I chuckled. "Today's game went exactly

how I'm hoping the rest of them go. You were fantastic out there, and, Damien"—I pointed to our rookie QB—"proud of you most of all. You're learning, listening, and it's showing. Good job."

He dipped his chin and was shaken by several other players slapping his shoulders. The room burst into encouragement and the young guy's face broke out in an ear-splitting grin, his cheeks turning fire engine red.

"Go home and rest! Replay the good you did today, and we'll be back here on Monday, proving once again that we're the team to beat this season!"

"Yes! Steel on three!" Cole shouted it, threw his fist in the air, and the entire team made the room shake as they joined in.

As soon as the team broke out of their chant, the coaches and I left them to their space. Jacobi, the team's offensive coordinator, was right on my heels. "You were right. We needed today."

"Now we just have to keep them focused. Meet in my office in a half hour?"

"We'll be there."

We'd taken to meeting after practices and preseason games immediately following. It helped keep us sharp, where we could all jot down what we saw, both good and bad, while it was fresh. Allowed us to spend more time on the opponents' films, too. Picking apart their own offense and defense.

I got to my office and tore off my game shirt, doused my face with water, and did a quick wipe down in my private bath before putting on a clean shirt. I'd have to do quick media interviews and be back to meet with the coaches.

Grabbing my phone from my desk, where I always left it during games, I swiped to check for messages. There was sure to be media and texts from management. I always avoided them during the game, which meant my phone was nowhere near me, but today, there was another reason to check my phone.

Ruby. She told me yesterday she'd let me know by tonight what she planned to do.

My hand shook, making my phone wobble when I saw her name in the string of unread messages. Ignoring everything else, I clicked on hers first.

I'll accept if you lower the salary to $50k. Move in before Amelia gets there?

We'd discussed both options of her being settled before Amelia got there or giving me time with her first.

It was the money that tripped me up. What was her *deal* with money and taking it from people who offered? Especially if what she was doing was a hard damn job.

Whatever. I needed her.

She'd get a hefty Christmas bonus. I wasn't going to argue about the money.

Move in tomorrow night. Take Monday night off, though, so I can have the night alone with her.

Her reply was almost immediate. Good thing since I needed to get to the media room. *Sounds good. See you then.*

A smile broke out on my face. I quickly wiped it away.

Yeah, I was smiling because I'd found someone to help with Amelia, but even I was too self-aware to lie to myself.

I was going to see Ruby again, and that made me happy.

I was so royally fucked.

I CONSIDERED NOT TAKING the job. I considered backing out after I accepted. If I'd had any luck getting a job that paid nearly half of what Logan was offering to pay, I would have jumped on it.

Maybe.

I had a bachelor's degree in art history. I also had no experience working with children outside the fact Jassen and I practically raised ourselves and the time I spent with Luke and Brittney. Surely, there had to be more qualified candidates, but there was something about the way Logan's face melted when he spoke about his daughter.

He *adored* her, and it was clear he missed her like crazy.

And yeah... maybe the fact he was so damn hot and sexy and made my stomach flip and my knees wobble had something to do with taking the job.

Which was also why I should have backed out of it.

It was a phone call from my best friend, Gina, who still lived in Portland, and a text message I received after that had me sticking with it.

Gina, because she was my number one encourager and

thought me being attracted to my soon-to-be boss was hysterical. "Can you call him daddy, too?" she'd playfully asked.

I'd snorted out my glass of wine through my nose. "No. And ew…"

I'd called her a bitch. She'd laughed in my face and after we hung up, Paulie texted.

I miss you. What are you up to?

Was he insane? He had to be. Texting me a month after he'd cleaned out my savings account and then taken off with all his things and half of mine, and he thought he could text me?

Fuck him. He'd screwed me over in more ways than financially and I wanted nothing to do with him.

I blocked Paulie's number, something I should have done the day I booked a flight to Nashville, and then rage packed the few belongings I still owned that Paulie hadn't stolen.

After my bags were packed and I made sure the guest apartment was clean, I headed down the stairs, threw my things into the back of my car, and headed to my brother's house.

They were finishing up dinner, and Jassen was loading the dishes while Molly wiped down Luke's and Brittney's hands and faces.

"You just missed dinner," Molly said, smiling at me.

She'd had more energy this weekend and had barely taken a nap when she came home from Jassen's game yesterday. All good signs. Made me not feel like a shmuck for saying I'd help her out and then bailing.

"Need anything to eat?" Jassen asked. "I can warm it up for you."

Stress and nerves had filled my stomach all day, making me not feel hungry. It'd be smart to eat, but I wasn't sure I could bring myself to do it. "No, thanks. I'm good."

"You sure?"

"Yes, big brother. I'm sure." I rolled my eyes and kicked the back of his knee.

"Hey! Good thing that's not my kicking leg."

"Good thing you're all big and strong and there's no way little old me could hurt you, huh?"

Jassen glared at me, teasing. He wiped the look away and replaced it with worry. "You'll be good, right? We're close if you need us."

"You're treating me like I'm moving into my first college dorm all over again."

"Well, you looked scared then, too."

Then, I most likely did. Did I now? I glanced at Molly and she shrugged. "You kinda do."

Wonderful. There was nothing to fear. I could play with kids. I could teach Amelia the ABCs and watch *Frozen* and *Tangled* as much as she wanted. I'd had a summer of getting used to kids and their schedules and moods. One child would be a walk in the park.

"Well, whatever. I'm nervous, maybe, but not scared. It'll be fine. Logan seems like a nice enough guy, and he assured me Amelia is a sweetheart."

The nerves weren't for the daughter.

The nerves were for the dad. What in the heck was I supposed to do in his *house*? Especially tonight, when it was just going to be us?

He'd texted me yesterday and said he thought it'd be a good idea for us to become more comfortable with each other. That way Amelia would settle quicker.

Of course he was looking out for his daughter.

But being comfortable with him? I'd had a half-dozen dreams last night that gave me a variety of very inappropriate ways for us to get comfortable.

Three times I woke myself up, throbbing, sweating. The first two times, I resisted taking care of that sensation, the third I caved, and when I had slipped my fingers beneath my panties and made myself come, it'd been a man a decade-plus older than me on my mind.

Bad Ruby. Very, very bad Ruby.

"All right, well, give me a hug." Molly opened her arms.

I rolled my eyes but went to her. "I'll be back tomorrow."

Or maybe I wouldn't. I'd have the night off, and I could do whatever I wanted to do tomorrow. Maybe I'd go out for a drink, get back to his house after she was in bed or something. He wanted to spend the day with her alone on Tuesday, but then thought we could all do something for dinner.

I had less than forty-eight hours to prepare myself to get over this ridiculous, crush-like attraction.

I could do it.

———

Unlike Friday, when I showed up for the interview, this time, Logan was waiting for me outside when I pulled up his long driveway that led to the four-car sideloading garage. He was sitting on the small stoop on the side door that would lead directly into his kitchen. My ten-year-old Corolla was vastly out of place in this neighborhood, which hadn't bothered me before, but the way Logan's brows arched as I put the car in park and turned off the engine made me grip my steering wheel tighter. He was still staring at the car like it was a deathtrap as I popped open my trunk and gathered my suitcase and large duffel bag out of it.

I'd been a college student with six-figure student loans. We couldn't all drive Bugattis. Not that I knew what he drove.

I might have slammed the trunk closed harder than neces-sary and he jumped.

"Need any help?"

"This is it."

"I'll get them."

He hurried down the cement steps, and once again, he was casual. Athletic shorts, well-fitted T-shirt. I gripped my things tighter. To keep my balance, not because I didn't mind help.

Okay, so I hated help. Accepting it didn't come naturally to me, which was why I'd asked for less money.

What fool did that?

Me. I was the fool.

I was definitely looking like a fool when Logan reached me, arm outstretched to slide the duffel bag off my shoulder, and I was staring at him, not moving.

"I can take them."

"I know." He grinned and damn him for doing it. "Let me help anyway."

Refusal burned my tongue, but I was being ridiculous. There was no reason to fight with my boss over helping me with luggage.

"Fine." I sighed and slipped off the straps of my bag. He took it from my arm, and his knuckles brushed down my forearms as he did.

I tensed. Heat singed my flesh and goose bumps pebbled where his hand brushed against mine. And oh shit... there was no way he noticed. Please tell me he didn't notice.

He glanced up at me. Those eyes like iron landed on mine, but they weren't cold this time. No way.

I stepped back and left him to grab the handle of the suitcase. Rubbing my arm to wash away the sensation was pointless. It remained long after I turned to avoid looking at him.

One stupid touch.

One stupid touch and it had to be *obvious* how that affected me.

But... what had it done to him?

I shook my head and rolled my shoulders. "Okay. So, if you can take those to my room, I'll just... spend some time unpacking?"

He was still watching me. The heat in those eyes was a smolder instead of that flare of inferno I first saw. Or maybe it was me. Maybe I was the problem and seeing things that weren't there.

Logan cleared his throat and wrapped his other hand around the handle of the suitcase.

"I'll follow you to the room we agreed on for you."

I'd be upstairs, two doors down from Amelia. The one next door might have been preferable, given my job, but she was four, not an infant, and the room I chose overlooked the backyard oasis and not the driveway.

I was still at the top of the stairs, close enough I'd hear if she needed me.

The bonus was Logan's bedroom was on the main floor, on the opposite side of the house. Once Amelia went to bed at night, I planned on reading in my room.

I could read every night for hours. We'd hardly ever see each other.

Easy.

This was going to be *so* easy.

———

Turned out, it didn't take me all that long to unpack the bags I brought. I could only rearrange my clothes in the closet and the empty dresser so many times and restack my bathroom supplies in the shower and on the counter before it would be obvious I was hiding.

The bedroom was as simple as the rest of the house. A white wood bed frame sat on one wall with matching white nightstands and dresser. All done with a simple shaker style. There was a circular mirror over the dresser, framed in gold, and the curtains were a dusty blue and white floral pattern. The bathroom was equally simple. White cabinets, marble counters, and gold hardware, the home was definitely newer and updated to the current styles, but it was all... white. Bland. Empty. Like Logan had either moved into a pre-furnished home or pointed his fingers at a catalog and said get me one of everything that will match all over the house.

I needed more life in the room. There definitely needed to be more life in Amelia's room, although Logan had assured me that was coming.

Footsteps pounded up the wooden stairs outside my room and I stopped adjusting the few books I'd brought with me and set on the dresser. For now, they'd have to work for decoration.

A quiet knock on the door followed soon after and I wiped my hands down my sides.

No reason to be nervous. None at all.

I opened the door and Logan was leaning against the wall across the hall. He'd been scrolling on his phone and glanced up when I stood in the doorway.

"Hey," he said and flashed me the screen on his phone. "I thought we could order dinner? Maybe have a couple of drinks. Get to know each other a little bit? That is, if you're done unpacking..."

It was really too damn bad I hadn't brought three more bags I had with me. But this was why I was here now. He didn't want us to seem like complete strangers to Amelia.

I'd agreed. Now it was time to put my money where my mouth was.

Spend time with my boss and prove I could do it without wanting to dive into his lap and ram my tongue down his throat.

I could do that.

Totally.

"What were you thinking of ordering?"

As long as it wasn't seafood...

"Sushi?"

I wrinkled my nose. I couldn't. "You should probably know now that I'm deadly allergic to shellfish."

"Really?" His brows arched in surprise. "Oh."

I leaned over to where I'd left my purse on the bedroom dresser and pulled out my extra EpiPen. I always kept one near a kitchen and one on me.

"No joke." I held it up for him to see.

"All right. No sushi, no shellfish of any kind in the house. Got it. Anything you want to eat?"

It was late. I hadn't eaten all day and I'd already passed on dinner with Jassen and Molly. I still wasn't sure my nerves would allow me to eat much, but it'd give us something to do.

I had to get used to being around him at some point.

"Know of any good burger places yet?"

He smiled, a full-out, panty-melting kind of smile that made me curl my hand around the doorframe to stay standing. "I know just the place."

I HATED SUSHI. I figured all women loved it. At least most of the women I knew back in California did. Vanessa could have eaten it every single day of her life and never grown tired of it. Even Amelia gobbled up the California rolls Vanessa gave her. The only reason I offered it was to make Ruby happy.

Not at all something I should have been considering.

My heart had squeezed strangely tight when she brought up getting burgers instead. Burgers I could definitely do.

"What's Cowbell?"

We were in the kitchen, and I'd placed my order for my own meal, knowing the exact place I wanted to order food from, before handing my phone over to Ruby.

"Some local place. Walked out of the dentist last month, saw the restaurant across the street, and went in for some lunch. I've been there so many times now they know me."

She glanced up from my phone with a smirk on her face. "That can't possibly be because you're the Steel's head coach and you've been all over the news?"

"I thought you said you didn't pay much attention to football?"

Her blue eyes rolled in a circle before she went back to

scrolling through the phone. "Yeah, I'm not like some super fan, but I watch the news. I have no idea what to order. It all looks so good. What'd you get?"

"The quesario."

Fried onion rings. Queso. Monterey jack cheese and fried onion strings. My mouth watered at the thought of it.

"Hm. I'll get that, too. Extra onion strings."

She handed me back my phone and I put in her order.

"You sure?"

"Sure, I'm sure. Why? Should I not?" She reached for my phone. "Are you messing with me and that's one you hate?"

"No." I held my phone to my chest. Her expression was priceless. "I wouldn't do that, and I was only asking. Chill."

"Chill," she huffed with a smile that was so sweet. "That's almost at the level of telling a woman to calm down and we all know what happens then."

I definitely did. Learned that early on in my marriage, most definitely. Still, she was smiling. Laughing, and for once things weren't awkward, so I couldn't resist. "Absolutely, they become completely reasonable, are able to think logically and within a conversational speaking volume."

Her eyes widened to saucers and by the time I was done, her jaw was practically unhinged. "Are you kidding me?"

"Careful, that sounds like you might get a little shrieky in your voice..."

"You... you... are..."

She sputtered.

I finalized the order and set my phone on the counter. "I'm messing with you, Ruby. Calm down."

Steam practically billowed from her ears as she pressed her lips together.

I grinned shamelessly. Damn, she was cute when she got angry. I'd have to remember that.

Or... no. I wouldn't. Making her cuter was not what I needed to do.

Too bad she couldn't look ugly while angry.

"You're a menace." She shoved her pointer finger in my direction. "That was mean."

"I'm not always nice." I shrugged. "Ask my ex-wife."

Ouch. I cringed as soon as the words came out of my mouth and Ruby's expression switched to sadness.

"Ignore that. Ignore me." I waved it off. "That was, well... true. Vanessa would probably say I wasn't all that nice, but I shouldn't have said it."

"I don't know." She shrugged and chewed on the inside of her cheek. "Can I ask what happened? I mean, I figure Amelia will say something about her mom. It'd be nice to know what to say to her."

"Ugh. Yeah, but I need a drink for that conversation."

"You drink during the season?" Her voice rose with surprise.

Nice to know at least one of my players didn't. Several did, and I didn't really care as long as they weren't getting drunk in the hotel the night before the game. What they did after game time or on their days off was their business. As long as it didn't affect their performance, I didn't really care. Some coaches did, though.

"I'm not the one taking the field. And I'm not planning on getting drunk."

"Right. Of course." If I wasn't mistaken, a pale pink rose on her cheeks.

"Want one?"

"A drink?"

"Yeah, you're old enough, right?" It was a shot at her age. Probably rude to do, too, but with her looking so damn cute in my kitchen, the reminder helped.

Too young for me. Way too young for me. My employee. I

would *not* be the creepy guy who banged the nanny, despite the thought of it sending a spark of lust to my groin.

She scrunched up her nose. Adorable. Absolutely adorable. "Yes, *dad*. I'm old enough to drink, but I'm good for now. Maybe once dinner comes, if that's okay."

"My house is your house." At least temporarily. "Speaking of, I do have someone who does all my shopping for me. There's an app we use, so I can add things to it as I run out. Nanette delivers everything on Thursdays. Any food we run out of or anything you need, you can put on there. Remind me to show you later."

"All right. Thanks."

I turned to the fridge to grab a Heineken. "And you, too."

"That's all right. I'll handle my own stuff."

I shut the fridge and turned to her. She had that uncomfortable look on her face. The same face she made when I offered to help with her luggage. Help was hard for her to accept.

It shouldn't have bothered me as much as it did, but I *wanted* to help her. I knew little of Jassen's personal life, but he hadn't made it a secret his mom wasn't that great, and he had no dad in his life, ever. He hadn't talked about his sister all that much, but that just meant Ruby grew up the same way.

The independence I understood, but I wanted her to lean on me.

Or against me... on me... beneath me... there were a lot of positions I'd thought of Ruby in the last few days.

I opened the beer and took a healthy swallow. Those thoughts needed to be banished from my brain immediately.

"So, Vanessa," I said. Nothing cooled me down faster than thinking about her. Especially this last week.

"Your ex...?"

"We were married for ten years, happily married for probably five of them." I didn't have a traumatic story. I didn't suddenly despise women and obviously Vanessa wasn't going out on some revenge tour against men or anything. "There's no huge story. We grew apart. Had Amelia and things changed. I was busy all the time, had just started coaching in the pros instead of college, and my focus was on my job and then being the best dad I could be. Like I said, I wasn't always a nice guy. I can admit, looking back, I pushed her to the side. It was football, my daughter, then my wife, and she still wanted to be number one. She should have been."

Ruby's lips pulled into a frown, but there was no judgment.

"Jassen's always said he wanted to ensure Molly knows she comes first, above everything, so I get that, but still... you were busy then. A baby and a *new job*? Shouldn't there be some grace to adjust, too?"

"A five-year grace period?" I smirked as I asked. Truth be told, I'd pushed Vanessa off to the side and then naively believed she was okay with it. We rarely fought. She'd never started a fight demanding my time. She grew quiet, sure. Asked for dates and my time.

To me, she'd appeared totally okay with the scraps I was giving her, even when I realized I was doing it, and didn't change. It was easier to keep taking advantage of her that way than make the effort to change.

Ruby's lip curled. "You have a point. So, what? You got the job here and she said nope?"

"Yep."

"Really?"

"She used more words, but that was basically it. I came home, excited to tell her about it, had already started looking at homes out here, planning schools for Amelia eventually, that kind of thing. She didn't want to leave her family and friends out there."

"That must have been hard for you. For Amelia."

"It's hard for me because of Amelia, yeah, and I hate coming home to an empty house. I miss the noise."

Maybe that was why I'd wanted Ruby to move in tonight. One less night of being alone. Of the silence. That was the hardest thing about not having Amelia, and even Vanessa. The clatter of glasses on a counter, water being turned on and off, her banging around in our bathroom. I never realized how much noise people made living their lives until everything was completely silent.

Even hearing Ruby moving around in the room upstairs had made me smile. The distant echo of doors closing. Muted footsteps. She must have tried the faucet and showerhead and ensured the toilet worked because the water had turned on and off several times.

"You look like you need a subject change."

"Please, for the love of God, yes."

I was rewarded with another blindingly bright smile.

Stunning.

Ruby Moore wasn't cute or adorable, she was stunning.

I was in serious trouble.

———

"Mmm. Oh my God. Amazing."

Hell. World's worst torture. Ruby and I were having opposite reactions to our burgers. Or, more to the point, I was having a *reaction* to hers. She moaned through every bite like an orgasm was on its way and every time she groaned, *oh my God* flashed in my mind of how she'd sound when I was the one making her do it instead of a burger.

While she had her eyes closed, biting down into, admittedly, the world's most amazing burger, I reached down to my lap and adjusted myself. If she made these sounds every time she ate, I'd have to start giving her privacy.

"This is incredible." She set down her burger long enough to pick up a napkin and wipe the edges of her mouth. "I could kiss you for knowing about this place."

Could she? Those full lips on mine? I wasn't sure I could say no.

Shit. It was the delicious moans that sounded more like pleasure from sex than food that had my head spinning.

"Sorry." She blushed and took a sip of her water. "I didn't mean that literally."

"Obviously." Shame. I finished my own burger and started on the fries. "I know you and Jassen both said you just recently moved here. How long has it been?"

Her blush was still staining her cheeks. It couldn't be possible she was actually thinking about kissing me. Right? No way. She had to look at me and see some old guy with a kid.

I'd force myself to believe it for as long as it took.

"I moved out here in July. Hot as hell and totally different than Portland."

"You were in Oregon? That's a move as large and different as mine."

"Yeah. Well, I didn't have much left for me there." She shrugged, lips pulled down, and the blush didn't only fade away, she paled further.

"I thought you moved to pay off student loans."

"I did. There were also some other factors..."

Her face scrunched up again, and she drained the rest of her water.

Clearly, not a topic she wanted to discuss. It wasn't any of my business. She was here and helping with Amelia. It should have been all I cared about.

But I was determined to learn the real reason because clearly, her brother didn't know either. And if they were as close as they'd both led me to believe, then something happened to Ruby to chase her across the country.

A guy probably, I guessed. And I wanted to figure out who

he was and pummel him into the ground for hurting her. And then thank him for being an epic dick that caused whatever happened to land her in my path.

"Tell me about Amelia," Ruby said quietly, almost sadly. "Teach me what she likes and what she loves."

It only confirmed my suspicions. It wasn't only money that caused her to move out here. Maybe not a guy. But something happened to have her looking so damn sad and hurt. There wasn't a damn thing I could do about it, either, and I hated it.

It was also none of my business. Outside of her taking care of my daughter, there wasn't anything in Ruby's life I needed to be concerned about.

"HER FAVORITE COLORS are neon orange and lime green. She despises pink and black. Says the two colors together give her a headache."

I chuckled along with him. This was what I needed. Time to learn about Amelia. Something else to focus on other than Logan's full lips and the way his eyes lit up when he talked about his daughter. Amelia was my *job* and it was time to get to know all I could about her.

"She loves unicorns and flowers, which should be obvious from the chaos currently going on in her room."

"Her room?" I hadn't seen it when I unpacked, and the other day it'd been empty.

Logan nodded. "Yeah. I had all her furniture and things delivered yesterday. You can go peek later, but if pink and black give her a headache, her new room might give her a migraine."

He scrunched up his nose. And shook his head. "Regardless, she's playful. Definitely not shy, although I have no idea how she'll be with you. Vanessa stays home with her, so she's never had many babysitters or nannies or anything outside my parents. I think she's brilliant, but I figure most parents say that about their kids."

"But she's more brilliant than theirs, right?"

He nodded seriously. "Obviously."

"I know you said you wanted me to look into preschools, but since the year has already started, that might be kind of tough to find an opening. Is there anything else she likes? Any other activities you've put her in?"

"She's been in gymnastics and soccer. I can help find places, though. I'm sure there are people on the Steel's staff or players with kids who might have recommendations."

"That's okay." I didn't mind the work, and it'd give me something to focus on. Luke and Brittney wore me down when I was with them through the day, but how hard could only one child be? "Or if you find places, I can call and get her in. I'm at your disposal for whatever you need..."

His eyes flared before he wiped it away. It took a second to realize how that sounded and I refocused on my burger. Great. One meal with the guy and I'd already made things sound sexual twice.

I was rocking this nanny thing.

Jassen cleared his throat. "I know you're here for the money. I'm not an idiot, but I'm still thankful you're willing to help me out, Ruby. It means a lot to me."

The flutter of praise shouldn't have dipped so low in my stomach, making me press my thighs together. At least he couldn't see that.

"You're welcome. What else do I need to know?"

Logan walked me through what he knew of her typical daytime routine. I grabbed my phone and started jotting down notes, including finding a pediatrician and a dentist and all that good stuff in case something happened.

We finished dinner and I helped clean up. The quicker I got used to moving around his space, I figured the quicker I'd be more comfortable there. Somehow, we worked well together, as if it wasn't our first time.

And yeah, I knew I was younger. Knew he'd had years of being an adult, a husband, and a father, but it still surprised me how easily he worked to clean up the kitchen, wiped down the counters, loaded the dishes.

No guy I'd ever dated had managed to so much as scrub their toilet more than once a semester.

The fact Logan did it all only made him more attractive. *Crazy*.

Maybe I needed to get laid. I hadn't thought about sex at all since Paulie, but my hormones were running in high gear if a man wiping down a counter made me all swoony.

Gina couldn't visit fast enough. A weekend at the bars around guys my own age was going to be needed.

Soon.

"Do you mind if I get that drink now?" I blurted it out of nowhere, right as Logan was bent over the kitchen table, ass filling out those shorts perfectly and those calves giving me wicked thoughts.

Yeah. I needed to go have a crappy hookup that would probably lead to a lackluster performance before I jumped my boss.

"Of course." Logan tossed the washcloth into the sink and headed to his butler's pantry off the kitchen. "What would you like?"

He waved to the wall on one side. Three thick floating shelves held as much alcohol as a liquor store. The shelves were framed by two sets of cupboards, glass doors, and every kind of drinking glass you could use. He might as well have run his own bar out of his pantry. Beneath the counter were two fridges. Sodas and sparkling waters and beers filled one, and the other was full of wine.

"I like to be ready for anything," he said when I dragged my surprised gaze off the hidden bar that could entertain his entire team for an evening.

"Well, you're certainly ready to turn into an alcoholic."

He chuckled, shaking his head. "What would you like?"

"Chardonnay, please, but I can get it."

He ignored me, crouched down, and after rolling several bottles to check the labels, he pulled one out. "This good?"

I bought and drank double bottles of Costco's store-brand wine. Whatever he had in his fridges had to be better. Not sure how it could be worse. "I'm sure it's great, Logan. Don't forget I've just been a poor college student."

"Right." That grin again. He meant nothing by it. Couldn't have. But I still reached out and grabbed the counter to hold me up.

Maybe I needed to go see a doctor. Get my weak knees checked out.

Logan grabbed the electric bottle opener from the counter and while he opened the bottle of wine, he turned to me. "So what did you go to college for anyway?"

Ahh. This was the topic I could talk about all day long. And all night. My passion for art sometimes drove even Gina crazy, and she and I had met in our Intro to Art History class in Portland.

"Art history."

I anticipated the surprised look before it came, but it was common. I was used to it. It wasn't the most common thing and most people who I told my major to assumed I wanted to go into teaching.

"That's not something I hear a lot."

I snorted and reached for the glass of wine. "No offense to you or any of the people you're usually around, but you've spent your professional life around athletes. That and art don't usually go together at all."

"Ah," he teased. "Is that a little bit of judgment I hear in your voice?"

I rolled my eyes. "Tell me I'm wrong and I'll apologize."

"Fair point. But I'm interested. Come sit with me outside and tell me about it?"

Talk about my passion for art while overlooking his serene backyard with the sun setting? He'd probably never get my ass off the chair, and I'd bore him to sleep on the back patio. Even knowing that, I didn't resist.

"Lead the way."

I stepped back. He grabbed another beer from the kitchen fridge, and I grabbed a napkin to use as a coaster on our way.

Once we were settled on his furniture, I relaxed. Hues of oranges and purples colored the sky to our right, and the shadows and covered patio kept us in the shade. Logan flipped on ceiling fans that whirred to life above his outdoor seating area and I melted into the cushions.

"I know I said this the other day, but your backyard is absolutely gorgeous. Quiet, too." Besides the cicadas and crickets coming to life, there was only the sound of a commercial jet somewhere in the distance. Ducks floated on the lake and across it, I could barely make out the shapes and shadows of two people standing on paddleboards.

"We didn't have much of a yard where we lived in California. Vanessa got the house so Amelia didn't have to move, but one of the things I was excited about moving out here was this kind of life. Quieter, land to roam and play and explore. I can't wait for Amelia to see it in person."

"You haven't seen her yet?"

"I flew back before training camp started and spent a couple days with her, but she hasn't been out here yet. We FaceTime and that kind of thing, which reminds me I'll need to give you Vanessa's number so she can call Amelia."

"Of course." That shouldn't be awkward at all at first.

"I've shown Amelia the home and backyard on the phone, but I wasn't expecting her to be out here for another month. My parents were going to bring her on our bye week in early October."

God. That was still over a month away and he hadn't seen her in a month. "That has to be hard."

I couldn't imagine how Jassen would do not being able to see his kids. Traveling for weekends was hard enough on him.

"It's hell. And so I don't sit here and wallow in how much I miss her, tell me about your degree. What do you plan on doing with it? What drew you to it?"

"Fourth grade field trip."

It wasn't a story I told everyone, but Logan knew Jassen. He had to know *some* of what our childhood had been like. Jassen never bothered to hide it, but I'd always been more cautious about opening up.

"Really?" Logan kicked his feet up onto the coffee table between us.

I was too short to stretch my legs like he was doing, but I bent my legs, curled my toes around the edge of the table, and relaxed further into the furniture.

"My fourth grade class took a field trip to the art museum one day and I fell in love." It was as simple as that and way more complicated. I sighed, thinking of that day. The peace in the museum, the gentle, happy feeling and soft, tender smiles that radiated from every adult who perused the art. My classmates and friends had been quieted several times by the parent who went with us, but I'd gotten so lost in the art and in my head I'd almost missed the bus to head back to the school. "Jassen and I didn't grow up with a lot, you know that, right?"

Logan nodded. "I know some."

"Our mom wasn't around a lot, and by a lot, I mean, there'd be days we wouldn't see her."

"In fourth grade?"

I huffed. "Since well before that. Jassen was cooking me

SpaghettiOs for dinner and he couldn't have been more than eight. And he's four years older than me."

"Four..." Logan said the age and it hit us at the same time. His brows rose in disbelief and then anger hardened his tone. "You were *four* and your brother was taking care of you?"

He was angry. On *my* behalf. It wasn't the warmth from the outside air heating my skin, but the way he was looking at me, with all the shock and fury of a *good* parent. One who'd protect his child, his daughter, not abandon her.

Most surprisingly, not a hint of pity. I wouldn't linger on that part of the conversation to allow it to show. So we had a crappy upbringing. It wasn't the worst I'd heard about, and we'd done okay despite it. Or maybe because of it.

"The museum was quiet." I sipped my wine and waited until he blinked away his anger to refocus. I took a second to do the same. "It was quiet and peaceful and there was this, I don't know, gentleness as soon as you walked through the building I'd never felt before. I could have lived in that museum and been happy. That summer, I started making Jassen take the bus with me to go into the city and we'd spend all day in the museum and the library next door. They were free. Sometimes they had kids' activities going on. And I was hooked."

I shrugged, like it wasn't all that impressive or anything, and it really wasn't. But we'd been ten and fourteen, way too young to be alone on a city bus.

"I think you're fortunate," Logan finally said and *that* surprised me.

"Fortunate?" I laughed.

"Yeah. Not too many people find their passion at such a young age and have it follow them through their life."

When he put it that way, he wasn't wrong. I'd always been more passionate about art than Jassen had ever been about kicking some pigskin around.

"So that's what I want to do. Get my master's in Art History and become a museum curator. Find art, work on the exhibits and collections, and I want to give tours to kids. Make it fun for them so more people will find the beauty and solace in art."

That last part was my own personal mission. I'd never told a soul and yet it fell from my lips so quickly, so easily, I didn't have time to keep it inside.

I sipped my wine and stared out at the lake and the darkening sky, feeling the weight of Logan's gaze on me for far too long, far too intensely to be able to find the courage to look back at him.

But it was there, pressing against me.

"I'm honored to be a part of your journey, even if it's only with finances."

I chuckled. It couldn't be helped and when I braved a glance back at him, he wasn't smiling.

"I'm serious, Ruby. And while you're with Amelia, please make sure you take her to the museums in Nashville as much as possible. Let her see that excitement and passion on your face you show when you're talking to me."

My eyes burned. Out of nowhere, emotion sparked. He almost looked *proud* of me, or impressed, and that was silly. He was far older. Had seen way more than I had. Had lived a life of far more excitement. "I will," I told him, and I meant it.

But it'd be for Amelia as much as me. If I spent too much time away from art, a part of my soul started to shrivel.

"Can I ask you something else? About your mom?"

I took a hefty drink of my wine and groaned. "If you have to."

"I guess it's not about your mom, but your dad. I take it he wasn't ever around?"

I should have known it was coming. It was still a surprise. Not that he was curious. Most people usually were. The surprise came from the fact Logan was no longer relaxed. At some point, he'd planted his feet on the patio and leaned forward, fully invested. Fully serious.

And while I usually blew it off, laughed about the completely shitty hand Jassen and I had been dealt, I couldn't do it. Not with Logan being so intense.

"Jassen's dad was around for a while. He came and went long enough I remember him bringing him bringing us Christmas gifts one year, but that was, gosh... I was maybe five then? I have no idea who my dad is. Not sure my mom ever knew."

There'd been a time I would have lied. Would have hidden that truth. It was in high school when I told a friend's parents about my parents and had seen the way they shut down around me. I'd gone from a friend of their daughter's to someone they kept an eagle eye on whenever I was around. Too afraid I'd steal something, probably, but that had never been the case. It had, though, been my first introduction to knowing I'd be judged forever for the choices my mom made.

"I didn't know," Logan said, and his voice was a quiet rasp. Thick with regret.

"Jassen and I are all we've ever had, but that was always enough. He went to college and even with his scholarship, he worked. He sent me money until I was old enough to get my own job. Where we grew up, we knew a lot of people who had it a lot worse."

The family who lived in the upstairs apartment from us had an asshole dad. Every night, he stumbled home and beat his wife and kids. We hadn't been abused... we'd been ignored and neglected.

Some would say it was all the same, but I knew better.

I'd had it golden compared to a lot of the other kids in our run-down apartment building. At least my mom had always managed to pay rent, kick out any guy she brought home who leered at me. There were many I knew who wouldn't do that. She might not have taken care of us, but she protected me from the worst things that could happen.

She was a shitty mom, but she wasn't the worst. By far.

————

Campfires and pine trees surrounded me, smothered me in a cocoon of warmth, and then I was being settled on clouds. Weighed down by the soft, luxurious feel of them.

A deep voice rumbled in my ear, creating a cascade of shivers down my arm. "Go back to sleep, Ruby."

Oh... *oh*... I was neither in the clouds nor near a campfire. This was Logan.

I forced my eyes to open and caught his gaze in the darkened room. He must have flipped on the bathroom light to let a glow light the room because the door was open behind him. "You... you carried me to bed?"

What the hell for?

Oh... the night. The patio. I'd talked about my mom and refilled my wine before he brought the bottle outside in a bucket of ice with a couple more beers. We'd spent more time talking about Amelia. About football. He'd chuckled at the basic questions I'd asked him and lit up the night sky with his smile when he told me stories about Amelia. And somehow, I'd fallen asleep.

How embarrassing.

"Thanks for keeping me company, Ruby. I had fun tonight."

I blinked and forced my eyes to open. I was so sleepy, but he was standing over me, and oh dear... those lips of his.

Keep *him* company? That did sound nice. I'd had fun, too.

"Night, Logan. Tonight was nice."

In the distance, a soft *hum* sounded. Maybe it came from him. Maybe me. Sleep was pulling me under and then I felt a warm brush over my cheek. I curled deeper into the pillow as he draped the covers over me.

"Night, Ruby. Sleep well."

I woke hours later, to the sun seeping in through the lightweight blinds. The gentle hum of the air conditioner. It took me a second to remember where I was, and once I did, I immediately rolled over.

"Oh God," I groaned into my pillow. I'd fallen *asleep* while talking to my boss, and he'd *carried* me to bed like I was some child.

What a horrible first impression to make. A nanny who couldn't handle her alcohol and fell asleep in the middle of a conversation.

He was probably going to fire me. Especially after telling him all the stories about my mom. There was no way he'd trust me with his daughter now. I might as well pack my bags and slink back to Jassen's. Hell, maybe Portland.

Not good. Not good at all.

CHAPTER 8

LOGAN

I SHOULDN'T HAVE CARRIED her to bed last night. Hell, I shouldn't have stayed on the back patio after Ruby fell asleep. I'd gone inside to use the bathroom and when I returned, it was clear she was asleep. I should have nudged her awake right then, gotten her to bed. Instead, I turned on my heels, went inside to grab my iPad, and I spent hours watching practice and game film, reviewing the lines and plays. Tweaking the strategy for the final preseason game. I filled my notes app with reminders and things to do and specific players to speak to as soon as we hit the field and made more notes to go over with the offense and defense coaches.

And I did all of it while creeping on Ruby like a pervert. Long, uninterrupted glances while she slept with her head back on the outdoor couch, head facing the backyard, gave me a complete view of her body, the way her lips parted as she breathed, and the gentle rise and fall of her chest.

Yeah. That was bad enough.

But deciding to pick her up and carry her upstairs like she was my child? Or my wife?

Crossed the line. One hundred percent. And the fact I *touched* her cheek, brushed my finger along her temple once I had her in that bed because I'd wanted to lean down and see if her lips were as soft as they'd looked all night?

Goddamn, I needed my head examined. Perhaps I should go back to the nanny agency and find some grandmother figure who'd teach Amelia how to crochet and knit and bake or something.

Ruby was a distraction I didn't need and one I couldn't afford.

I'd spent all day thinking of her, the feel of her body in my arms. The way that once I tried to wake her up and she didn't move an inch and I held her in my arms, she'd curled into my chest. The way she glanced at me in that bedroom, half asleep, eyes barely opened, and given me a smile that had my heart tightening.

She was beautiful, so much wiser and confident than I'd been at her age. And she seemed so kind, so gracious. So forgiving. The way she'd talked about her mom, her life, and she never once seemed angry or bitter.

She wasn't only way too young for me to be thinking these things about. I was beginning to think she was way too good for me.

A week. I'd give this time before I made any final decisions. There was nothing I could do with Amelia's plane already landed, at the gate, and I was pacing back and forth where they'd exit soon. Nothing could change except for my resolve to stay away from Ruby as much as possible. I'd given her the night off so I didn't have to worry about seeing her. She'd be back sometime tomorrow, so she and Amelia could meet. Amelia would change everything.

She'd keep Ruby distracted and help me keep my focus. She'd be the icebreaker I needed, because hell, my little girl had already been through enough. She didn't need me to screw up with her new nanny and lose someone else in her life.

"Daddy!" My cheeks split into a smile as soon as I heard that sweet, loud voice. I couldn't see her behind the crowd of people, but she must have seen me because soon, little hands were shoving people out of her way.

They glanced down at her, scowled, and then smiled because who could not smile at the tiny little bundle of waist-length, curly blond hair demanding she get through them.

And soon, she was there, running to me with her little back-pack flopping behind her, and I crouched down to grab her.

My favorite arms in the entire world wrapped around my shoulders and the heels of her feet dug into my hips.

"Daddy! You're here and I missed you and the plane ride was so much fun and even if I was scared, the lady who sat next to me was so nice!" I was racing to follow every one of her rushed, shouted words when she cupped her hand over my ear and whisper-shouted, "She even gave me extra pretzels and cookies even though she said that was a no-no!"

"Did she?" I leaned back, brushed her hair off her cheeks, and hugged her fiercely.

Behind her, a flight attendant smiled at us, headed directly toward me. "Please tell me you're Mr. Caldwell."

"I am. Thank you so much for keeping my daughter safe." I held out my arm to shake her hand and the woman took it.

"My pleasure. She's a treat."

"So were those extra cookies!" Amelia shouted.

Her volume rose and fell with her sleep schedule. Maximum when she was awake, zero when she slept was pretty much all we'd ever gotten out of her. But missing it? Not hearing that raspy little shout all day long, God, I missed my little girl.

The flight attendant gave her a shocked look and glanced around. Several adults were hiding smiles or brazenly dishing them out. Amelia charmed everyone.

I had no reason to be worried about how she'd react to Ruby.

"Here's her other carry-on, Mr. Caldwell." The attendant

slid her neon green suitcase to my side. "I'm told there will be luggage to pick up in baggage claim for her, as well."

Vanessa had included that in the flight information she posted, but I appreciated the reminder. "Thank you…"

"Reanna."

"Reanna. Thank you again for watching over her."

Her smile was genuine. "My pleasure. Bye, Amelia, you have a super fun time with your daddy and new friends, okay?"

"I will! Bye, Reanna!"

Reanna gave us a low wave before she turned back to the plane's boarding ramp. Passengers were still unboarding, so I grabbed the handle of Amelia's suitcase and pulled us out of everyone's way.

I set her in a chair, crouched down in front of her, and plopped my hands to her cheeks. Pulling her, I peppered her chubby cheeks with kisses until she laughed and squealed and cried out for me that it was too many.

"I can't help it. They're kisses for every day I missed you so much."

"Mommy's in Itawy."

"I know. But you'll see her on the screen like you and I had to do, and she'll be back before too long."

"And then she'll be back here?"

Back here? Did she think Vanessa was moving back with me when she came back? The airport wasn't the place to have this talk, and I might have misinterpreted, but in case that's what she meant, I stood and held out my hand. "How about we get your things and then we can get home and you can finally see your new room?"

Her little hand clamped onto mine, so small she could hardly wrap around my palm. I squeezed her tight.

"Yep. Mommy said it's big enough for everyone to live in. She said it was pretty."

Another frown pushed at my lips. And again, I ignored it. A

crowded airport was not at all the kind of place to question Amelia. She'd had a long day and a wild few months. She had to be confused. I knew Vanessa thought the home was pretty because she'd told me, and even if she hadn't, she would have made sure to have a positive attitude about it for Amelia's sake. Trip to Italy aside, we were both fixated on doing what was best for our daughter.

"It is pretty, *and* I have a friend staying with us for a while for you to hang out with while I'm at work."

"Like Brownie?"

Brownie was the neighbor's dog in California and every time Amelia stepped outside, he came to the fence, wagging his tail and panting with excitement. He'd stay in one single spot until Amelia came back in. Never barked, never scared her or ran up and down the yard, just sat, waiting for her to come say hello to him and keeping an eye on her while she played.

"Um. Well, sort of? But she's a person not a retriever. And maybe you shouldn't compare Miss Ruby to a dog when you meet her."

"Why not? Dogs are great!"

Yes, yes, they were. And so was Ruby, but I still doubted she'd be excited about that.

Small, quick feet dashed through the house and all the irritation and sadness I'd had over the last months about living alone evaporated as Amelia's squeal bounced off the high ceilings and walls and her feet thundered straight to the backyard.

Her hands slapped the glass doors and made a squeaking noise as she tugged her hands down the glass. "Wow! Daddy! That lake is so much bigger than on the phone, and the pool is so pretty! Can we go play in it? Can we? Can we?"

She jumped on the floor and kept squeaking her hands

against the glass. A forty-minute car ride home of her constant chatter and now all this excitement and I was desperate for a nap.

Yeah, I loved my daughter and her excitement, but I was *far* out of practice with the constant energy she had zipping through her. I scrubbed a hand through my hair and fought off a yawn.

"What if I show you the house first? Maybe we can have a snack or some dinner? See your room? Then after we eat, we'll go swim."

"I wanna swim in the lake!"

"I think the lake is more for boats and stuff right now." I hadn't even checked to see how deep it was. But I didn't have a dock or a safe swimming area. That was put on my to-do list in the spring. She turned to me, shoved out her bottom lip, and her gray eyes turned to saucers. "But I never swam in a lake before."

"No pouting." I reached for her, picked her up, and threw her in the air. She squealed and I settled her on my hip and bopped her in the nose. "I need to make the lake safe for you first and it's not ready. But maybe we can get a canoe or something so we can be out on the water sometime."

"Today!?"

"No. Not today. Maybe when Papa and Nana come to see you?"

"They're coming? Here!? But I just saw them!"

I had no doubt they were all hands on deck with helping Vanessa with Amelia, but they hadn't said anything to me about seeing her recently.

"You did?"

"Yup." She nodded. "Mommy went away and they stayed with me."

"You mean today? On her flight to Italy?"

"No, Daddy silly. Last time!"

"Last time?" I shook my head. I hadn't heard a single word about Vanessa going out of town and that bothered me. We'd agreed to total honesty about our lives, at least when it came to Amelia due to the distance. She had a right to live her life. I wouldn't judge her for that. But not telling me she was leaving my daughter alone?

And my parents didn't tell me, either?

I scratched a mental note to call them later and set Amelia on her feet.

"Come on. Let's go see your room, find your swimsuit, and then we'll order pizza so Daddy doesn't have to cook. How does that sound?"

"Great!"

She tore her hand out of mine and raced toward the stairs. "Bet I can find my room faster than you can!"

God bless fathers with daughters who had unending energy. I only hoped that didn't translate to sass and attitude in her teenage years.

Hours later, Amelia was finally worn out from the swimming and racing around the house. We'd eaten pizza and I managed to wrangle her into the bath. Her hair was dry, brushed, and she was settled in her pajamas. We'd unpacked her suitcases. Well, I did the unpacking. Amelia took the time to point to where she wanted everything to go while having a bounce party on her new bed. I'd tucked her in, read her countless books, and once she was finally asleep, I stayed sitting next to her on the bed.

I snuggled Amelia to me and buried my nose in her hair, inhaling the scent of her shampoo, grateful I didn't have to keep seeing her only through a phone screen.

Everything in my little world was currently perfect, and I'd make sure it stayed that way.

Distractions of Ruby be damned.

"HE *CARRIED* ME TO BED, Gina. There's no coming back from this."

"Well, you better find a way to come back from it. You're working for the guy."

"Ugh. It's so humiliating." I still couldn't get past it. Logan hadn't just woken me up after I'd fallen asleep. He carried me to my bedroom in his house like I was a child. Maybe his child. Like I was so young to him he thought he had to take care of me. And on our first night together?

"Maybe he didn't think anything of it."

"Then what was with that finger brush?" I swore my skin still burned where he'd brushed my hair off my cheek. I wasn't sleeping then, not really.

Gina laughed. "I don't know what you want me to say, girl. If I tell you it's no big deal, you insist it is, and if I tell you he wants you, you tell me I'm crazy."

"I'm going crazy, that's for sure." I was in the bathroom at my brother's house. Since I'd just come back for one night to give Logan and Amelia the day alone, I'd camped out in their guest room instead of the apartment. I had Gina on FaceTime, propped up on the bathroom vanity, and was fixing my hair before I had to get in my car and drive back to Logan's.

I was a nervous wreck to meet Amelia and face Logan again, and Gina wasn't helping.

She leaned toward her phone screen and applied mascara to her eyelashes. "You're not crazy, you're nervous."

Ugh. She knew me so well. "And embarrassed."

She scowled at me and laughed again. "All right. So you're crazy, embarrassed, and nervous. Have you heard from him? Has he said this won't work?"

"No."

"Then who cares. Show up, love the heck out of his little girl so he sees how good of a nanny you'll be to her, and then both of you can forget whatever silly thing happened between you."

"That's not so easy when I want to jump his bones every time he walks into a room."

She pointed her mascara wand at the screen. "Don't do that. At least not until you know he'll catch you and then take over."

"Argh!" I tossed a hair tie at my own screen. "You're impossible."

"That's why you love me."

"Not today, Satan."

Gina picked up her phone, fluffed her blond beachy waves, and spun in her bedroom, headed toward her closet. "Okay. You want him. You have a crush on the guy. Big deal. Do you know how many grooms I come across a year who are like, the hottest freaking thing in the world? I swear, some of them are so damn sexy I've stuttered and blushed my way through the event and it was their *wedding* day. It's perfectly acceptable to find someone attractive. It's also perfectly normal if they occasionally show up in your dreams. Or you have a little daydream fantasy about them."

I hadn't quite thought of *that* yet. "Thanks for putting that thought in my mind, Gina. Really appreciate it."

"It's happened to me. And you'll be close to him. It will totally happen if you don't go find someone else to date, and still might even if you do find someone to date."

"I don't want to date anyone." The very idea of getting back on dating apps or having to go out to bars or clubs or anything like that turned my stomach. It was so much easier to date when I was in college, when I could run into guys on campus. Of course, that was where I met Paulie and that didn't work out so well for me, either.

Yeah, I wasn't nearly ready to start dating again, and meaningless hookups were never my thing.

At least I'd packed my favorite, never-failed-me-yet toys.

"Then suck it up. You've got this."

I inhaled a breath, staring at my reflection in the mirror. I'd dressed to impress Amelia in a cute spaghetti-strap summer dress. The heat was still unbearable, and knowing her favorite colors, I figured she'd appreciate the green dress. It was modest, hitting me right at mid-thigh, and had ruffles around the top of my breasts and a flared bottom. It was cute, summery, not sexy in the least, and surely a sweet four-year-old would like it.

My hair was pulled back. The top half was secured in a cute bun and I'd straightened the rest of it. The humidity would frizz it out in no time, but for now, I was dressed and ready to go.

Back to where I'd practically burrowed my face into a grown man's chest and inhaled the scent of his cologne.

Nope. Nothing to be embarrassed about at all.

"Hey, Ruby?"

"Yeah?"

She peered at me through the screen. "Everything will be all right, you know?"

My chin wobbled and I squeezed my eyes closed. She was the only person I knew who wasn't snowed by Paulie. She hadn't hated him and the theft of all my cash along with the revelation of who he really was came as a surprise to us both, but she'd been there with me through all of it. Would always be there for me.

I opened my eyes and blew her a kiss. "You're right. I've got this. Thank you."

"Damn straight." She nodded once and then smirked. "But if you do jump your boss's bones, make sure you give me all the details because I've looked that guy up on Google and he is F-I-N-E, *fine*.

"You're a brat." I ended the call to the sounds of her belly laugh, laughing along with her.

Way to help me out, Gina. Now I had to hope and pray I didn't think of him when I fell asleep that night, in my private room... in his home.

No. I wouldn't.

There would be absolutely no thinking of bone jumping.

I was there for Amelia and the money.

No bone jumping allowed.

———

This time when I pulled up to Logan's house, he was not outside waiting for me. I took the extra second to steady myself. Remind myself that this was a job. He was my employer. And he was well over a decade older than me. And I was his player's younger sister. All of those things made my crush on him completely ridiculous.

I would never act on it. Would never jeopardize my job or Jassen's relationship with his coach.

I had this in the bag.

I only hesitated at the door, finger raised to ring the doorbell. Technically, I lived there. Did I have to knock anymore or could I just walk on in?

I pressed the doorbell. Maybe he'd appreciate knowing I was there instead of barging into whatever he and Amelia were doing. Logan hadn't specified what time he wanted me to return, just that he wanted me to give them the day together and then we could all get together for dinner.

It was five o'clock, early enough I figured he wouldn't have fed her yet, but when I left, Molly and Jassen were getting started on their family's dinner.

The door opened, and once again, I hadn't prepared myself for Logan Caldwell. Not nearly enough. And this time the universe had to be playing with me because he didn't open the door dressed in his typical T-shirt and shorts with his tousled hair and full gorgeous lips.

Oh no... this time, he was naked.

At least the top half, except for the kitchen towel slung over his shoulder.

"Uh... hi... I'm back?"

Logan's eyes, those dark iron-ore eyes, blinked slowly, and then those freaking great lips curled at the corners. "You don't have to keep ringing the bell, you know."

"Right. Of course not." Because I lived there and all.

He swallowed, and I followed the path of his Adam's apple, straight to the divot between his collarbones. The man *really* needed a shirt on.

He blinked and stepped back, but not before he took in my dress and quickly yanked his gaze back to mine. "Come on in. Amelia and I are cooking dinner. She's excited to meet you."

"Sorry. Am I overdressed? I wanted to impress Amelia."

"You're perfect." He cleared his throat and I jumped at the door slamming shut behind me. "Dressed perfectly. She'll love it."

He headed off to his kitchen and lifted a hand, swiping it across his forehead.

That meant nothing. Just a slip of his words. Or innuendo like I'd done the other night and didn't mean. Right?

"Right," I whispered to myself and slipped out of my sandals.

Leaving my purse and overnight bag at the door, I followed the path to his kitchen, where the most beautiful, gorgeous little girl I'd ever seen in my life was kneeling on the kitchen counter island, hands on her thighs.

She was dressed in a white, one-piece swimsuit covered in cherries and her hair fell all the way to the counter.

"Amelia, meet Miss Ruby. She's the friend I was telling you about, remember?"

"Yup." She nodded and grinned at me. And *wow*. I hadn't looked up Logan like Gina had, but maybe I should have. This little girl was absolutely stunning, and when she smiled, she flashed me a whole mouth full of little white teeth. Her mom had to be *gorgeous*. "Like Brownie, right?"

Logan coughed, covered it with his fist, and I was certain also trying to hide a laugh. "More like Nana and Papa when they watch you."

"Oh." She crunched up her nose. "Are you going on vacation too, Daddy?"

His smile that had appeared vanished. "No, sweetie. We talked about this. Daddy has to work, so you're going to stay with Ruby while I go to work. Remember?"

"I can go to work with you like I used to sometimes."

I stepped into the kitchen. "I can take you to your daddy's work sometimes, sure, if he says it's okay."

Her tiny pink lips pressed together, and she gave me a quick once-over. As she did, she frowned and turned back to Logan. "I'll go with you every day. We don't need Miss Ruby."

"Oh," I whispered, and *ouch*. Denied and brushed aside by a four-year-old. I looked at Logan for direction, but he was watching his daughter, as stunned as I was.

"Sometimes you can come, and sometimes you can come to my games if you want to, but I'm sure Miss Ruby will have you doing all sorts of fun things during the day."

"Like what?" She'd effectively dismissed me, didn't even look at me while I walked around the kitchen island.

Logan was swiping butter on bread and there were stacks of cheese nearby. On the stove, a pot simmered with something. I went for a subject change instead. Maybe getting her off the idea of not seeing her dad during the day would help.

"Are you having grilled cheese and soup for super?" I asked Amelia. "My nephew Luke *loves* grilled cheese."

"I like pizza better," she replied and twisted so instead of sitting on her knees, she was sitting on her bottom, legs hanging off the counter. The turn put her back to me completely.

So... this wasn't starting off great. I flashed Logan wide eyes.

He cringed and smiled down at her. "We had pizza last night, and we can have it later again this week and next time, we can make it here so you can do the dough, okay?"

"Can I watch TV?"

Logan's brows rose, but he set down the bread and knife and helped her to the floor. "Sure, Amelia. I'll let you know when dinner's ready."

"Not hungry," she murmured and ran off to the living room.

I waited until she'd grabbed the remote, working the television clearly not a struggle for her, before turning back to Logan.

"I'm so sorry," he whispered, peering at his daughter. "She's been great all day and we've talked about you coming. I don't know what happened, but she's usually so much more friendly."

I knew what happened. His daughter just had her mom go to Italy with another man and then when she finally got her dad back, another woman walked in. She was only four. How was she supposed to understand everything that had happened in the last year?

Hoping that was the case, I gave Logan a look I hoped was full of assurance.

"It'll be fine. Give us a few days to get to know each other and I'm sure she'll come around."

WELL, that was not at all how I wanted the night to go, nor did it go in any way I'd expected.

I finally tore myself away from Amelia at ten, hours after I usually put her to bed. She needed more books. She needed more snuggles with Dad. She needed another glass of water, and then she needed me to fix her sheets because they were itchy and angry. Eventually, she begged me to sleep with her, and since I hadn't seen her or hugged her or climbed into her bed in months, of course I said yes.

I had no issue with any of her procrastinating sleep. She was still in a new house, in a new bedroom, and was clearly dealing with changes she couldn't express. The problem was the way she'd treated Ruby all night.

If she wasn't scowling at her, she was outright ignoring her, and no steps Ruby took helped.

It could have solved my own Ruby problem. Clearly, Amelia wasn't responding to her new nanny. It gave me the perfect excuse to go back to the nanny service, find someone else, and get rid of Ruby, but I didn't think it was a Ruby issue.

I sensed it was more a woman-in-dad's-life issue, even if

Amelia was reading that all wrong. Vanessa and I had never been the kind of parents who wanted to give in to every whim, every tantrum, everything she wanted. We wanted her raised being grounded, even if she already had more than anything Vanessa and I had growing up. We'd always been aware of it and therefore took extra effort not to spoil her outside birthday and Christmas. Fortunately, she was four, and she didn't know any different, but that day would come and I hoped when it did, she'd understand her privilege.

That being said, if I gave into this tantrum now, I'd teach her nothing about adversity, unfairness, and even the anger and sadness she was feeling but not expressing correctly.

The problem was, I was going to have to leave her tomorrow with a stranger she clearly didn't want, and I didn't have the time to sit and talk with her more about any of this.

I wanted to do nothing more than go downstairs, grab a drink, and forget the night. Work wasn't even on my mind.

Unfortunately, Ruby was.

Through the night, her smiles had dimmed, her shoulders slumped. I knew she wasn't taking it personally, but Amelia had been so cold, Ruby had felt it. I at least needed to make sure she wasn't ready to pack her bags and hightail it out of here quite yet.

I knocked on her door. Light shone beneath, so I knew she was awake. She'd skipped off to her room before I told Amelia it was time to get ready for bed, and I knew it was to give my daughter and me time together. Thankful for it then, it hadn't been necessary.

There was shuffling, a quiet knock of something from the other side of the door, and then it opened.

Ruby stood in the doorway, hair pulled up and piled on top of her head, and to my utter surprise, pale pink glass frames were perched on that slim, perfect nose. She also wore an oversized T-shirt, and I didn't dare glance farther south to see if she had shorts on, or any that were at least visible. Her legs had been tempting enough in the dress she wore earlier.

I crossed my arms across my chest to prevent myself from reaching for her. "You okay?"

"Of course."

A lie. Obvious with the way she scrunched her nose and glanced toward Amelia's room before responding. "That was really rough. I wasn't expecting Amelia to be like that."

"You don't have to apologize for your four-year-old daughter, Logan. She's been through a lot in her little life."

All true things. That didn't make it okay. "Regardless, I'm sorry about that. Hopefully, she'll adjust quickly."

Her smile wavered, and doubt shone in her ocean-blue eyes. "I'm sure she will."

Her confidence matched mine, and I should have probably left, but after the night, I didn't want to be alone, worrying about how I was failing Amelia any more than I wanted to think about all the small comments she dropped about Vanessa. "Can we talk? About the rest of the week?"

Ruby's eyes widened and she darted her gaze to her bedroom and back to me. "In here?"

With only a bed to sit on? Absolutely not.

"Downstairs? It's a busy week, so I'd like to run through the schedule with you."

"Sure. Give me five minutes?"

"Perfect."

Less than five minutes later, I was sitting at the kitchen table, scribbling down not only Amelia's normal routine, but my schedule and all the numbers Ruby would need to know to get ahold of me. I never took my cell phone onto the practice field with me, so she couldn't reach me that way. It'd probably be better to print it out, too, or something, but I hadn't thought that far ahead. Hopefully, my writing was legible for her.

She entered the kitchen and went straight to the fridge,

refilling a water jug she'd carried around with her most of the night.

She took the chair across from me, and I didn't glance up until she was fully seated, legs hidden beneath the table. She wore the same oversized, pale yellow shirt she had on earlier, so large it draped off one shoulder.

No bra strap in sight.

I focused on my laptop and pushed the notebook in her direction.

"Wednesdays are the team's busiest and longest days once the season really starts. I know I told you I'd be able to get Amelia up and ready in the mornings, and I will most days. But I need to be at the facility by seven tomorrow."

"Okay. Can I have that pen?"

I slid it toward her. She scratched out something I wrote and rewrote it in her own hand.

"Can't read it?"

She glanced up and that pretty nose of hers wrinkled, making her glasses bounce on the bridge of her nose. "Your penmanship says doctor not coach."

I chuckled. "Not the first time I've been told I was better suited for prescription scribbling."

"I can get the numbers you wrote down. Those at least make sense. I'm assuming you won't have your phone on you?"

"Not while I'm on the field, no. In meetings and times like that, I might, if I remember to grab it, which I'll try to do for a while in case you have questions."

She scanned the sheet of paper, flipped a page, and when she looked up at me again, she was blushing. "Maybe just walk me through everything else again and I'll write it?"

"No problem," I said, once again laughing.

God, she was cute. And fun to be around. Once Amelia warmed up to Ruby, I had no doubt they'd become fast friends.

I shook all the thoughts of her beauty away and walked her through everything I'd already written down.

When we were done, Ruby surprised me by saying, "I called all the local preschools today."

"You did?"

"Yeah, figured I should get started on that, but you were right in that they're all full. I was able to get on the waiting list for a couple of them, though. Can I show you them?"

"God. Yes. Please." It was a relief. And impressive. When I asked her to call, I hadn't meant immediately. But a waiting list was better than nothing.

I pushed my laptop toward her, and she brought her chair closer to me. She leaned in, and once again, I got the over-whelming urge to dive my hand into all that hair. Ocean sunrises and salty air made my head swim, along with the idea of Ruby in a bikini that I couldn't squash before she froze, turning her head in my direction.

"Is this okay?" she asked, and God, I swore her voice was gravelly. Huskier than normal.

"Of course."

She bit her bottom lip, turned back to the computer, and *fuck me sideways*.

This was a disaster waiting to happen, and I'd gone so long with using my hand for pleasure, I wasn't sure I was strong enough to resist.

Two damn days she'd been in my home, not even, and I was already losing it.

This was not good. Not good at all.

I cleared my throat and pushed my chair back. A cool drink would calm me down, give me a second to get my shit together. I grabbed a glass and filled it with lemonade I usually kept on hand for Amelia. By the time I returned to the table, Ruby had put space between us again and had the laptop facing where I'd been sitting.

"I pulled up the three I was able to get on the waiting list. The first one is closest, but when I was looking at them with Molly, she and I both liked the third the most. But you can look and decide."

I quickly flipped through the open tabs and then favorited them so I could look more into them later. If she'd looked at preschools and had Jassen's wife involved, I trusted them completely. "Thank you for this, truly. It's one thing that's been on my mind and I really appreciate it."

She leaned back in her chair and gave me that blindingly bright smile again. "You're welcome. Now"—she leaned in, arms on the table, hands clasped together—"tell me *all* of Amelia's favorite foods and meals so I can get her to fall in love with me."

"Bribing my daughter through food?"

She shrugged and gave me a quirky little grin. "Seems to work on all the men I know, and they have the same mental capabilities as a four-year-old."

"Ouch." I laughed. "Damn, that's harsh. Those must be some men you've been around."

Her smile instantly fell, wiped to a straight line, and the light in her eyes vanished. "Yeah... guess so."

I'd said something wrong again. Something I wanted to fix, but before I could, she was standing from her chair. "I should probably get to bed. If you could leave me that list, I'd be grateful."

She was hurt, and it'd been something I said. And since I didn't know her well enough, there was no easy way to fix it. "I'll make sure I type and print it so you can read it."

There was a faint hint of a smile on her when she glanced back at me over her shoulder. "Good night, Logan."

"Night."

"Daddy!" I barely had time to crouch low before Amelia's body came slamming into me, arms around my shoulders. I picked her up easily with one hand on her bottom, still holding on to my bag with the other, and carried her farther into the house.

"Hey there, sweetie. Do anything fun today with Miss Ruby?"

It'd been well over a week. So far, she hadn't said a single nice thing about her nanny, and instead, changed the subject. In that week, Ruby looked more tired, sadder, but every time I caught the first glance of her, she gave me a warm and hopeful smile.

"Maybe today will be the day she cracks," she'd jokingly muttered to me this morning.

Apparently, today was not that day because Amelia pushed her lips out. "We did nuffin' fun."

I carried her into the kitchen and set her down on the island, where Ruby was wiping down the island counter.

Despite Amelia's unhappiness with her nanny, I couldn't bring myself to call the service and find someone better. Mostly because I knew this was Amelia's issue, and it wasn't anything to do with Ruby. On her part, my home had never been cleaner, my kitchen never smelled as good when I came home, and she'd taken to writing out a list of everything they did during the day, everything she attempted to bribe Amelia with, including treats from a gas station, a trip to the library, and many days spent swimming in Jassen's pool with his kids.

She was having plenty of fun, proven by the smiles she gave when Ruby took pictures of her when she wasn't looking. She just wasn't willing to admit it.

For that, and the fact I'd grown to like Ruby's company even more, I wasn't getting rid of her.

Ruby rolled her eyes and shook her head at me behind Amelia's back.

"Nothing fun?" I asked and grabbed the piece of paper on the counter. I scanned the list. There were always the typical activities Ruby did during the day like morning cartoons, coloring books, reading books to her. One day she'd taught Amelia how to make slime, and even though Amelia said she thought it was gooey and icky, I'd caught her playing with it several times in her bathroom before I went to help her with a bath.

Something caught my eye on the list, and I gave Amelia wide eyes. "You played in *dirt* today?"

She held up her hands, dirt still stuck beneath a few of her fingernails. "Miss Ruby said we needed a garden."

"Well, that sounds fun."

"She made me plant stuff." She crossed her arms and huffed. And for real, my daughter was so damn cute even when upset it was hard to fight the smile and take her seriously.

I nodded equally serious. "Sounds absolutely miserable and horrific."

"It wasn't *that* bad," she said, and almost like she realized what she was admitting to, she flipped her head around and looked at Ruby. "But it was not *fun*."

"I know. I'm sorry I made you plant a garden that will bring you lots of butterflies to chase when the flowers grow big and tall and full of fun colors. It will never happen again."

Had to hand it to Ruby. She spoke to Amelia like she wasn't desperate to get this girl to like her as well as remind her of what was coming. Amelia gave her a look like she didn't know whether to argue with her or not, and that alone was progress.

"A butterfly garden?" I asked.

Ruby cut in. "It's probably too late in the year, but they're perennials, so they'll come back next year, and when we were playing in the yard the other day, I felt sad for those empty garden beds. I also planted some herbs. Figured it's too late in the summer for most things, but you should still be able to get some fresh herbs out of it."

"Yes, I'm sure they're miserable too," I teased her.

"Boxes can't be miserable, Daddy." Amelia tugged on my arm.

I couldn't do anything right today. I kissed her forehead, set her on the floor, and waited until she ran off, ignoring the last remark.

"No better today?" I asked Ruby after Amelia disappeared up the stairs to her room.

"She was actually doing okay, laughing and being silly with me when we went to the store to buy the seeds and dirt, but Vanessa called when we got home and were preparing for lunch."

"Did you talk to her?"

"Vanessa?"

"Yeah."

"No, as soon as I saw it was her, I handed the phone to Amelia. But after they got done talking, she told me the garden was dumb and she pouted while we tried to finish it up."

Okay, so she missed her mom. That made total sense. "Did she say anything?"

"Vanessa said she was coming back here when her trip was over. Amelia hasn't wanted anything to do with me since."

"*Here* here?" I pointed my finger toward my own floor.

Ruby shrugged and pressed her lips together. "That's what she said."

"Damn." I rubbed my hand across my forehead. "I need to get ahold of her. I've tried calling, but with the time difference, it's been hard. She's called me back when I don't have my phone on me. I'll call her this weekend and figure this out."

I'd felt better after talking to my parents last weekend. They assured me they'd only stayed at Vanessa's house one night while she had a date. It'd helped relieve the worry I had about some of the things Amelia had been saying. Simple miscommunication. It had to be. But somewhere along the way, my little girl was getting the idea Mommy was moving back with Daddy, at least that was how it felt, and it always happened after she talked to Vanessa.

"If it makes you feel better"—Ruby smiled—"she didn't *hate* her French toast this morning."

Her favorite breakfast. Ruby had made it three times and every time she made it, Amelia told her it wasn't good and Daddy's was still better. The first morning I'd left them alone, she'd refused to eat it, saying she hated it.

I made it for the next morning, she downed three pieces, and then I gently reminded her she didn't *hate* French toast.

"Small mercies." I grinned.

Her smile stretched. "She has her first gymnastics class tomorrow. We bought her another leotard this morning and trust me, she liked that."

"Well, I haven't met a woman yet whose attitude isn't improved by a little bit of retail therapy."

Ruby laughed then. "You know us so well."

I didn't. Not women in general. And I didn't know everything about Ruby, but everything I'd seen from her so far?

That, I *really* liked.

"You two ate, I'm guessing?" I asked. Changing the subject had worked so far whenever I started thinking about Ruby.

"Macaroni and cheese, a while ago. I ate with Amelia."

"Need something else? I'm going to go change and grill some burgers."

"Please. And thank you."

It wasn't the first time we ate together, but only the second. Amelia ran to her room after I got home. I changed, made some dinner if Ruby hadn't made dinner and left me extra. Ruby usually took off to her room to hide then, too. And I knew she was hiding. As soon as Amelia was out of my sight, Ruby took that as her cue to leave me alone, too.

But it was getting harder to want that.

It was dinner and some burgers, maybe a beer before I spent an hour with Amelia before putting her to bed.

What would it possibly hurt?

CHAPTER 11

RUBY

THE LAST WEEK and a half had been a new form of hell I hadn't at all been prepared for. From the way Logan initially spoke of Amelia and her personality, I hadn't expected to go from being completely ignored to being treated like I was in the middle of a hostile encounter. She was a child. I understood that. But I wasn't sure I'd ever been around a child whose words made my heart hurt.

They were easy to brush off, but I was only seeing glimpses of the little girl Logan so clearly loved and I was beginning to wonder if it'd be best for everyone if I wasn't around. All things I planned to bring up to Logan when I could, but considering how Amelia acted around me, I'd made myself as scarce as possible, so I didn't upset her further.

And today's phone call with her mom? That had been a turning point. Amelia had actually smiled at me this morning when I brought up the idea of a butterfly garden. She'd shouted "*Yes!*" so excitedly I thought she'd forgotten she didn't like me, but she quickly smothered her excitement, shrugged, and went back to, "Fine, but my mom doesn't like when I'm dirty."

I promised to clean her up to make her mom happy and off we'd gone.

And then the call with her mom happened. The smiling happy girl decided dirt was stupid and flowers were dumb approximately thirty seconds into talking to her mom and Vanessa said, "I miss you too, honey, but I'll be back there with you and your dad soon."

My own brows peaked at the comment, the way she said it. It left me wondering if Vanessa was regretting not moving to be with Logan. No wonder Amelia was expecting it.

All of which was none of my business, and I forced myself to remember the money he was paying me. I couldn't turn it down and walk from Amelia quite yet. Couldn't go back to job hunting and not getting basic cocktail waitressing positions. None of them would pay as much anyway.

Which meant I was stuck in a house with a little girl who despised me, and her father who still made my pulse speed up every time he laughed or I caught a whiff of his campfire and cedar cologne.

Yes. A new form of hell, indeed.

Like currently having to sit across from Logan at the outdoor table where he decided he'd eat, with absolutely nothing around to distract me. I had a direct view of his tousled curls, his unshaven scruff, and those full lips. The stretch of his shirt over his chest and the low, deep rumble of happiness he made with every bite of his burger.

"So, outside the call with Vanessa from today, anything else I need to know?"

I shook my head and forced my gaze to meet his eyes, which was equally horrific to my pulse. He was so intense. So serious all the time. The few moments I'd made him laugh had felt like a birthday present.

"No. She didn't complain about the breakfast I gave her, and at one point she asked if I'd swim with her later."

It'd been a huge step for Amelia to invite *me* to do something instead of going along with whatever I suggested.

"Did you?"

"No. We were going to go after lunch and after we'd cleaned up from the garden."

Understanding struck and he arched a brow. "Ah. Maybe you could join us tonight."

And be around Logan while he wore nothing but swim trunks and laughed and splashed with his little girl?

My ovaries couldn't handle it.

"I think I'll—"

"Don't avoid us," he interrupted me, knowing exactly where that train of thought was going. "She has to get used to this."

"I know." And I did. "But that doesn't mean she isn't confused and doesn't want time alone with you. You *have* been gone from her daily for months."

He frowned, even if I'd tried to make that last part as gentle as possible. "You're right. I'm just... the season starting. The stress on my shoulders. I thought this adjustment would be easy and worry-free and it's—"

"DADDY! Swim with me!?"

Amelia barreled through the back door onto the patio in a soft yellow swimsuit with white stitching at the edges, towel looped over her arm. She didn't so much as glance in my direction as she ran to her dad, climbed into his lap, and brought her hands to his cheeks.

"Please, Daddy! Swim with me?"

He looked down at his daughter and kissed her nose. "Hey, sweetie. Remember when Mommy and I have talked to you about interrupting people? If Daddy or Mommy are talking to an adult and you have something to say, you say *excuse me*, and wait your turn?"

"Yep."

"Well, I was talking with Miss Ruby, and I'd absolutely love to swim with you, but we're having a conversation, so I need you to wait, okay?"

Her nose scrunched. "But I want to swim."

"I know." He spun in his chair and set her on the patio. "But I'd like to finish eating and then I need to get changed, so if you want to swim with me, you have to wait until Miss Ruby and I are done talking, and then let me get ready."

"It's okay—"

"Don't." He cut me off, holding on to Amelia's hand so she couldn't run off quite yet. His dark look was enough to have me stuck to my chair. "Interrupting is never kind, and I apologize for just doing that to you now, but Amelia can learn. Can't you, sweetie?"

He turned to her and smiled. She shrugged and brushed her bare toes over the cement patio. "I guess. Sorry for inneruping you, Daddy."

"You're forgiven. Want to go grab a popsicle and bring one out here so you can eat that while Miss Ruby and I finish up?"

"Popsicle before swimming? Yes!"

She ran back to the house almost as quickly as she'd arrived outside.

I nibbled the inside of my cheek. There really wasn't anything left to say, anyway.

"Hang out with us. If you don't want to swim, stay outside and read a book or play on your phone, but it does her no favors if she sees you hiding from us every night."

"I'm not," I sputtered.

I was, though, a terrible liar.

"No?" That brow arched and a flutter went off in my chest.

"Fine," I agreed.

Watch Logan throw his daughter around in a pool half-naked.

How hard could that be?

———

I pretended to read while I snuck glances at Logan.

I'd been right. Not only was watching him hard, but his entire body was also defined and hard. The way his abs rippled and his biceps popped when he threw Amelia through the air was enough to have me pressing my thighs together.

The water dripping off his hair, the way he shook it back all while laughing at something Amelia said made my toes curl into the lounge chair.

By the time they were done playing in the pool and Logan had ushered her inside after forcing a reluctant, "Good night, Miss Ruby," in my direction, I was ready for a drink.

Which was exactly what Logan found me doing in the kitchen when he returned, faster than usual.

Thankfully, fully clothed and rubbing his hair with a towel.

"Oh God. A drink is just what I need tonight."

He grabbed a beer from the fridge while I tried hard, so very hard, not to notice the way his shorts cupped his perfect backside.

"Amelia went to sleep that quickly?"

"She was yawning and tired. Kept it to one book. Any chance you'll sit outside with me again?"

Ahh... the first reference to the last time. If he could brush it off, so could I. "I promise not to fall asleep again."

He shrugged and bent down, coming back up with a bucket. He filled it with ice and while the clatter rang through the room, he smirked at me. "Didn't mind it the last time. Wouldn't mind it again."

Well, damn.

Good thing he was bringing all that ice. I'd probably need to dump it over my head. That is, if I heard him correctly.

I was still gaping at him when he turned, grabbed my bottle of wine, winked at me, and plunked the bottle into the bucket.

He winked! There was no way to miss that. What in the world was going on?

Next thing I knew, he was at the back door, sliding it open. "Are you coming? Or am I drinking this wine alone?"

Uh... he thought he could get me moving by threats of drinking my wine?

He was right.

I scurried right after him, directly into my next form of torture.

When did I become a masochist?

Tonight. Tonight I became a masochist because I was following him outside, and it had nothing to do with the bottle of wine he held hostage.

My phone buzzed in my hand. I glanced at it and promptly tripped over my feet as I read Gina's text.

Bang the boss yet?

"You okay?"

I jerked my head up, cheeks on fire from the visions that assaulted my brain at Gina's text.

"Yeah. Everything's fine." I waved my phone in my hand. "It was a text from my friend Gina.

"Oh?"

"Yeah, she is an interior designer out in Portland and was just asking me how everything's going here."

A small smirk grazed his lips. "Did you tell her you're working for a tyrant?"

I nodded as serious as I could be given the embarrassment still stinging my cheeks. "Absolutely, yes."

As gracefully as I possibly could, I dropped onto the couch in the same spot where I sat last week and once again pressed my feet to the edge of the coffee table. Logan was still chuckling as I took my first sip of wine. For several minutes, we sat in the peace of the outside. No noise other than the chirping of bugs starting to awaken for the night. It was peaceful, calm. And the exact antithesis of what was swirling inside of me.

The more often I was around Logan, the more I was starting

to really like him. He was kind. Generous. Nothing made him smile larger than his little girl. He was thoughtful. Passionate about his job. He cleaned up after himself and cooked his own meals. And he was so damn sexy every time I saw him, that first glimpse of him stole my breath. If I was writing a list of qualities I'd look for in a husband or partner, he'd check off every single one I could think of and still have so many I'd never considered.

And there was not a chance in hell he felt the same way about me.

Fortunately, I didn't pass out on the couch again.

Unfortunately, I didn't get to feel Logan's arms around me or have him carry me to bed.

We talked about the team. I asked him questions about the transition from player to coach. We even spent time talking about what life was like for him out in California and how it was different than here.

We noted a lot of similarities from moving from the West Coast to the east. When conversation stalled, I'd taken the rest of the wine inside and fallen asleep before I could finish a chapter of my current dark fantasy romance read.

I woke up rested, able to get in a quick workout in his home gym I'd taken to using while he was getting Amelia awake and ready in the morning.

"Well, I think that's the prettiest little leotard I've seen, Amelia."

Her lips rolled together. I was learning that was when she was trying not to smile. She glanced up at Logan, who was screwing the lid on his coffee cup, before heading out the door and he rose two brows at her.

She turned back to me, shuffling her feet. "Thank you, Miss Ruby."

But she didn't sound happy. And she didn't sound all that thankful.

I gave the same look back to Logan with brows arched and he nodded in the direction of the front door.

Following him there, he had one hand on the doorknob, the other holding his coffee, and he bent down and whispered, "I talked with her this morning about being polite even if she's sad or frustrated and that our words matter. Hopefully, that helps her get through the day for you."

I doubted it, but he was trying, and truthfully, she was thawing toward me. It'd only been a week, after all.

"We'll be fine, Logan. Get to work."

"Have a good day." He leaned in, and before I could process what he was doing, he was leaning back, and the burn of his lips on my cheek was searing straight into my brain.

"Uh." He blinked at me.

"Uh," I repeated.

Both of us gaped at each other.

Had he just..? "Did you..."

"God. I'm so sorry. So sorry, Ruby. It was just, we're at the door, and we're talking, and it..."

His fumbling and his own pink-stained cheeks made laughter erupt from me.

Oh my God, he'd *kissed* me like he was saying goodbye to his wife or something and how humiliating. How hilarious. "It's okay. Really. Go."

I stepped back and waved my arm toward the door, gesturing for him to leave. Could this get any worse?

"We'll talk about this later," he said, and he looked so upset, so mortified.

"We are talking about this *never*," I told him and put my back to him. I lifted a hand in the air. "Have a good day at work, Logan."

"Fuck," he whispered.

I was near tears.

He sounded pissed.

This was hysterical to me. Only the man I wanted could kiss me without thinking because he had me confused with... whatever... or whoever...

"Be good, Amelia, and I can't wait to hear all about your tumbling today!"

The door closed behind him, and Amelia popped around the corner to the kitchen.

"Did my daddy kiss you?"

And oh dear. She was *not* happy.

The hilarity of what happened vanished. "Sometimes friends give each other kisses on the cheeks."

"So you and my daddy are friends?"

"Yes, and I work for him."

Perhaps if I made it seem like no big deal, because I knew that kiss had been *no big deal*, even if the soft imprint of his lips was now a brand on my cheek, Amelia would forget about it.

Her round eyes narrowed, and she frowned. "I don't kiss my friends. But my mommy and daddy kiss each other all the time."

I was sure that wasn't true, based on what Logan had said about his marriage, but I certainly wasn't going to argue with her. Instead, I shrugged and headed to the kitchen to make my own breakfast.

"Mommies and daddies kiss too. And in some places, like France, people kiss each other's cheeks when they say hello and goodbye."

And could we please stop talking about kissing?

He hadn't meant it. It was obvious. The whole thing was... a slip of the lips or something.

No big deal.

And I was definitely *not* telling Gina or anyone about this. She'd have a conniption.

After I put my bagel in the toaster, I turned back to Amelia. "So tell me your favorite thing to do at tumbling classes."

"Are you going to kiss me?"

"Me?" I jolted and looked over my shoulder at her where she had her arms crossed over her chest, squeezing herself tight.

"Daddy said you were going to be my friend, but you don't kiss me like Daddy kissed you."

We *really* needed to get off the kissing train.

I crouched down in front of her. "I'd like to be your friend, Amelia. But we don't have to be friends *today*, and I would never kiss you or do anything you don't want me to do. But if someday you think we're close enough friends and you'd like to give me a kiss on the cheek, I'd sure like that. Okay?"

God, I wanted to reach out and touch her. Assure her everything was going to be okay, and all I wanted for us was to get along. Before I could think of the right thing to do or say, she shrugged.

"Maybe. Can I get my shoes on?"

We didn't need to leave for her tumbling classes for thirty minutes, but if putting her shoes on distracted her from any further kissing talk, I'd let her do anything she wanted. "You bet."

She ran up the stairs and while she was gone, probably making a mess of her room and digging through a bucket that held at least thirty pairs of different shoes, I slathered cream cheese on my bagel. Ate my bagel. Cleaned up the kitchen.

And I didn't spend a single second thinking of that kiss and how I wished it could have been real.

I KISSED MY NANNY.

I kissed my fucking nanny.

I kissed my nanny in the most embarrassing way possible, without thought, like we'd done it a million times before.

I kissed my goddamn nanny like she was someone precious to me.

I kissed my nanny... and I didn't have a single regret about doing it, except for *how* I'd done it.

And she'd laughed at me.

Laughed so hard I thought she was going to fall right over.

And yeah, okay. That *was* embarrassing and horrible and awkward and nothing breaks awkward tension like a good old laugh fest, but my *God*.

I couldn't stop thinking about it all day. The softness of her skin. The smell of that fucking salty air that was driving me absolutely insane.

All last night when she sat next to me, I'd wanted to move closer to inhale it better. The occasional whisper of a breeze that sent it in my direction hadn't been enough. It'd only started an itch I couldn't scratch. A desire I knew was wrong, but I was having a hell of a time fighting against.

And then I'd gone and done it.

I kissed the nanny.

What in the freaking hell was wrong with me?

"Hey, Coach! How's Ruby doing?"

Oh fuck. I dropped my head and stared at the turf beneath my shoes.

Of course. Of fucking course. Of all the players to hit the field first, I should have been prepared for it to be Jassen. He was *always* one of the first guys out here, and I'd come out here early to clear my head. Fat lot of good it was doing me.

I couldn't clear my head because *I. Kissed. The. Goddamn. Nanny.*

I kissed Jassen's sister. My player's sister.

"Uh... hey, Jassen. She's good. Real good. Awesome really. Wonderful." Fuck. I needed to stop talking.

He gave me a look that said enough words without saying any, most of them being *what the fuck?* "All right... you okay?"

"Yep." I grinned. Felt feral stretching across my face. "Never better. Awesome really. Yep."

Awesome really. Because I've never said that before in my life and now I've said it twice.

Get your shit together, Caldwell.

"How's Molly feeling?" I asked. "Morning sickness improving?"

The furrowed brows on his face, warranted considering I was acting like a clown, loosened. "Better. Yeah, for sure. Still tired and stuff, but she said Ruby and Amelia coming over has helped her some. They doing that again today?"

"Not that I know of. Amelia starts her gymnastics classes at some point today." I didn't tell him Ruby usually left me a schedule of what they had planned. She usually only noted the bigger things, so the garden yesterday had taken me by surprise, but she hadn't mentioned going to Molly's again.

Although again... I'd spent the whole day thinking of kissing my nanny and not much else.

"Cool. She like that kind of stuff?"

It took me a moment to realize he was talking about Amelia tumbling and not if Ruby liked her lips on mine.

"Um." I scratched the back of my neck. "Yeah, or she used to anyway. She's been a bit... moody... since she's been here."

"Understandable, though, right?"

"It is. Doesn't mean I like it."

His answering smile was full of understanding. "That's because you're a good dad and you care. But Ruby's doing okay? Has she said anything at all about Portland or anything?"

"No. Why?"

"Just a feeling I get." His gaze stalled on a half-dozen defensive players heading to the field. "She was dating this guy, and he called looking for her the other day. Said he couldn't get ahold of her, but I don't know, didn't sit well with me at all. She mention anything about that? Anything about Paulie to you?"

I was already shaking my head. Even if she had, if she wanted to talk to her brother, she would have. I was learning Ruby didn't keep a lot of things to herself. She'd insinuated being hurt or something, but I wasn't spilling her business if she hadn't done so already. "Never heard of him."

Which wasn't a lie, but now I knew who hurt her. *Paulie.*

"All right." He turned back to the field. "All right. Thanks."

"Not a problem. Go get warmed up."

"Aye aye, Coach." He gave me a two-finger salute from his temple and jogged off.

Perfect timing because the guy I needed to see the most was walking toward me, helmet in his hand held loosely at his side, red jersey on.

I glanced down.

Cole's ankle was still wrapped, beneath his shoe and over

and around the top, but I heard from the trainer this week it was healing well.

He hadn't fully dressed all week, and stress from the first game of the season barreling down on us eased at the sight of him.

"How's the ankle?"

He lifted his foot and rolled it in a circle. "Not bad. I'll stay light today, but Morgan said I can practice if I feel like it."

"Good. I'll keep you as a backup to Damien, but we'll make sure you get some reps in. You still working with him?"

Cole grinned. "Does getting him drunk playing cornhole last weekend count?"

"No," I deadpanned. But at this point, I'd take whatever worked. "Anyone on the team having any get-togethers before the game next weekend?"

This team was always together. Hell, Cole lived next door to Davis Hall, our team's best running back. Davis's wife had a baby last spring, and Cole's wife, Eden, was currently pregnant. Far as I knew, Davis and Cole usually rode in to practice together.

"Why? You want an invite?"

I wasn't usually invited. I'd only been to one and that was mostly to get the team used to being around, but player get-togethers were just that, for them. "Not for me. Thought it might help Amelia get to know some of the kids, though."

"She's here? Since when?"

This was when I missed being a player. I'd always had fifty guys around me, knowing all my shit. But as a coach, that circle tightened and shrank. And frankly, the other coaches and I weren't besties like the players tended to be. We were strictly coworkers who worked well together.

"Yeah." I scratched my cheek. "Something came up with Vanessa, so I have her for the next few months."

"Damn. Hard time for a change for her."

"Exactly. I don't need to come or anything, but if there's something, if I could stop by, maybe drop her off for a little bit... I figured if she got to know some kids, it'd help make her go to the family room on game days easier or something."

Ruby was working for me, but I didn't expect her to come to the games and sit with Amelia if she didn't want to. The woman had to want her own space and life at some point.

"Yeah, man. I honestly haven't heard, but hell, that girl could definitely use some friends. I'll see what I can do."

"Don't do it on my account."

Last thing I needed was to be known as some needy guy.

Cole shrugged it off. "Not much of a leader if I don't take care of the whole team, that being you if you need it. And kids are always included."

He slapped my shoulder and jogged off, straight to Dawson Butler, who was stretching in the end zone. It was less than a minute later when Dawson lifted his head in the middle of a deep side lunge and met my gaze.

One quick nod, and I knew Cole had already talked to him.

Dawson had trusted me when I was hired. He was still the hardest nut to crack, but that one nod meant a lot.

It was better than his scowls.

I refocused my head on practice. The team had already done their lifting and exercising, mostly on the bike to keep their limbs loose. And after we spent the next couple of hours working out final kinks, running plays until they became muscle memory, we still had hours of film to watch.

We might not have a game this weekend, but we had eleven days to be game ready at their champion level. Eleven days left to prove to myself and the team that management didn't make a mistake in hiring me.

I might not have any idea what was going on with Amelia. I might not be able to stop thinking about Ruby despite myself, but football...

Football was my life.

I could do this.

———

My phone pinged and I reached for it while I shoveled a mouthful of noodles from our team's Asian buffet dinner into my mouth.

One quick swipe of the incoming text and I was grinning and choking down my dinner.

Amelia's face lit up the screen. She was standing with her legs apart, one foot pointed out, one hand in the air and her other hand on her hip. Her smile was the smile I missed every day she wasn't with me and hadn't seen much of in the last week, and her eyes were bright. Sparkling.

Happy.

Another text followed.

She had so much fun at gymnastics. Teacher said she's so advanced they might have to move her up a level.

Tell my girl I'm super proud of her. Does she need a special dessert to celebrate?

Bribing her with food, Mr. Caldwell?

It was the same thing I'd said to her last week, and it was innocuous enough, but it was the Mr. Caldwell that made my blood race. I could see it. Ruby, on her knees, looking up at me, *"Anything I can do for you, Mr. Caldwell?"* while those slim, tanned fingers reached for my waistband. Her naked, legs spread, feet planted on my bed, while asking, *"Like this, Mr. Caldwell?"*

God. Damn. And after that stupid, silly, and ridiculous kiss this morning...

My dick was hard. I was hard in my office like a teenager

who saw a flash of cleavage for the first time and I was growing powerless to stop it.

Absolutely I am. I replied, because I wasn't an animal.

I could keep my baser instincts and reactions to her in check. For now.

At some point, I might blow it, but it wouldn't be via text.

She says chocolate chip cookie dough, but we can stop and get it.

I'll get it.

Ok. Oh... she smiled at me today. Twice. Progress.

Progress, indeed. Hopefully, once I talked to Vanessa, which I planned to do first thing in the morning, I'd be able to figure out the rest of some of Amelia's struggles, and the rest would follow much more smoothly than it had already.

Leaving work early. Be home soon.

Because why would I stay behind my desk, thinking of my nanny, when I could enjoy ice cream with her and my daughter and enjoy them both in person?

Yes, sir.

She probably didn't mean anything by it. Was most likely just being her sassy, smart self.

But that *sir*. God, she had no idea what she was doing to me. What she was starting.

Yeah. I was going home to my nanny.

———

The house was completely quiet when I walked in. A stark change from how it'd been all week, I would have wondered if Amelia and Ruby were gone somewhere, but her car had been in the driveway. After dumping three different flavors of ice cream and two fresh boxes of popsicles into the freezer, because I was a sucker for treats and my daughter was too, I went searching for them. There was no movement out by the pool, so I headed upstairs. I only went up there to put Amelia to bed. I didn't need the temptation of being on the same floor as Ruby any more than necessary, so I'd avoided the floor as much as possible.

But their whispers grew louder the closer I got to Amelia's room. A giggle sounded from far away and my chest swelled.

Amelia was giggling. With Ruby.

I was grinning as I pushed open the door to Amelia's bedroom, but it was empty. Not a single toy or shoe or piece of clothing in sight, almost like it was empty.

Had to be Ruby. My girl was messy. She could throw her entire toy basket across the room and step on it for weeks if we let her. Another quick peek proved they weren't there, so I left her room and headed back toward the stairs.

Maybe they were watching a movie in the theater room. Or in the workout room?

Another giggle and I spun back around. No, they were in *Ruby's* room.

I almost didn't enter. Shouldn't have, but her door was open, and I couldn't help myself. Outside the first night Amelia was here and we were all together, I hadn't even glanced in Ruby's bedroom's direction. I was laser focused. Amelia's room. Downstairs. No side-eyeing the bedroom where the nanny was doing who knows what, wearing who knows what in her bed.

I stepped closer, put my palm on the door, and when I found her room empty of the occasional giggler, I frowned.

Damn. Light shone from beneath her bathroom door. That was too personal, right? Too much of a boundary crossing?

Somehow, my feet took me in that direction anyway, and I paused before the door.

"Think my daddy will think I'm pretty, Miss Ruby?"

Something clattered on the bathroom surface. In her rich,

soothing voice, Ruby said, "I think your daddy always thinks you're pretty. Do you know why?"

"Cuz he's my dad and he has to?"

"No." This time, it was Ruby's giggle. "Because you *are* pretty. You have wonderful hair and very pretty eyes, but did you know it's not your hair or your eyes that make you pretty?"

"It's not? Mommy says she gets her hair done to be bootiful."

"Well, nice hair can make a woman feel pretty. Sure. But prettiness really comes from inside, in your heart, and how you treat people. You're nice to people, right?"

There was a beat of silence. "Most of the time, I think."

Another of Ruby's giggles. I should have backed away. Left. I should have given them this moment, but my chest ached to see the expression on both of their faces. I wanted to see the seriousness in Ruby's as she imparted wisdom to my daughter, and I wanted to watch Amelia soaking it up.

I couldn't without ruining the moment. Something had broken through with them today, and I needed to give them this.

"Well," Ruby said, and her voice was softer. Lighter. "We can't be perfect all the time, but I think you're nice. And I know your dad does. He says wonderful things about you and how you treat your friends, so I know you're pretty on the inside, too."

"Oh."

A moment. She whispered something I couldn't hear, but then there was Ruby's equally quiet, barely audible, "You're welcome. Now, blue eyes or purple?"

"Purple!" Amelia cried out.

I backed away and went back downstairs.

A few minutes later, I was in the kitchen when Amelia's thundering steps echoed through the large, vaulted ceiling and preceded her down the stairs and into the kitchen.

She arrived in a swirl of her body, arms flying out as she spun in circles, and a lime green tutu around her waist. Wearing the same leotard from earlier, she looked like two Skittles mashed together as she danced her way across the kitchen floor to me.

"Daddy! You're home! Did you bring my ice cream?"

I crouched down and scooped her into my arms. "Oh..."

Purple eyes indeed. And bright pink cheeks and light red lips.

Makeup. They'd been putting on makeup, one of Amelia's favorite things to do with her mom.

My heart hurt at the same time relief rushed through my body. She missed her mom, and Ruby was able to help her. Thank God I wasn't doing this all on my own.

In contrast to how Vanessa and Amelia would play with makeup, Ruby followed in Amelia's footsteps, much quieter, much slower. I was looking down at Amelia, so I noticed her feet first. Bare feet with teal-painted toes, I dragged my gaze up to say hello to her, and when I did, choked on my own laugh.

Ruby's lips were pressed together, eyes enormously round, and her finger was in front of her lips, telling me to be quiet.

My brows rose high on my head.

"Isn't Miss Ruby beautiful, Daddy? She let me do her makeup and hair!"

"She did a *great* job, didn't she?" Ruby asked and spun in a slow circle.

From the front, her ebony hair was perfectly straight, loose and long, but from the back, there was a maze of tangles and attempted twists, all pressed to her scalp with over a dozen, neon-colored hairclips and barrettes.

"It's, um..."

"I did it myself, Daddy!" Amelia squealed. Her feet kicked at my hips, and she pushed at my shoulders, so I set her on the floor.

"Aren't we both so pretty?"

Do you think Daddy will think I'm pretty?

Somehow, being pretty was more important to her than being beautiful.

I glanced at Ruby, then at Amelia. "Absolutely, honey. I think you're the prettiest girl I've ever seen in the whole wide world."

"And what about Miss Ruby? Did I make her look pretty?"

Ruby's hand came to her mouth to hide her own laugh.

Couldn't blame her. Amelia had definitely made her look *something*. It was more clown-like, but still.

"You did, Amelia," I said, and I couldn't tear my gaze away from the surprise sparking in Ruby's. "Miss Ruby is also very pretty."

I meant every word.

The blush that rose on Ruby's cheeks told me she liked it.

CHAPTER 13

RUBY

HE CALLED ME PRETTY.

He called me pretty in a way that wasn't amused and for his daughter's benefit. He called me pretty like he couldn't *not* call me pretty and feel okay about himself.

It shook me the entire night and was still shaking me while he was upstairs putting Amelia to bed. After that comment, nothing else was said. He barely looked at me while he grabbed the ice cream and he and Amelia both had dessert. He then sat and asked me to join him while we watched the live animation *Beauty and The Beast* movie together.

It was a typical, normal night where I didn't feel the need to hide to give them space and wasn't in a hurry to run off and hide from him. It was so normal, it was comfortable. Like I was sitting in my brother's living room with my own family.

Familial and comforting... if I could stop the runaway train running loops inside my brain, that was.

He called me pretty like he meant it.

Or the tension strumming between us every time he glanced in my direction. Which wasn't often, but happened, and I couldn't *not* feel it because I'd definitely been sneaking looks in his direction, too.

He kissed me this morning like it was second nature.

He called me pretty like he meant it.

I was stewing on the entire strange day, all over again, when he came into the living room and plopped back down on the couch.

"Seems like you should have taken Amelia to her gymnastics class last week."

He chuckled. He wasn't wrong at all. Whatever break-through I had with Amelia came after her class. Of course, she hadn't talked to her mom today either, so I wasn't holding my breath quite yet that the tides were turning.

I was walking in from the kitchen with two water bottles when he came down the stairs and I took one to him, setting it on the coffee table near him.

"Thank you." He didn't reach for his water. He leaned back on the couch, tipped up his chin, and swallowed. "We should probably talk about this morning."

We definitely should.

No way I wanted to. If I could go back to pretending to forget it happened, I'd be better.

"Before we do that, any chance you can help me get these hair clips and barrettes and pins out of my hair? I can feel the tangles turning to cement and if I don't get them out, I'm going to have to shave my head and I *really* don't want to do that."

Amelia had insisted I keep them in all night, so I couldn't do anything when she was awake. And when I tried to remove them on my own, I could only get out two before I learned the rest were knotted in there too tight.

"Sure." Logan chuckled.

Which brought me to my next problem. "Um... where do you want to do it?"

His brows arched, and I was pretty certain we had the exact same thought in our minds.

Shouldn't have made me feel crazier, should it?

Was this *man* attracted to me? There was no way.

"Have a seat, Ruby." He spread his knees on the couch and sat up straight.

Oh dear *God*. He wanted me in between his knees? His thighs that close to me. His hands shoving through my hair?

This was a bad idea. It had to be.

He smirked. "I promise I won't accidentally kiss you again, too."

A laugh bubbled free. "I thought we weren't going to talk about that."

"Figured we should get it out of the way." He gestured with a dip of his chin to the floor in front of him. My knees turned to jelly as his expression changed. "Come on. Do you have anything for your hair?"

I had a comb and detangling spray in the kitchen. "Yeah."

I ran to grab it, my knees wobbling and my heart thumping the entire time.

Oh God. Sit on my knees in front of him, where I'd be *so* close. So close to him. It was that or in the downstairs half-bath. Where he'd have to be behind me, and I'd be able to see his expression, stare at his full lips.

Facing away from him was infinitely better.

I returned, stared at the space between his knees, and quickly collapsed into it, sitting on mine so my back was to him.

"Well," he huffed. "This is quite the masterpiece my daughter made today."

I chuckled and cringed as the first sting of something stabbing into my scalp radiated through my head.

"Some of these are going to hurt," he said quietly, but he was focused on the task.

"I know," I whined and curled my hands into fists so I didn't reach back and make anything worse. "She asked if I'd do her hair because her mommy always made her look pretty and I couldn't say no."

"Of course not. Thank you for that. I can do basic pigtails and things, but Vanessa always took extra time with her."

"Yeah, well, after the nest she left in my hair, I'm wondering if it was her way of getting back at me."

Another hiss from the pain escaped my lips and I was most likely wearing off my teeth enamel from grinding them together.

Logan's hand curled around my shoulder, and he squeezed. "I'm sorry."

"It's fine. Keep going."

I was getting used to living with pain. Sure, it'd been my libido in overdrive this last week, but the pain searing through my scalp was cooling down that problem.

Logan went back to work, and every few seconds, tossed a barrette or hairclip or bobby pin onto the table.

Soon, the pile grew. There wasn't much to say, much to talk about, while he worked. He murmured his apologies and I kept groaning in pain.

It was when the final clip was out, and he sprayed the detangling spray in my knots Amelia attempted to braid that my sounds changed from winces of pain to groans of pleasure.

He was slowly, methodically working through my hair, but his fingers were pressed to my scalp, holding me still, and the comb felt delicious running through it.

Was there anything sexier than having a man's hand in my hair? I wasn't sure there was.

"Oh, that feels so good." I groaned from the sweet relief of the pressure against my head and then my eyes popped open.

Logan froze, fingers tense in my hair. His legs, legs I'd been trying not to stare at and failed massively many times, did the same.

Oh no. I'd made a *sex* sound. If I could bury my face in my hands and escape the humiliation, I would, but Logan went back to work.

"I plan on calling Vanessa first thing tomorrow," he said, and oh yes.

Talking about his ex-wife and Amelia was a perfect distraction.

"About Amelia?"

"More about what she's been saying to her so I can figure that out. Hopefully, today was enough to get her back to her normal self, though."

I grinned. His little girl had been absolutely *adorable* in her class.

"Let's hope. I was really impressed with her. I don't know a lot about four-year-olds, but the way she can already do flips and stuff blew my mind."

"Yeah. Vanessa put her in gymnastics as soon as she could walk, it feels like. She used to love practicing on her balance beam we have at our, well, my old house."

"You should get some of those things for her here." His fingers were slowing and the pain started to lessen. The comb ran through my hair with only a few snags. He'd be done soon, and I should have been preparing to move away, but I wasn't quite ready for it to end.

"I hadn't even thought of it. I'll look into it."

A minute later, he tossed the comb on top of the pile of discarded clips.

A breath rushed from me.

"Torture over," he murmured.

"Thank you—" I stopped, froze with my jaw slack as Logan's hands dug into my hair, my scalp. And then he started massaging my head.

"I think I'm good now," I rasped. My core was pulsing in between my thighs, and I swallowed a large cotton ball in my throat.

His hands slowly ran through my hair and he curled both of

them around my shoulders. He kept massaging. Kept rubbing. It was the worst stress-relieving massage ever.

His hands on my body did the opposite.

"Logan?" I asked. And nothing else.

"I promised you I wouldn't accidentally kiss you again." His voice was a whisper by my ear, and I shivered as his warm breath slipped down the column of my throat. "But I thought about that kiss all day today."

Oh dear *God*.

"I..." I had nothing to say.

"You can say no," he murmured, and his lip brushed the lobe of my ear as he spoke. His hands were firmer now. Thumbs digging into the nape of my neck made my head swim with desire. With the need to flee. He created an overwhelming sensation of wanting to lean back against him and see where this took us.

To trouble. That's where it would take us. Nothing good could come from anything happening between us, but as those thumbs kept working and the heat spread south, tightening my nipples and heating my core, making me grow wet, I wasn't sure I was capable of coming up with reasons why it'd be so bad.

"Logan," I forced out his name, and it hit the air like a whisper, quickly vanishing.

One of his hands slipped from my shoulder, to the side of my neck. His thumb pressed against the soft spot beneath my chin, and he tipped my chin up and back until I was facing him.

His iron dark eyes were molten lava, his full lips parted. And for the first time, I didn't hold back on the urge to push that wayward curl off his forehead.

His eyes feathered closed at my first hesitant touch and he licked his lips.

"You can say no," he repeated. "Tell me you don't want this. I'm not forcing you, won't. We can walk away from this and nothing has to be said about it."

All sensible, responsible options.

"I know," I rasped out and chose none of them.

I leaned forward, barely a centimeter closer to him, but he caught it and took it as the consent it was intended as.

The first brush of his lips against mine sent searing heat tumbling down my spine, almost choking me.

The second, firmer touch, had me twisting on my knees so I could get a better taste.

And the third time his lips brushed over mine, I was up on my knees, clinging to his biceps to steady myself.

"Fuck," he groaned against my mouth, and then he *kissed* me.

His hands cupped my jaw. His tongue ran along the seam of my lips. They parted for him, and I tilted my head for better access.

He might have moaned again. It could have been me. As he swept his tongue inside my mouth, against mine, the ache in my core grew painful and I pressed my thighs together to relieve the ache.

Logan's hands pushed back to my hair. Those same fingers dug right back into my scalp and he leaned back on the couch, bringing me with him until I was scrambling to my feet, leaning over him and then straddling his waist.

It was so quick, so fluid, and I was so lost to the feel and taste and the heady scent of his campfire and dangerous nights cologne, I barely registered the movement until the hard, firm press of his erection was at me.

"Oh," I whimpered, rocking against him.

"Shit, that feels good," he muttered and dove back for more.

We were clinging to each other, a mess of animalistic sounds and moans, and when I rocked against him again, my entire body shuddered. One of his hands dropped to my lower back and he held me against him.

"Take what you need," he whispered, lips pressed to my throat, sucking on that sweet spot that made my pussy clench and my brain sizzle.

"Logan…" I was clinging to his shoulders, head thrown back. Still rocking, but… "So close."

And I couldn't be embarrassed this was happening so quickly. I'd been on the edge for the last week and a half, too afraid to take care of myself for fear he'd hear. Or *know* his nanny was growing a massive crush on him.

Now, I was free to enjoy it, and with Logan helping me along, pressing his hips into me, yanking me against him, the swirling heat in my spine intensified at my sex.

My orgasm came fast, my body trembling, and I pulled him off my throat and slammed my mouth against his right as my climax hit. I cried out into his mouth, my entire body vibrating with the intensity as I shook and came on his lap like a teenage girl instead of his employee.

Oh shit… what had we done?

The aftershocks of my orgasm were still sizzling when I buried my forehead into the crook of his neck and cursed. "Shit."

He did the same, holding me tight to his body. He wrapped his arms around me and kept me cemented to his hard chest. I was drunk on this scent and the thunder of his heart beating against my chest, even as I knew it was best to move.

"I can't believe we just did that on my couch," he whispered against me, laughed, and when I sat up, he almost looked embarrassed.

If he wasn't going to freak out about this, my own could wait.

"You didn't…" I gestured between us.

"Later. I'll take care of that later, trust me."

"I can—"

"Another time." He cut me off with a hard kiss that left my brain rattled. The man could *kiss*.

Reality returned as I blinked, caught sight of us in the reflection in the windows, and I cringed.

We should not have done this. Definitely should not have done this out here. "Amelia was sleeping, right? Because I don't need another awkward conversation like this morning."

"What conversation?" Brows dug in close together on his forehead and his fingers at my hips gripped me firmly.

"Oh." I tucked a lock of hair behind my ear. After what had just happened, that silly little kiss didn't seem so important. "She saw you kiss me earlier. Kept asking me about it."

"She saw *us*? Why didn't you say anything to me?"

Gone was his racing heart and his possessive hold on me. He shifted, slid me off his lap, and stood so quick it gave me whiplash.

"Because it was nothing," I said. "I obviously knew it was a mistake and more instinct than anything. I said lots of friends give their friends kisses on cheeks. It was sweet actually..."

"My daughter seeing me *kiss* you is not sweet, Ruby. And if something like that happens, it should be *me* explaining it to her." He jabbed his finger to his chest and spat the words out with so much venom I was speechless.

My mind spun for entirely different reasons than it had been only moments ago.

A jump into an ice bath couldn't have chilled me down further and I stood from the couch. It took me a second to readjust the shirt he'd just so effectively twisted and wrinkled before I nodded. "Right. Well, then I'll make sure there's no chance of that happening again."

On legs that were still unsteady from that kiss and the orgasm and the whiplash after, I left the room.

I was at the bottom of the stairs when Logan said, "I didn't mean it like that."

I gripped the banister of the stairway railing and looked at him over my shoulder.

His regret was clear, but the trouble we could create if we let that happen again was, and I wouldn't be someone's dirty little secret. Not ever again.

"I'll see you in the morning, Logan. Good night."

MY DICK WAS STILL HARD. My hands burned with the memory of the feel of her body against me, and my brain would never forget the sounds Ruby Moore made when she came while trying to keep quiet.

I overreacted, and I hadn't taken a second to think, but with her body trembling against me while I was fighting off coming in my pants like a twelve-year-old boy who got his first glimpse of a stolen porn magazine, hearing my daughter could have seen us, *had* seen me kiss Ruby early, had knocked me off my feet.

Amelia had already been through so much. Seeing me with a woman was the last thing she needed in her little life, and I was a shit father for even making that first move with Ruby.

Shit. This had all been my doing anyway. I handled it wrong from the beginning of the night to the end. Hurting Ruby's feelings was the cherry on top of a pile of shit I started all because while I was playing with her hair, listening to her make those noises, my dick decided it'd be best for him to start making decisions. Between those sounds, her soft, silky hair, and the sting of salty air and beaches in my nose, I'd fucked up.

I went to go after her, follow her up the stairs before we could end the night like this, but giving her space was the right thing to do. I wasn't sure I was still thinking clearly, what with my dick still wanting to know exactly what she felt like. Going into her room *now,* with what we'd just done such a vivid memory in my brain, wouldn't be smart.

I was a father. Her employer.

It was time I started making smarter decisions about all of it.

Tomorrow.

Tomorrow I'd get ahold of Vanessa, talk to Amelia about what she saw, and heal things with Ruby.

Ironic how I was having trouble with all three women in my life and the only common denominator was me.

I huffed a laugh, scrubbed my hands through my hair, and turned toward my own bedroom. It wasn't nearly time for me to go to sleep. I still had work to do. Films to watch. Plays to tweak.

But I wasn't going to the bedroom to sleep, and I wasn't going to be able to focus on work until I took care of my own pressing needs first.

Water sluiced down my back. A smarter man would have taken a cold shower, but I was doing enough idiotic things, I didn't stop myself from soaping up my body. None of it erased Ruby's beachy scent from invading my senses. I could still feel her. Still see her as she lost control, the way she threw her head back and then used my mouth to swallow her cries. The way the heaviness of her full breasts pressed against my chest as I held her and rocked her against me.

Goddamn. I'd wanted a kiss, not a full-blown make-out session in my living room.

All of this had been my fault, from the ridiculous kiss in the morning to me forcing myself not to shove down my shorts, peel hers off her tanned legs, and sink into her.

In a room where my *daughter* could have seen.

Fucking hell, I was a mess. And still, knowing it didn't stop me from reaching down, wrapping my hand around my thick length and pumping. I slammed my other hand to the tiled wall and squeezed my eyes closed. Visions of ebony hair and starlight eyes assaulted me, made my thighs tense and my knees shake.

Ruby's smile and sarcastic little quirk of her lips when she made a joke played along with one of mine. The hopeful look in her eyes when Amelia was kind to her.

Goddamn. I groaned, already hard, so damn needy, primed from the way Ruby had used my dick to get herself off, and my orgasm raced down my spine, coiled in my balls, and I let loose, biting down on my bottom lip hard enough to bleed to stop myself from screaming out her name.

The pain mixed with the pleasure of finally allowing my own release made my head spin and my gut clench until the water washed it away.

Pressing both hands to the tile, I dunked my face in the shower's spray, dropped my head, and stared at the floor.

Tomorrow.

I'd fix everything tomorrow so we could go back to how we always should have been.

———

I hadn't slept. I'd done a bang-up job of tossing and turning all night. I'd only taken care of myself one more time, something that should have been medal-worthy considering the number of hours I spent hard, unable to stop thinking of Ruby. Not giving in every time my dick stirred with interest was my punishment for continuing to think about her that way, but somewhere around the time of the sun starting to rise, I gave in.

It'd only make the day worse if I walked out to the kitchen with another hard-on for Amelia or Ruby or anyone to see.

Besides, there were things to do, and since I hadn't done a lick of work last night, sleep would have to wait.

I climbed out of bed, threw on clothes, and headed out to the kitchen. A cup of coffee and then a phone call to Vanessa were the priority of my agenda. I didn't realize I wasn't alone in the kitchen until I headed to the coffeepot to find it already filled. Hot.

Barely empty.

"I was up early."

"Jesus." I gasped, hand flying to my chest, and spun to find Ruby at the kitchen table across from the island. She was sitting in the fucking dark. No wonder I hadn't seen her.

"Sorry. Didn't mean to scare you."

"It's all right." I probably deserved it, anyway. "What are you doing up?"

She hmphed, then went back to her coffee, staring out at the pool and beyond.

Right. Conversation wasn't necessary. I deserved that too.

I waited until I made my coffee, and put the whole milk I used for creamer back in the fridge before I risked it and took a seat at the table on the far end from Ruby.

She didn't glance in my direction, but there was a twitch in her nose, showing her annoyance that I'd stay so close to her.

"I'm sorry about yesterday. The morning and last night."

Her head tilted to the side. Her hair was down, twisted into two full braids, and all it made me think about was how soft it'd felt against my harsh and calloused palms. "Which parts?"

"Excuse me?"

"Which parts are you sorry about? The part where you fixed Amelia's rat nest in my hair, the part where you practically begged to kiss me and had me ride you on your couch—"

I choked on my first sip of coffee. "Jesus, Ruby…"

She continued, unfazed. "Or the part where you turned into an asshole after over an innocent comment?"

It wasn't innocent. Amelia had *seen* us, and I'd risked it happening all over again because as soon as I had Ruby in between my knees on the floor in front of me, I'd completely forgotten Amelia existed.

Based on the firm press of her jaw and the daring look in her eyes, correcting her wouldn't go over well.

"Definitely the asshole after part," I told her. She turned back to the window, shoulders slumping before I said, "But the rest shouldn't have happened either."

I tried to gentle my words, but I still caught the flinch.

"So you regret it." It was a statement, not a question.

Goddamn, I needed to learn how to be a better man and quick, because I told her the truth, knowing it was the absolute wrong thing to say. "No, I don't regret any of it, Ruby."

Her eyes sliced to me, cold as ice.

I continued. "I think there are a lot of reasons why it should haven't happened, why it should never happen again, and I don't think you can argue that with me."

She opened her mouth to do just that, I assumed, but I kept going because I was a dumbass who hadn't slept and couldn't stop myself. "But trust me, if things were different, there'd be nothing stopping me from throwing you down on this table, having *you* for breakfast, and spending the entire day with your legs wrapped around my waist until you forgot your name."

Her cheeks flushed, lips parted.

Someone needed to come kick my ass for saying all of that.

"And I don't regret that, either, as much as I should." I stood from the table and palmed my phone. I had a phone call to make and a mess to clean up. Hopefully, I did this next one better than I'd just done with Ruby. "But that doesn't mean I'm going to do it."

She gaped at me, long after I left the kitchen.

I felt the weight of her stare on me until I was down the hall, out of her sight.

And I still smelled the goddamn fucking beach.

———

One good thing about Vanessa being in Italy with another man was that it was the sole reminder I needed to erase the visions I'd so casually had and thrown out to make Ruby suffer right along with me.

I was not a good partner. I was not a good husband. I was too selfish. Too in my head about the things I wanted and enjoyed and not nearly thoughtful enough to take into consideration what was good for other people.

I steamrolled through life, doing what I wanted, taking care of me first.

The very fact my ex-wife, a woman I'd loved for a long time, was answering my phone call while on some sort of extravagant holiday with another man named Renaldo, was proof of that.

"It must be early there," Vanessa said as soon as she answered the phone. "Is Amelia okay?"

I didn't warrant a "Hello, how are you?" anymore.

"Good morning."

"It's afternoon here."

It was too early to do the math. Six hours ahead, seven? I always forgot and definitely hadn't been thinking about it before I called.

"Whatever. Listen, Amelia's fine, I promise. She's sleeping, but there's something I need to talk to you about. Do you have a minute?"

"Of course. What's up?"

My ex-wife was gorgeous. A cheerleader in college, we'd met through friends at a football party. She'd stolen my breath immediately, but it wasn't her looks that had captivated me from the first sight of her. It was her smile. Her laugh. She was friendly to everyone. I wasn't sure I'd ever seen Vanessa be rude to anyone, even after I started playing professional football. Money didn't change her or her morals. She was full of goodness and sunshine, sprinkling it in her wake everywhere she went.

It was why her trip, leaving Amelia so suddenly, threw me. It was also why I couldn't fathom the things Amelia said were true.

There was no way Vanessa had any plans to come back and be anywhere close to me.

"Amelia's been saying some things that have concerned me."

"Oh gosh. Like what?"

I scratched my jaw, pacing back and forth in front of my office window. The sun was just rising, making the lake shine as steam gently lifted from it from the heat. Normally, it soothed me.

Not today. Not with how epically I'd already screwed up.

"Well, she's made a few comments, even from the day I picked her up at the airport. Things like when you get done in Italy, you're coming back *here*."

I tried to stress the here.

"To the States? To her? Of course I am," she scoffed, like I was the one being ridiculous.

"No, Vanessa." I blew out a breath. "I think she's taking whatever you're saying and believing you're coming back *here*, to my home. To me." I forced myself to choke out the last part.

We hadn't ended on horrific terms. It was cordial. Probably the politest and easiest divorce anyone in the Los Angeles area had ever taken care of.

Through the phone, Vanessa groaned and then laughed. "Logan. She doesn't."

"She does. She's said the same things to Ruby, her nanny."

"I know who Ruby is, Logan. I've talked to her when I've called."

Of course. "That doesn't change—"

"I'm so sorry. Maybe we should have a family call or something? But you can't honestly believe I'd be on vacation with Renaldo all while planning on trying to get you back when I return, do you?"

I hadn't, even if the comments made me wonder. "I'm not a

four-year-old girl whose mom left for an extended vacation at the drop of a hat and whose dad moved across the country all in six months."

"Well, when you put it like that, it sounds like we've totally screwed up our daughter."

She mumbled the words in her quiet, playful tone.

"I just want to know what you've said, so I can help her understand."

"Nothing. I can't think of a thing. I guess, I don't know. I figured when I got back, maybe I'd stay for a little bit so I wasn't just showing up and whisking her away or anything. But I've always been planning on staying at a hotel. Not your place or anything."

"So you *have* told her you'd be *here*."

"Well, yeah, but not like that. I'm so sorry, Logan. I guess I wasn't thinking."

"It's fine." I ran a hand through my hair. "That at least gives me something to say to Amelia when she brings it up again. There's something else you should probably know."

And I probably should have clarified what the conversation about kissing had been like with Ruby and talked to Amelia, but Vanessa had taken to calling Ruby before they went out for the evening, so I had no doubt it'd come up later.

"Um, she sort of..." God, this was embarrassing. "She sort of saw me kissing Ruby. On the cheek." I quickly clarified, but now I was thinking of her cheeks. Of how it'd felt so *normal*.

"What? Logan, you're not—"

"Nothing's going on. It was a mistake. I was at the door, leaving for work. We were talking about the day, the gymnastics, and it happened. It felt like..."

Like I was kissing you. Like I was saying goodbye for the day to you...

"Oh..." Vanessa mumbled. "Well, that's—"

"Embarrassing. And dumb, I know, for a thousand different

reasons. But it sounds like she kept asking Ruby after I left why I was kissing her cheek, so I wanted you to know in case she brings it up."

"Well, what'd Ruby say to her?"

"Something about how sometimes friends kiss on the cheek."

"Well, there you go. No biggie."

It didn't feel like *no biggie*.

It felt like something huge.

It wasn't Amelia's reaction I kept thinking of when I thought about the kiss.

It was the fact I wanted to do it again. On purpose. And not only on the cheek.

"Yeah." I cleared my throat. "No biggie at all."

And shit. Vanessa knew me too well to not hear the doubt in my tone.

"Unless. Is it?"

"She's the *nanny*, Vanessa. That's all."

"Okay, then. When I call later, want to stay on the line so we can work out the stuff with Amelia?"

"Absolutely. Just text me first."

I could practically see her grin. "I always do. And, Logan?"

"Yes?"

"The nanny is *really* pretty, even if she's a bit young."

The call ended with her tinkling, teasing laugh I'd heard that first night all those years ago and couldn't resist.

This time, it made me want to throttle her.

I was not going to bang my nanny.

At least, not again.

CHAPTER 15

RUBY

...IF THINGS WERE DIFFERENT, *there'd be nothing stopping me from throwing you down on this table, having you for breakfast, and spending the entire day with your legs wrapped around my waist until you forgot your name...*

I couldn't believe he said that!

I couldn't believe he had the audacity to walk away without following through on it after he *did* say that.

I should have gone to my room and packed.

I should have followed him right to his office and told him I quit.

This wasn't fair.

He couldn't tease me and regret it. He couldn't throw out all those ideas that made my panties wet and force fantasies I'd spent all night trying *not* to have and then walk away.

The man was infuriating, and I'd already been thrown into a game with one ex I hadn't wanted to play. I was not *in the mood* to be invited to another.

Even if this new game sounded a hell of a lot more fun than Paulie's.

"Ugh." I groaned and grabbed my pillow off my bed in my room where I'd gone to hide as soon as Logan closed the door to his office. Throwing it across the room, I grabbed another one. Then a third. I tossed all twelve pillows on my crazy, beautiful, comfortable bed and threw them all around the room until I was breathless, head spinning.

This was dumb. All of it. Moving to be with Jassen. Leaving Gina. Letting Paulie drive me out of Portland.

I hadn't made a single smart decision in the last three months, but I was a smart girl, damn it.

I was a smart woman. I had a decent head on my shoulders. I wasn't overly cynical or naively innocent. I had a plan. I didn't *need* to be in Nashville, or staying with Jassen, to see it through. There had to be a different solution than this merry-go-round.

I would eat you...

Oh God. That familiar pulsing started. I clenched my hands into fists.

Screw him.

Screw Logan Caldwell.

He'd started this, and I was going to end it.

Games and hidden dirty secrets be damned, he had things to answer to.

As much as I wanted to stomp down the stairs to expel more of my frustration, I was aware enough to think of Amelia. So I didn't slam my door open like my adrenaline demanded and I didn't stomp down the stairs like a child throwing a tantrum.

No. I took a moment.

Gathered myself. I washed my face and slipped my hair out of the braids I put them in last night to hide away the pine and fall scent Logan's cologne had left behind. I changed out of my oversized pajama shirt and yoga shorts, and I slid into an easy-breezy, olive green T-shirt dress. It was modest, casual, and even though it was loose, it made my breasts look fantastic.

Ready as I'd ever be, I stopped outside Amelia's room to make sure she was still sleeping, even though I knew the girl loved to sleep and it took Logan at least a half hour every morning to wake her up. On a Saturday, she'd sleep for hours, yet.

I headed down the stairs, keeping an ear out for Logan. He'd gone to his office when he walked away from me, but he could be anywhere now. A quick peek told me he wasn't in the kitchen, so I turned down the hallway that led to his office, the movie room, and weight room.

His office was first, door closed, and a quick check told me he wasn't on the phone. I didn't bother knocking like I should have. Instead, I opened the door, slipped in, and closed it behind me.

He was standing at the wall of floor-to-ceiling windows, staring outside when I entered, and when the door closed, he jerked, spinning in my direction.

I settled my back against the cool wood door to calm my racing heart. A fruitless endeavor. I was already breathless at the sight of him.

"You're my boss," I stated.

"What are you doing in here?" he asked, without acknowledging what I'd said. I could understand the confusion. Hadn't stepped foot inside this room since I'd been in the house.

I ignored him like he had me and restated, "You're my boss."

His jaw ticked and he scratched at his scruff. "I am. But—"

"And I'm probably way too young for you."

Those dark eyes flared. "You are."

It came out as a growl and I watched with rapt attention as he crossed his arms over his chest. His own breathing depended.

"Ruby…"

"I don't care." I pushed off the door but forced my ankles and legs to stay steady despite the blood rushing to my head and parts farther south.

This was an epically horrible idea, but this time, it was *my* idea.

"I don't care about any of it. All the reasons why this is bad. I want you to do to me exactly what you described earlier."

...if things were different, there'd be nothing stopping me from throwing you down on this table, having you for breakfast, and spending the entire day with your legs wrapped around my waist until you forgot your name...

A shiver rolled through me before I could stop it, and I licked my lips. Goose bumps sparked on my arms, and I fought the urge to rub them away.

Logan was glaring at me. Jaw popping, tension tightening his shoulders. His nostrils flared and he shook his head. "Ruby."

I took another slower step forward until I was so close to him I tilted my head back to meet his gaze. And then I copied his words from last night. "Tell me you don't want this and I'll leave."

He cursed. Dropped his hands to his sides and clenched them into tight fists. Veins popped on his forearms, a map of power that vanished beneath the sleeves of his STEEL T-shirt. A map I wanted to trace with my tongue.

Indecision warred on his face, and it only increased the weight in my breasts, the slight sting of pain in my nipples as they hardened under his glare, and the throb at my sex.

I was desperate for him.

Desperate for the promised pleasure I knew he'd give.

Before he could back out, step back into reality and become sane, I asked him, "Are you planning on dating anyone while you have Amelia here?"

"No," he all but growled.

And it was so delicious my toes curled into the rug beneath my feet.

"I don't want to date anyone, either. Not since..." I shook my head. Paulie wouldn't be brought into this. "Not for a while."

"That doesn't mean this is right."

I took that last minuscule step forward and placed my hand on his chest. His heartbeat pounded beneath my palm and when I brushed my hand over his pecs, he didn't stop me.

"No one has to know. We can keep this between us. Just sex, Logan. That's all I'm asking for."

His nostrils flared, and his Adam's apple bobbed on his corded throat as he smiled. "Just sex."

He sounded filled with doubt.

My own was creeping in. Was I seriously standing in my boss's office, propositioning him? Trying to talk this man into *fucking* me?

I thought of Gina. Of her confidence and the way she'd told me to bang him. And yes, yes, I was.

It was perfect. I'd be a secret again, but one of my own making. I was setting the rules. And no one was lying here.

Well, except for the lies I was telling myself.

"Just sex?" Logan repeated, and this time, he was reaching for me. His hand settled at my waist and he grabbed a fistful of my dress. "You're okay with that?"

I'd have to be. I licked my lips and lied. "It's all I want."

Someday I wanted more, but it wouldn't be from him and it wouldn't be now. I had no misconceptions about that.

A wicked gleam sparked in his eyes. "Prove it."

"What?" My head jerked back.

Logan grinned, and it was so evil, so wild, I almost stepped back.

Until he stepped back, shoved his hands to his hips, and stared at my stomach. "Lift your dress."

Oh holy insanity. The floor wobbled beneath my feet and my lips parted in surprise as I gaped at him.

"You want me..."

"I want to see you." He quirked a brow, but there was nothing playful about the way he looked at me. "You came to me, Ruby, but this will happen my way. Now, lift your dress or leave the room. The choice is yours."

On fire. An inferno heated my blood and my fingers shook as

I lifted my dress. It scraped up my thighs, making me shiver, and then cool air brushed along the seam of my thong.

Logan's gaze stayed glued to the apex of my thighs and he didn't make a sound, a noise. He might as well have been a statue until I had my dress balled with one hand at my waist.

He glanced up. "Take off your underwear."

I was going to die. He was going to kill me. I had never been so turned on in my *life*. I had never known a man who could instantly take such command of a situation.

This was hot as hell and it was possible my orgasm could hit from his words alone.

This time, I didn't delay. With my free hand, I slipped my underwear off my hips and shimmied out of it until the pale satin sat in a discarded pile at my feet.

And still, he didn't move except for the tip of his tongue that appeared at the seam of his lips.

His eyes met mine and he gestured for the desk. "Go sit at the edge. I haven't had my breakfast yet."

My knees wobbled. I stumbled while standing silent and Logan reached out, chuckling darkly, and grabbed my arm before I could fall.

I had to turn from him to head to his desk. He hadn't told me to drop the dress, and I debated. Yeah, I had a nice ass. But this was a *lot*.

Still, it wasn't discomfort swirling in my stomach. It was excitement. Arousal. It was the bone-jarring realization that Logan was most definitely about to do things to me no man had ever done before.

A light click echoed and I spun, but it was just Logan at the door to his office.

"Locking it. You okay?"

I nodded again, my throat parched and my lips dry. As I settled my backside against the desk like he'd said, Logan walked toward me, tearing off his T-shirt, and oh sweet mother...

I'd seen him in the pool. I'd seen those abs obvious beneath those athletic shirts he wore to work.

But this... this was for me. And the giant bulge in his shorts was *because* of me. Oh yeah... this was going to be the best, worst decision I ever made.

The coolness of the wood at my backside quickly warmed, taking away any relief from the heat thrumming through my veins as Logan stepped up to me. I spread my legs so he could press his body to mine and gasped when he cupped my jaw with his large, strong hands.

"I'm not usually so bossy, but you called me sir the other day and I haven't stopped thinking about what it'd be like for you to obey me like that."

Combustion. I was going to explode on the spot right in front of him at the admission. He'd *thought* of me.

I swallowed, grinned up at him, and licked my parched lips. "I think I really liked it."

"Can I check?" As he asked, one of his hands drifted down my cheek, down my arm, drew small circles on my thigh with his thumb. "How wet are you for me?"

"Soaked," I admitted and closed my eyes.

He leaned in. Pressed his lips to mine and whispered, "Prove it. Spread those legs a little bit farther for me."

I took a chance. A huge one. Larger than the one I made when I walked down to his office. I did as I was told and whispered, "Yes, sir."

His mouth slammed to mine and his tongue dove in on another guttural sound that slipped from his throat into mine. He tasted like coffee and desire, and I drank him in while his hand settled on the inside of my thigh. He brushed his fingers up and down my thigh, making me breathless, igniting the need to move, to grind against him, but every time my hips rolled, his fingers moved farther away.

Until finally. *Finally*, he pressed a finger to my slit.

I moaned with pleasure as he grunted against my mouth and tore his mouth off mine. His forehead pressed to mine, and with our ragged breaths mingling together, we both watched him slip a finger inside of me. It came back soaked with my arousal and Logan cursed beneath his breath.

"So wet for me."

"More," I begged. My hands were wrapped around the sharp edges of his desk, digging into my palms, and yet I didn't let go. I didn't take what I wanted and didn't dig my hands into his hair. Didn't grab his shoulders for support. Didn't slide my hands over the expanse of his chest.

I took what he gave me, sliding that one finger in and out of me, ensnared in the fascination that covered his face while he drew circles around my exposed and swollen clit.

And then he pressed his hands to my knees, left me empty while he sank to his knees in front of me.

"Feet on my shoulders, Ruby, and make sure you stay quiet."

"Oh God," I panted, listened, and this time Logan didn't tease. He wasn't gentle and he wasn't slow.

He helped me get my feet on his shoulders, and I threw my head back, bit into my bottom lip as he leaned forward and swiped his tongue down the length of my slit, from front to back and front again to swirl his tongue over my clit.

And then he *ate*. He used his mouth to devour me in a way I'd never been touched before. He added a finger, two. He twisted them and thrust them with force deep inside of me before crooking his fingers all while his mouth and tongue did wicked things. To my clit.

It was moments. Who knew how quickly, but I was so primed, so ready for him, and had spent all night wanting him so badly, I came on a cry and clamped a hand over my mouth while my orgasm shattered me. He tore me apart, and that explosion I was so certain of detonated behind my eyes in sparks of pleasure that had to be inhuman. My thighs shook and Logan clamped his hands onto my hips while he kept *eating*, kept drinking me in, and bathing me with the desire he had to make this good for me until I fell back, slamming my elbow onto his desk before I collapsed on top of it and he finally, slowly, brought me back to the atmosphere, to our current state, and to reality.

I gasped, absolutely panting, when he stood in between my legs. There was no way I could move and his mouth shone with my wetness. The pain of my elbow hitting his desk was beginning to throb when he shoved his shorts below his hips and wrapped his hand around his hard, thick, and long dick that had a drop of moisture gathering at the tip.

"Lift your dress above your tits."

My hands trembled as I did, and then he was there, hips shoving my legs wide open, my legs wrapping around his waist, holding him to me.

Logan stared at me, gaze dropping to my breasts, my stomach, my sex he'd just destroyed for any other man, and pumped his dick with his hand. I licked my lips, watching how he liked it. Long, hard strokes followed by quick, shorter ones, focused on the engorged head of his dick. He leaned forward and slammed a hand to the desk right next to my head.

I twisted and kissed the inside of his wrist, all while keeping my eyes on that gorgeous, swollen dick and when he grunted, I tore my eyes back to his.

"What the fuck are you doing to me?" he groaned, came, and his seed splashed all over my stomach and my breasts.

He stayed that way, gathering his breath, and it gave me time to gather my own senses. He released his dick, gently curled his hand around my hip, and smiled up at me. "You okay?"

I was. I was more than okay, all while being terrified.

I had started this. I had wanted this.

But could I live with the consequences?

"I'm all right," I finally whispered.

"Good." Logan grinned, squeezed my hip, and brushed his mouth over mine. "Because we are definitely doing that again."

I laughed against his mouth and soon we were both chuckling. At least, until we glanced down and saw the drying mess he'd made all over my stomach.

"Um. Do you have tissues or anything? Because I was really hoping to wear this dress today."

Logan glanced around. "Shit. Stay here."

He quickly dressed, left the office, peeking down the hall, and in the seconds he was gone, worry hit me.

Would that reality slam back into him? He'd just had sex with the nanny, been completely inappropriate while his daughter slept upstairs.

I prepared for the rejection that could come, but when Logan came back into the office and locked the door, he wore a sheepish smile and carried a towel.

"You still okay?"

He came to me as he asked and began cleaning my skin.

"I'm good. You?"

"I think this is a really bad idea, but I don't want to stop."

A valve released the pressure gathering in my chest and I grinned, able to sit up again, and covered my lap with my dress. "Same."

"We'll need to keep it hidden from Amelia."

"I agree."

"And your brother—"

I lifted a hand and stopped him right there. "My brother never has and never will know *anything* about my sex life."

His phone rang, screen lit up on his desk.

"Speak of the devil." Logan's face paled as he reached for it. "Hey, Jassen? What's up?"

"Hey, sorry to call you, but is Ruby around? I tried calling her, but she didn't answer. Is she sleeping?"

We were close enough I could hear every word my brother spoke, close enough to watch the fear slack Logan's features.

"Um. Not sure? I've been in my office."

I pressed my lips together and gave him wide eyes.

"Oh. All right. Well, I can tell you. Talked to Cole last night and since Molly's feeling okay, we're going to host a Labor Day party. Thought you being there with Amelia wouldn't be weird if Ruby was there, too. That cool?"

A party? Labor Day? My brows furrowed. Logan reached out and smoothed away my confusion with his thumb.

"Sounds good, Jassen. We'll be there."

He hung up and stared at his phone. "Thank God he didn't call five minutes earlier."

I burst into a laugh, and Logan's own chuckle followed.

"A party?"

He grinned, shameless. "Want to be Amelia's and my date?"

His smile faltered as the words registered. It wasn't a date. I was the nanny. Logan and I would never have a date.

I pushed through the unease and smiled back, jumped off the desk and kissed him. "You bet I will."

LOGAN

AS SOON AS Ruby stepped into my office, I was sucked into a vortex, completely consumed with her. As soon as she said she didn't care that she was my nanny, and that we could keep this *thing* between us just sex, a switch I hadn't known that existed inside of me flipped on for the first time.

Maybe it was the fact she was younger. Maybe it was because she was my employee. But watching Ruby follow my commands, strip for me, and hold her dress and spread her legs all because I *told* her to?

It was the hottest sexual encounter of my life, and that had been before I touched her.

Now, I was standing there, staring at her, while we ate a *real* breakfast back in the kitchen and waited for Amelia to wake up.

I was simply going to ignore the fact I was fucking a woman I paid, in the house where my daughter slept. She'd never know. We'd be careful.

"You're kidding me," I told her. "After what we did in there and decided, you're leaving?"

I had my finger shoved in the direction of my office.

Ruby reached across the island and pushed my arm down.

"Calm yourself. I was planning on giving you and Amelia the weekend alone anyway."

Well, yeah. That was always the plan. But that was before. Before I got lost in between her thighs and tasted her. If I didn't have to be a dad, I would have spent all weekend doing that over and over and over again.

Now she was taking that away from me. I didn't know whether to pout like a child not getting a toy or demand she stay. Given how well she obeyed earlier, I figured there was a fifty-fifty chance she would laugh in my face.

"You only have so many weekends with her, Logan."

"I know that, but you said... wait. Are you sure that you're okay with what happened? You're not leaving to avoid this, are you?"

"No." She laughed and shook her head. "And I know Jassen said on the phone that Molly's feeling better, but they're now apparently having some party."

"Yeah." Me and my big damn mouth. "That one's on me."

"What do you mean?"

"I asked Cole if anyone was getting together this weekend. Thought it'd be good for Amelia to meet other players' and coaches' kids before the season. He said he'd figure something out."

"Well, then this is your own fault, isn't it?" She wadded up her napkin and tossed it. I caught it easily and tossed it right back at her.

She batted it away.

"You can go over early on Monday to help set up or some-thing." I was starting to pout. How ridiculous. I'd gone seven months without sex and now I was whining because I wouldn't get to eat pussy for three full days.

"I'll go after lunch, and you'll survive."

She came to me then, glancing toward the stairs and the hall to double-check before she leaned in. "Is this okay?"

The kiss? The risk?

We'd said sex not playful kisses and teasing in my kitchen. I didn't care.

"Yes," I grunted and hauled her to me when her lips pressed against mine. "Leave me for the weekend if you must, but you better be prepared and rested up for when you get back Monday. I'm going to spend all weekend thinking of ways I can torture you for this."

She shivered in my arms and winked. "Yes, sir."

It was playful. It still stirred something in me. Made my dick perk up.

Damn her for teasing me and leaving me. I slapped her ass and let her go, moving back to my breakfast.

It was two and a half days.

I'd be fine without Ruby. Without her smiles and her body and her moans and kisses.

I was fine without a woman for months. A whole weekend was nothing.

———

Vanessa wiped tears off her cheeks, and I dropped my head into my hand, groaning. "Well, that went well."

Outside, Amelia was curled into a ball on the lounge chair. Feet pulled up to her bottom, head dropped to her knees. Her little arms were wrapped around her shins, holding her together.

Of course she had to hold herself together. Her mom and I had broken her.

"I'm so sorry. I honestly had no idea she was getting those ideas from the things I said." Vanessa sniffed and blotted her cheeks.

The family Zoom call had *not* gone well. Started when Amelia asked when her mom was going to say goodbye to

Renaldo and ended with us explaining, as gently as possible, that Mommy and Daddy were not going to live together again.

"I want you both!" she'd screamed and then had run out the door.

"I can come back and see her, at least spend some time with her."

I was staring at my daughter. I hadn't yet found a fence company to come put a safety one around the edge of the pool and with Amelia's state, I didn't trust her not to do something dangerous like fling herself into the pool without her swimmies on.

"I think that would only confuse her right now, don't you?"

"Like I have a clue. See what I've already done to her?"

In all fairness, my job and my decisions had *done* this. I faced Vanessa and shrugged. "I think we can both agree it's not you who did this to her."

"Whatever. We worked until we didn't. I should have had a care for her, though. She cried for five straight days when you left. I should have anticipated this happening."

"Thank you, Vanessa. Rub salt in the wound, please."

She rolled her eyes. "That's not what I meant and you know it."

"I know." I wanted someone to lash out at, though. Someone to blame for making my daughter cry.

Unfortunately, that person was me.

God, I was fucking screwing this up.

"So what now?" I asked.

I could at least *solve* the problem instead of continuing to dwell on it.

The only good thing to come out of this conversation was knowing where Vanessa stood with certainty. The morning conversation had helped, but hearing her apologize to Amelia cemented it. She wasn't trying some sneaky way to see if we could work things out. She'd simply said a few things that allowed a little girl to have hope.

And we crushed it.

Awesome. We were awesome at this parenting thing.

"I'll be more cautious with my words," Vanessa assured me. "And I'll call her more often if you think that would help. I know she's so little, but can you get her an iPad or something that's just hers so we don't have to keep communicating through your phone or Ruby's? Something that's hers so she can talk to me whenever she wants? And you too, of course?"

"We'd always agreed no electronics until she was older."

Vanessa gave me a sad smile. "We always used to agree on a lot of things."

"Ouch." Damn. She hadn't been trying to be harsh, but the accusation slammed into me like a pile of bricks anyway.

She pressed her lips together. No apology for it, and I shouldn't have expected it. She was right. We used to agree on a lot of things.

I changed the game on her and she adjusted to the new plays.

"It's not a bad idea," I finally admitted. She could call my parents whenever she wanted to, and Vanessa's sister and brother in California. She missed their kids, who were around her age. "We should have thought of it earlier."

"Things change, we adapt."

"Wow." I looked back at Amelia and grinned. "You are so much more chill now than you used to be."

"Oh fuck off"—she laughed—"that's fighting words and you know it."

I did. But we were laughing. And it felt good. I hurt Vanessa. She hurt me, but we'd found common ground in order to get past that.

That common ground was now sitting on the chair, legs

crossed and hands in her lap. Her gaze was on a canoe moving slowly along the edge of the lakeshore.

Something I'd promised her.

I held up my hands, palms out. "I cede this round. I'll get Amelia an iPad and will let you know when it's set up and everything."

"Wow." She stuck out her tongue. "Look at you, being so reasonable these days."

"Brat," I teased her right back. "Have fun with Renaldo."

"Oh, I do…"

I gagged. No man needed to have innuendo tossed his way about his ex's sex life. "Too far and you know it."

"I'll call Amelia tonight to check in. Is that okay?"

"We'll be here."

But first, we had some serious shopping to do.

———

Amelia went ballistic, bouncing off the walls of the house and then in her booster seat when I brought up the idea of going to buy a boat. We stopped at REI first since it was closest, and the salesperson suggested a kayak might be easier for her to help paddle. They were easier to maneuver and lighter to move in the water, especially the paddles. They were out of stock on two-person kayaks, so we filled up the bed of my truck with a half-dozen other items, including inflatable stand-up paddleboards and paddles. Four life jackets for adults and a couple for Amelia. When I mentioned my part of the lake shore didn't have a dock yet, the guy took us to their floating lounge docks.

"Not for permanent use, obviously, but they can be secured to the lake floor with an anchor. Gives you a little bit better access to the water and might make it easier to board the kayak. Can always be pulled up and out of the water if you want it."

The floating dock was eight feet by twelve. Plenty of room.

So the floating dock went into the cart as well. Along with ropes and anchors to hold it in place.

It was when we were in the truck on the way to the Bass Pro Shops on the northern edge of Nashville when Amelia stunned me.

"Why did you buy three paddleboards, Daddy? When there are only two of us?"

"What?"

"Three boards. You bought three of them."

Had I? I had. I'd bought three because, throughout the store, I kept thinking of the way Ruby always sat facing the lake for her morning cup of coffee. Because the two times we'd had drinks outside on the patio, her gaze always drifted to the lake. Because when I was splashing in the pool the other night with Amelia and I convinced Ruby to stay outside with us, she'd set down her phone and stared at the still water. And when I thought of paddleboarding, I envisioned Ruby out there with us.

And if I was being completely honest with myself, I'd bought the teal blue life jacket because it reminded me of the ocean.

It was four hours since Ruby left our house to head to her brother's and my thoughts were consumed with her.

"Well, if one gets a hole or something, we need an extra." I lied to Amelia for her benefit. Not mine.

I hadn't even realized I'd bought the damn thing. Somehow, I included her in my life and with activities with my daughter like it was the most natural thing.

It wasn't natural, it was dangerous.

She was leaving at some point to go off and chase her own dreams, meet her own needs.

I had my own list of needs to take care of. Raise Amelia. Win football games. Earn the trust and respect of not only my team, but other coaches and teams in the league.

I didn't need to be consumed with a young woman who

would eventually leave both of us. What we were doing was fun, not permanent. It'd be best if I remembered that.

We drove to Bass Pro Shops, and like she'd done before, Amelia unbuckled herself from her car seat and hopped out of the truck before I could get to her.

I took her hand and reminded her, "You need to stay with Daddy, okay? This store is big and I can't have you running off."

"Okay, Daddy!"

I gave her promise an entire thirty seconds.

As soon as we walked inside, Amelia's jaw dropped and excitement relit in her eyes. "Boats! Look!" She pointed out some fishing boats. Way too big for us and probably too big for the lake we were on. "Can we go see them?"

Climbing wouldn't help anything. I took her over and helped her climb up one of the ladders to get inside. She ran straight to the captain's chair and pretended to steer the boat.

I pulled out my phone and took a picture and sent it to Vanessa.

Seeing her daughter smile after the tears that ended her conversation would make her feel better.

"Good afternoon. Can I help y'all?" A salesman, Steve stamped on his nametag, sauntered up to us.

"I want a boat!" Amelia cried out from her spot in the driver's seat. Not too far off in reality.

"We're looking. Came to get a kayak."

"And fishing stuff! We can go fishing too, right, Daddy? Papa says he loves fishing!"

I turned back to the salesman. "We're here for a kayak and fishing supplies, but I think we'll wait on boats for a bit."

"Sounds good. Let me help you get started. Name's Steve."

He held out his hand and I shook it. "Logan. Thanks for the help."

His eyes flared with recognition before he stumbled back. "Happy to help, sir."

I shouldn't have been surprised. It hadn't happened that often, but I wasn't wearing a hat to hide myself and I'd been plastered all over local and national news for the last month. Critics were gearing up to tear me down. Fans were ready to build a shrine or waiting to bury me six feet deep.

"Amelia, let's go get your kayak. Come here." She jumped out of her chair and climbed down the ladder. I swung her down the last two rungs and held her hand.

"You're the new coach," Steve said, and his voice had turned shaky.

Definitely a fan of the team. "Yep. Happy to be here, too."

"Well, shit." He flinched. "Sorry. My bad. But this is exciting. Glad I can be the one to help you out today, Mr. Caldwell."

"Daddy, how does the man know your name?"

I opened my mouth to explain, in the way I usually did. *Daddy has a job and sometimes he's on TV, but he helps football teams play better.* At least, I tried.

Steve beat me to it. "Well, how couldn't I, pretty little lady? Your daddy here is the best football coach Nashville's seen. We're going to be winning lots of games with him at the helm."

Her blond brows furrowed. "What's a helm?"

"It means he guides the boat safely," Steve explained with a smile that said he was used to kids and their questions.

Amelia looked up at me and frowned. "But you don't have a boat and you play football."

"That I do, sweetie. That I do."

"Then how can—"

"Kayaks," I said loudly. Too loudly. Steve hid his laugh behind a cough and Amelia forgot about helms and boats, racing to the bright yellow, two-person kayaks hanging vertically along a wall.

"That one!" she cried. "I like that one cuz it's got seats so we don't fall out and sink."

I turned to Steve. "We'll take that one."

After getting us set up with paddles, two larger ones for adults and a lighter, shorter one that would work for Amelia, she then raced down the aisle where the fishing poles were.

"Look, Daddy! A *Tangled* pole!"

She shouted so loud, men in the aisle frowned at her noise. My glare had them returning to their business, but I still walked up to Amelia and reminded her of her inside voice.

"But it's *Tangled*," she whined in a half-whisper, half-shout. "Can I get it?"

She'd been right earlier that my dad loved to fish. His father had lived on a lake and we'd taken family vacations there all the time. I hadn't been fishing in twenty years and I had no idea if the lake we were on was even stocked with fish. Hadn't actually considered I'd have the time to enjoy it much during the season.

I still pulled my phone out of my pocket, pulled up Dad's number, and when he answered, I asked, "Hey, Dad. Amelia and I are at the store looking at fishing gear. Got any advice on what we need?"

My dad's voice boomed with happiness almost as loudly as Amelia had earlier.

At least I knew where she got it from.

Steve left me to the phone call but stayed close in case we had questions.

Thirty minutes later, we walked out of the store with a kayak and extra paddles. Fishing poles for a small army. We had two tackle boxes, a *Frozen* one for Amelia that clashed with her *Tangled* pole, but I was smart enough to keep my mouth shut. We had lures and spinners and fake worms and grubs for bait along with bobbers and weight sets. I'd thrown in gloves and pliers.

Our drive home had the kayak tied and strapped to the truck bed, the rest of it filled with everything else we had.

"I need more swimsuits," Amelia said as we drove down a street near our house and she caught sight of the Target sign.

"You have plenty."

"Both those are for the pool, not the lake."

Duh, Dad, might as well have been tacked on to the end of that sentence.

"Please? My pool suits can't get lake stuff on them."

She was smarter than I gave her credit for. Although Vanessa was the one who gave her the Target obsession.

I caught her gaze through the rearview mirror. She was smiling. Huge. She'd been happy all day. I knew it was temporary. She'd pushed down the anger and hurt from our talk earlier and that was sure to resurface all over again at some point.

But for right then, I'd do anything to keep that smile on her face.

So we went to Target.

I didn't buy her a swimsuit for the lake.

I bought her five.

And I would have bought her twelve if she'd asked.

———

I was dragging the kayak through the grass. I also had one of the paddles and two life vests strung on my arm. Next to me, Amelia was dragging her smaller paddle, huffing and puffing from the hard work.

Once we got home, I told her we could go on the lake if we let the dock and boards sit until after dinner or tomorrow so we could blow them up. They'd take too long and I'd rather our first outing be on the boat, not a board where I had to balance her and me both, while standing... something I'd never done before and wasn't all that excited about trying.

She'd been so happy about her new swimsuits, she hadn't cared, and while I unhauled everything into the garage, she ran inside and changed.

She came out in a white one-piece suit with small blue anchors on it, and a fist pumped in the air. "Ahoy, matie!"

Ruby's nephew Luke was in a pirate phase, so it wasn't the first time she used it. Just the first time she did it looking so cute with her hair in pigtails and the anchors stamped all over her.

"I need some help, matie," I'd told her.

Now we were almost at the water's edge, and I was dripping in sweat.

"This paddle is too heavy. You hold it."

She pushed it into me like I had an extra limb somewhere. I juggled the paddle and vests and the handle of the kayak and grabbed it.

"Good idea. How about you go scope out the best place for us to get on the boat."

"It's a kayak."

Right, right. My bad.

She scampered off. I cursed my decision to buy such a big yard. Dragging all this gear down the acre-plus of my property was a pain in my ass. If we kept this up, I was going to need a shed or something down here to store everything in. Lot of fucking work I was planning when I wasn't going to be living here the whole year. All the doubts washed away with Amelia's smile. She was crouched down at the edge, peering down in the lake, and when I reached her, she grinned up at me.

"Look. Baby fishes! We can fish here!"

I'd told her in the store I didn't even know if the lake had fish, but baby fishes were definitely a good sign.

"That's great, honey. Put your life jacket on, okay?"

"You bet! I'm so excited. This is going to be so fun."

She shouted every word, and her echo bounced back from across the lake. "Remember what I said?" I bent down and helped her with her clasps, tightening the straps around her belly. "If we're too loud, we'll scare the fish away."

"Got it," she whisper-yelled again. "I'm so excited!"

"Me too." I kissed the top of her head, put on my own jacket because I might not have been a good dad, but I was going to be a good example of water safety if it killed me.

"All right. I'm going to climb on. You keep those paddles close to the edge and once I'm settled, I'll get you in, okay?"

"You got it."

It took me three tries to get into the kayak. Steve had made it sound so simple. But the skinny stupid yellow banana-shaped boat wobbled back and forth so much I kept stopping.

Finally in, thankful I hadn't tipped the dumb thing, I had the paddles in my lap and was scooping Amelia into the front seat.

"Buckle up and pull it tight, okay?"

"Got it. Can I have my paddle?"

"Yep." I lifted it over her head and reminded her how to hold it. "If you get tired, you just put it in your lap, okay? But if you're not paddling, you have to keep the ends out of the water."

"All right, Daddy. Let's go. Anchors away!"

Anchors away indeed.

We moved slowly. It took a couple minutes to find our rhythm and Amelia's paddling efforts were more of a hindrance than helpful. Soon, thankfully, she gave up and rested the paddle in her lap and skimmed her fingers along the top of the water.

"Will the fishes bite my fingers?"

"Nope. It's too hot for them to be close to us. They like the dark water to stay cool."

"So if I'm swimming, they'll bite my toes?"

She sounded thrilled at the possibility.

"Maybe. But you'd scare the big fish away, so it'd just be those little baby fishies at the shore."

"Would their bites hurt?"

I reached forward and tickled the back of her arm. She squealed and rocked the kayak from giggling. "That tickles!"

"Those are baby fish nibbles. That's what it'd feel like."

"Hm. I might like that."

She went quiet after that. Out on the water, the heat didn't feel nearly as blistering as the walk to the lake had been. Course, I wasn't carrying fifty pounds of gear anymore either. We were several houses away from ours, Amelia still letting her fingers trail in the water, bending over to watch them when she said, "I think Ruby would like this."

"Yeah? You think?"

It was the first time she'd brought her up. Usually, it was Mommy, though.

My chest swelled with hope that Ruby truly had broken through with Amelia. It'd make the next several months so much easier.

"Yeah. She said she loves the water. Says it's peaceful."

"It is peaceful, isn't it?" There was barely a breeze, but the tops of the trees swayed gently. Birds swam in circles in the air and on the opposite side of the lake were two ducks swimming.

"I think it's my favorite place." Amelia sighed. "Think Ruby and I can kayak?"

"Absolutely."

"Good." She brought her hand out of the water and set it in her lap. We finished the kayak ride shortly after that, the small trek enough for one day, and on the way back to the house, she made us stop to water the gardens.

"Since Miss Ruby isn't here," she said, "we should take care of them."

"I thought you didn't like them?"

"Maybe I do." She pouted the words, not sounding really happy with herself over the idea, but I let it go.

Maybe, *maybe* what she needed to hear from both her mom and me, together, was that we were not getting back together. We were not going to live together again. As much as it'd hurt to say it and hurt to watch her pain, was it possible it was the best thing for her?

I SHOULDN'T TEXT HIM. It'd made me too needy and came across as too desperate. I couldn't have the man I'd made a *just sex* deal with twelve hours ago thinking I was already wanting more than that. I already knew Logan wasn't going to fall in love with me. I didn't want that, either.

My heart had been put through the wringer once before and I was in no hurry to put it on the chopping block again.

But that didn't mean I didn't spend the whole afternoon thinking about him. Thinking of the things we'd done. The things he'd *said*. The things I *followed*.

Hot. So damn hot it was scorching, and I'd be lying to myself if I wasn't counting down the hours until I could have that again.

Maybe leaving for the weekend was the worst thing I could do.

No, it was the best for Amelia, and she was my priority. She was who I was concerned about.

Which left me wondering how the call went with Vanessa.

And how she handled it after.

God, my thoughts had raced all day. More than once Molly and Jassen had to get my attention by calling my name several times.

"Everything okay with work?" she finally asked me over dinner of simple grilled cheeseburgers, corn on the cob, and baked beans. "You seem distracted."

"It's nothing. Work is great." I flashed her a smile that felt crazed and her responding look agreed.

I cleaned up for Molly. Jassen and her went and helped get changed into pool clothes. By the time Luke and Brittney were running around the backyard, I was drinking a glass of wine on their covered back patio and Jassen sat next to me when things went to shit.

"I've debated bringing this up, but Paulie called me last week."

"Excuse me?" I jumped so quickly from my seat wine splashed over the rim and onto my legs. "Damn it!" I brushed it off and took a large swallow. "When? Why?"

Oh God. He hadn't told them. Had he?

No, Paulie wouldn't. He'd lose too much and his whole shtick was getting people to believe he was a nice guy.

The greatest.

Barf.

Jassen's brows tugged in, and he scratched his clean-shaven jaw. "I don't know. Like on Wednesday? Tuesday or something? He asked for you, said he tried calling you and he couldn't get ahold of you."

"What'd you tell him?"

Not that it mattered. It wasn't like Paulie would come looking for me, but the fact he still tried to get ahold of me after everything he did made my blood boil.

"I said I'd let you know he called. But since you look like a ghost, why won't you be honest about what happened?"

I barked out a laugh. "Never gonna happen, just don't answer again if he calls. I blocked him."

"But why? You seemed happy..." His voice trailed off and we watched Molly at the edge of the pool, splashing her feet. Brittney was floating in a contraption with a ring around her to keep her out of the water and Luke was doing cannonballs into the pool from his other side, bouncing up and out of the water from the floaties on his skinny biceps. "It's all right if he wasn't the one, but you always said he was good to you and that you were happy. And then all of a sudden, you're here and not talking to him. I'm worried, Ruby. That's all."

"You're my older brother. That's your job. Or it used to be. Stopped being your job a long time ago."

I'd been on my own for four years after he went to college. He came home as often as he could, but I'd raised myself since I was fourteen.

"That's not fair," Jassen muttered, his lip curling.

"It wasn't supposed to be a dig. You're married with your own family. I was living a country away. Things happen."

"And Paulie is one of those things that happened?"

"We were together for a long time. I decided he wasn't the kind of guy I wanted to marry, so we broke up. Why does it have to be more complicated than that?"

But oh, it was. Because there was the theft when I kicked him out, sure. But the list of secrets he'd kept hidden from me for years still made me want to smash something. Namely his face into a wall. And I'd been the blind, naïve idiot who had the same horrible taste in men as her mom.

So yeah, I wasn't giving my heart to anyone again.

"Fine," Jassen muttered and took a drink of his iced tea. "Keep your secrets, but they have a way of coming out when you least expect them to."

Well, Jassen would never find out this one. I'd make sure of it. Or the other one I was now keeping from him.

He'd never look at me the same way again.

I went back to sipping my wine, now irritated and still wishing the phone in my hand would buzz with an incoming text.

I didn't want to be the girl who texted first, and after all, I'd told Logan he'd be fine for a few days without me.

No way was I acting like some needy little schoolgirl.

But I wasn't inclined to sit next to my brother, who would bring the judgment down on me with the holy book he loved to read so much, so I excused myself, filled up my glass of wine, and headed to their guest room, wishing I had gone back to their garage apartment instead.

———

I ended up taking a shower for lack of anything else better to do. It was enough to get over the conversation with Jassen. It was not enough to get over Logan. It was a shower where I'd remembered all the things Logan had done to me in the last twenty-four hours. A shower where I'd wished I'd also brought some toys with me so I could take care of the heat sparking through my body at the thought of them. A shower where, in the end, I said who gave a shit about the toys and used my own hand. My own fingers to touch me the way Logan had spread my lips, forcefully shoved two of his deep before flicking my clit with his thumb and then lapping at it with his tongue. It was enough to take the edge off, but it wasn't nearly good enough.

It wasn't nearly the same as Logan doing it himself.

And oh dear God... I froze, bent over in the bathroom, hair being dried with a towel, and stood abruptly.

What if Logan Caldwell ruined me for my own self-pleasure? There was no way. I'd never had a man give me an orgasm where I hadn't thought afterward, "I could have done that, and probably better, without all the hassle."

But oh... how he proved me wrong. From the bossiness to the touches. To the firmness and the sting of pain when he hadn't hesitated to do whatever he wanted to my nipples...

Oh man.

I was at risk of becoming a royal hot mess with this one.

This had potential trouble stamped all over it for reasons outside the logical ones he and I already talked about. Maybe this was a fluke.

Maybe I was distracted from the day with my brother. The conversation.

That had to be it.

There was no way Logan gave me better orgasms than I could take care of with a wide variety of tools. I refused to believe it.

I went back to drying my hair when my phone lit up and like the needy, silly little schoolgirl I was trying *not* to be, I dove for the phone before the first alert had finished the short ding.

Have a good day?

Okay. So at least he was thinking of me. At least he texted me. There were a dozen ways to play this. Did he want the sassy, confident woman who stormed into his office that morning asking for what she wanted? Which still... surprised the hell out of me.

Did he want the obedient, simpering fool who went weak in the knees every time she called him sir and his eyes flared with lust and dominance?

Or did he want the nanny? The friend to his daughter?

Simpering fool it was.

Can't stop thinking of me, sir?

If that was what he wanted, the sir would get a reaction. I bit my lip to contain my smile and tossed my towel onto the hook by the door. I'd made sure to lock the bedroom door, so I strolled to my bed and climbed beneath the covers, forgoing the pajamas on my dresser.

That mouth is going to get you into trouble.

Oh, if only he knew... But he liked this game, so I'd play along.

Maybe I like thinking of the way you'd take control of it.

I was wet. And it had nothing to do with the shower. A few simple sentences tossed back and forth, and my hand was drifting beneath the covers, cupping my full breasts and tugging on my nipple.

My phone screen lit up. A FaceTime call from Logan. I scrambled to grab my AirPods from the nightstand and popped them in.

I'd look silly and probably already did with my soaking wet hair and my unmade-up face, but there was no way I was missing out on this.

Instead of the bossy, in control man I experienced that morning and expected, as Logan's face cleared on the screen, he appeared more rattled.

Hair tousled. Scruff longer than normal. There was a puffiness beneath his eyes and a thin line from his lips pressing together.

My heart clenched. What if I'd judged this all wrong?

"Hey. You answered."

I squirmed beneath the sheets and kept the view above my naked shoulders. "Well, you called."

Silly man.

"Right." He chuckled, scrubbing his hair. "You're driving me crazy. All this *sir* stuff. You have no idea what it's doing to me."

"Oh?" Was it new for him? He'd alluded to it earlier, but still. "It's new to me too, you know."

"I hadn't." His voice was a thick rasp. Confused. Frustrated. My heart started to sting when he blinked and then glared at me through the screen. "If I told you what to do now, would you listen?"

Oh... well... "I guess that depends."

I was in my brother's house after all. I was also naked. On

fire for him. So damn turned on I could easily slip my fingers beneath the sheets and—

"I don't want you touching yourself this weekend."

He wouldn't. "You're joking."

"You're driving me crazy. I'm going to make sure you feel the same pain. Told you that mouth would get you into trouble." He gave me a wicked smile that had my toes curling into the sheets. "Will you listen?"

I could lie easily. He'd never know. There was no way. And yet...

"Fine," I grumbled. "But only if you do the same."

He barked out a laugh that was cold. Cooled me down the slightest bit. "Oh, Ruby. You're not the one in control here. We'll see you Monday."

The phone screen froze and blackened. I gaped at it, far longer than normal before I chucked it to the bed next to me and threw off the covers.

He was a horrible, horrible man. I didn't have to listen to him. I didn't need to do anything he told me to do.

So why was I stomping to the dresser and yanking on my pajamas instead of staying in that bed, naked, taking care of myself?

What did that say about me?

———

"Can you chop this up for the salad?"

Molly handed me cucumbers, broccoli, and tomatoes. The pasta was boiling on the stove and she'd already mixed the dressing for the pasta salad.

We started prepping for the Labor Day party yesterday, and today we were finishing up sides we wanted to ensure were fresh.

Since I hated cooking, I'd been put in charge of all the chopping.

"Yep. Would love to." I started on the cucumbers first, peeling off some of the outer skin. "It was really nice of you to volunteer to host this."

Especially since they were doing it for Amelia, and in a way, Logan. I hadn't spoken with him since that call on Friday night. Over two days and I was losing my mind. Over two days and I'd been walking around like I imagined a man in his late teens, ready to hump anything I saw. Even the cucumber in my hand tempted me.

I was strung tight, disgusted with myself, and yet every time I thought of Logan's words, the way he'd asked if I'd listen to him like it was important to him... I became so damn turned on to the point it was almost painful.

Last night, Jassen had walked into the kitchen where I was standing, head shoved into the freezer in an effort to cool myself down.

If Logan didn't give me relief soon, I was going to throttle him. Wrap my hands around his sexy, corded throat and choke the life out of him.

"Jassen said it'd be good for the team to have him around and be a bit more personal, too. And I'm sure Amelia could use some friends. She's still on the preschool waiting list?"

It'd been less than two weeks since I added her and wasn't surprised there hadn't been a change, but I'd hoped some child would drop out so she could start going.

"Yeah." I moved on from peeling to chopping. "And I know friends would be good for her, but this was still a lot for you to take on."

I glanced at her rounded belly, visible earlier with her third baby in such a short amount of time. She rested her hand there and smiled. "I'm doing okay. As long as I can get a nap afterward, it shouldn't be too bad."

"I haven't heard your morning puking session this weekend, so that's good."

Molly chuckled and drained the pasta water into the strainer in the sink. "Thanks. What a lovely visual you've given me."

It was true, though. She was still throwing up every morning, multiple times a day, before I left.

"And yes, as long as I stay away from chicken while it's cooking, or being forced to eat it, I tend to be all right these days."

"So Jassen's not allowed on his chicken and broccoli diet anymore?" My brother could live on that and rice during the season. Especially at the start of it when training was more intense.

"I've declared he can only eat it at the training center or in his car." Even then she made a face and I switched the subject from things that made her puke to her plans on starting a non-profit to help get athletic equipment into the hands of children in poorer areas and schools that typically used hand-me-downs. Especially with the safety necessary in sports like football, she wanted to make sure every child had equipment that would keep them as protected as possible.

"Do you need help to plan fundraising or anything? Or have events set up yet to raise the money?"

"No, that'll take a while. I have ideas, and I'm hoping to get in contact with some other professional teams like the Avengers to see if they'd be willing to help, but that'll take time."

"Well, let me know if you need my help. I'm happy to lend a hand wherever needed."

She turned to me with a soft but sad smile. "That could be months, Ruby. I thought you'd be gone by then?"

I'd planned to stay long enough to pay off student loans, recover the debt from Paulie, and then head to Graduate School. With the money I was getting from Logan, I could easily have all that taken care of and be ready to start in January with the spring semester. The school I was planning to attend in New York had delayed my admission for one semester.

But the reminder of me leaving made my stomach tighten. I was enjoying being here, being close to my family again. And there was Logan...

Nope. No way. I was not putting my life on hold for him. He wasn't planning on living here full-time anyway. Changing my plans would be foolish.

"Yeah," I muttered, and I might have started chopping the broccoli more harshly than necessary. "I guess I will be."

We moved on from pasta salad to piping the filling into deviled eggs. She made a street corn type dip while I shucked corn on the cob. We'd barely finished and wiped down the counters when the doorbell rang for the first time.

That was all it took for me to be distracted all over again.

Logan was going to arrive at any moment, and I was a turned on, simpering hot mess all over again.

Damn him and his demands.

CHAPTER 18

LOGAN

I HAD no intention of following the rule I set forth for Ruby. It wasn't even possible without walking around with an iron pole in my shorts the entire weekend. Not good in general, but especially not when Amelia and I spent most of the weekend in the water or on it. We were either swimming in the pool, fishing at the edge of the lake, or in the kayak, and I'd woken her up early on Saturday with the surprise I'd not only inflated the floating dock, but also one of the paddleboards. We went out for a morning ride, her sitting on her bottom in between my feet.

I declared that every morning I could, we would start the day exactly like that. There'd been something so calming about the morning paddleboard ride. Where the sun was rising, and the air was still. The glass was crystal and the only movement on it were the gentle wakes left behind from the board and my paddles. Ducks swam close to us, and a few turtles popped their heads above the water much to Amelia's enjoyment.

But after the ride was done and we were back in the house, I'd had to set Amelia up with a cartoon and breakfast while I went and took out my frustrations in the shower.

Every morning, I woke up hard, thinking of Ruby, wondering if she was doing what I asked her to do. Every night, I ached for her. It'd been tempting, so damn tempting to call her or text her again, but it was possible I was becoming a sadist. I not only *liked* the idea of her in pain, but my dick also got hard every time I thought of her choosing to listen to me over her own pleasure.

I'd never been this fucked in the head before, especially not over a woman or sex, but it was happening, and I no longer cared about stopping it.

As long as Amelia didn't find out or discover us, I was willing to explore this new need of mine with full abandonment. As long as Ruby was still willing to be along for the ride.

I saw her before she saw me. As much as I'd wanted to be the first person to show up, considering Jassen agreed to have a party for Amelia and me, I also wanted to make Ruby suffer.

Just a little bit longer.

A wicked grin twisted my lips as Amelia entered the backyard. Dozens of kids were splashing in the pool. The noise was chaotic. Women were mostly under the covered patio or lounging in the sun, watching them, and the men, like any typical American partying, were hovering near the drinks and the grill.

Amelia was sitting at the edge of the pool with Molly on one side of her and Maggie Hall at the end.

She and my running back, Davis, were married in the off-season, and she was now holding her infant daughter to her chest, tugging down on the pink and white brim of her sunhat.

"Daddy! There's Miss Ruby!" Amelia squeezed my hand and pointed to Ruby with the other.

"I know. Want to hand me your towel and sandals so you can go say hi or jump in the pool?"

Her hand squeezed mine together and for once, her voice wasn't at a shrieking, high volume level. "There are lots of kids in there."

"There are." I couched down and squeezed her shoulders. "Remember what we talked about? How Daddy helps coach all these guys here and their kids wanted to meet you? That way you can have friends to play with if you ever come to my games."

She scanned the pool and her eyes grew wide, face paled. Turning back to me, she put her hand on my arm. "I can stay with you."

She was nervous. Not unexpected. For as outgoing as she was, she wasn't used to large groups of children. One of the reasons why I so desperately hoped a spot in one of the preschools would open up. "Okay. You can stay with me for a bit or go see Miss Ruby."

"No. Your games. I'll stay with you."

I bit back my laugh and a smile, glancing toward the crowd. Ruby was facing away from me, so all I saw was the back of her head, but Molly and Maggie were laughing at something. She hadn't seen me yet.

Good.

"We'll talk about my games another time." Hopefully, that appeased Amelia. "For now, do you want to get a snack? Go for a swim? Or say hi to Miss Ruby?"

Her lime green Crocs brushed against the pavement and her nose wrinkled. She needed to decide soon. I wanted to be on the opposite side of the pool before Ruby saw me, so I gauged her expression.

The edges of Amelia's lips pushed down and she finally sighed. "I'll go see Miss Ruby and that baby."

"All right. Go on."

She headed in their direction like she was walking a plank, keeping a close eye on the chaos going on in the pool. I hurried around the pool, nodding hello to some of the wives I'd already met. There'd be time to talk later. I wanted to see...

Her cheeks turned a furious shade of pink and her ocean-blue eyes widened when Amelia settled her hand on her shoulder. Instantly, Ruby looked behind Amelia, asked her a question, but there was no hiding the desire, and quite possibly, the irritation swimming in her eyes as she found me across the pool.

I reached down and grabbed an ice-cold water bottle and lifted it in her direction.

Ruby's eyes flared and I was pretty damn certain her chest heaved with heavier breaths.

Oh yeah... She'd listened to me. I could tell from the way she bit down on the corner of her lip, glanced back at Molly and then at Amelia before her tongue swept along her bottom lip.

It was that easy. That one needy and wanting look from her and I chugged the entire bottle of water.

"Glad you could come," Cole approached, beer in one hand, wearing only red swim trunks. He held out his free hand and I forced myself to tear my gaze off Ruby's and onto him.

"Thanks for planning this. I really appreciate it. And your ankle isn't wrapped."

"It's good to be around us every once in a while, get to know us, so stop working," Cole said, smiling. "Ankle's fine. Don't want it wrapped if I get in the pool with Jasper."

"Where is he?" His son wasn't that much older than Amelia.

"Backyard." He gestured to the part of the yard where a handful of players and a half-dozen young boys were tossing around a football.

"And you tell me not to work." Mason Yeets, one of our wide receivers, who wasn't even a parent but was still here, was out there with them, tossing the ball in the air so the kids had to scramble to catch it.

"You tell Yeets there's a party, and he's not missing it. How you been? Where's your little girl?"

"Amelia," I told him and then looked back where she'd been. She was now sitting next to Maggie, her little mouth moving nonstop as her fingers played with the brim of the baby's hat. "Sitting with Maggie."

"Ah. All the kids are obsessed with Lulu. I'm not surprised."

I smiled at the way my daughter was so gentle with the baby, carefully sitting with her feet tucked under her. Ruby sat up from the edge of her pool and...

Fuck me.

She was in a bikini, and obviously that should have registered early, but it wasn't a simple, black or plain bikini. Red and white striped triangles barely covered her full, generous breasts and were barely being held up by a thin red strap wrapped around her back and her neck. Two tiny bows were tied at the curve of her hips. And there was no way, with how small the front of her bottoms were, that the back fully covered her ass.

My nostrils flared as I took in any of the guys who might have noticed her, who might watch her move, but of course... there weren't any.

Almost all the men here were married or engaged, and I was being a jackass.

I cleared my throat and tried to focus on Cole. They had thrown this party for me after all. I couldn't become a dick. "How's Eden? Is she here?"

"Nah. She was tired. Said she needed a break."

She was over halfway through her own pregnancy, and she had Jasper to chase around most days. "Bet she's glad Jasper's back in school. God, we love the day he goes back to school and then we're sad because he's not running around all over the house all day. How messed up is that?"

"Parenting is a special form of torture. I get it."

"Yeah. Cool you've got time with your girl, though. Jassen said his sister is a nanny. That worked out well for you."

"Perfect timing." In a dozen ways, many of which I'd only begun to explore. "She'll stay until Vanessa gets back from Europe. I'm glad she was able to step in and help out on such short notice."

"Amelia doing okay with her? That can't be easy. I know

whenever I get Jasper back from his mom's, it takes a day or so for him to adjust."

"It's been…" Hell. Incredible. Delicious torture and infuriating. "Amelia's coming around, I think."

"Hey, how's it going, Logan? Glad you could make it."

I turned to the familiar voice and caught the kind smile Jassen Moore always seemed to wear. "Thanks for doing this, and for Molly. I know she hasn't been well."

"She's getting through it. Amelia is suddenly scared of the pool or is something else going on with her today?"

She was now standing at the edge, her chest floatie draped across her chest, around her biceps. Ruby was clasping it at the back and bent down to speak to her. Her breasts swung, the sides visible from those damn, tiny triangles. She was a current, walking red flag and she'd pay for this teasing.

A quick sideways glance from her direction to me, a narrowing of her eyes, and a barely there and then gone wicked gleam in my direction proved she knew exactly what she was doing.

I fought down the urge to growl at her and tried to remember Jassen's question. Amelia. Right.

The whole damn purpose of today. "She loves the water. It's all the kids that make her nervous. She'll warm up."

As I said it, Molly called Luke to the edge of the pool. He swam straight to Amelia and clung to the edge of the pool. He was younger than her by a year, but she at least knew him from Ruby bringing her over here before.

She bent close to him, grinned, and then stepped back and settled her hand on Ruby's thigh.

"I'll be back," I told them.

I'd go check on Amelia, get in with her if I had to, but if we were here to get her used to these kids, it wouldn't do for her to avoid them all day.

The trek around the pool was short, each step of mine on the patio slow. Ruby caught me coming as soon as I took off and if we weren't careful, we were going to give ourselves away sooner than I wanted—which was never. But God, the way her eyes tracked every single one of my movements. The way I was having a hard time not staring at her tits.

She was fucking gorgeous. Lean, tan. Not overly toned, but soft.

And I knew the sounds she made when she was fighting back a screaming orgasm.

My chest tightened and I forced my jaw to unclench as I reached them.

"What's going on?" I attempted to smile down at Amelia.

She flashed me wide, scared eyes. "You mad, Daddy?"

"No, I'm not mad." I was fighting an erection I wasn't too pleased about, but I wasn't angry. "Need me to swim with you?"

"She can swim with me!" Luke shouted from his spot at the edge. "I told her, too."

"You like Luke, Amelia," Ruby said.

I glared up at her because I couldn't *not* when that summery, ocean scent hit my nose and her hair blew in the breeze.

A blush crept up her cheeks, but she rolled her eyes at me, at my display of carnal insanity, and turned back to my daughter.

"I can swim with you too, Amelia. See? Lots of people will help you if you need it."

"I can do it," Amelia said, and her tiny little hands curled into fists. She glanced down at Luke. "Can you move? I gonna jump."

"Do it super far!" he encouraged her, and I chuckled, despite the heat building in my groin.

"Here, this way." Ruby gently tugged Amelia farther from Maggie and Luella. "Jump over here so you don't splash the baby."

"Oh." She flashed worried eyes toward Maggie. "This good?"

"It's great, Amelia. Show Luella how high you can jump."

Maggie encouraged with her smile. She had a gazillion siblings living with her and Davis, and it shouldn't have surprised me she'd be good with someone else's.

Amelia jumped into the pool, making a splash and a squeal at the same time.

Once I saw she was safe and happy, I turned to Ruby. She was grinning and clapping for Amelia, but as soon as my lips were near her ear, her body tightened.

"Meet me in the downstairs bathroom in five minutes. I want to see if you listened to me."

Her jaw fell and her cheeks turned a hot pink.

I spun on my heels before she could say anything and headed back to the other side of the pool for more ice water.

I was going to need it.

———

Exactly four minutes and thirty seconds later, and I knew that because I set a time on my Apple watch, Ruby excused herself from where she'd been talking with Molly and headed toward the house.

My heart started racing and I downed the last of the water I'd been holding in my hand. Close to me, Davis and Cole were talking about the losses we had not only in the preseason, but this last week when we had to cut players to reach our fifty-three active man roster.

Talking like their coach, the guy who made all those hard decisions wasn't right next to them. They didn't mean anything by it, but this was why coaches and players didn't often mingle.

"Spanklo will be a tough loss," Davis said. "I felt like he covered well."

"Not fast enough off the line," I told them. "Trust me, that was a hard one to call." I hadn't slept for two nights, working with the rest of the coaching staff on our decisions. They sent me the list of players who they thought they should keep for offense and defense and special teams. The final call was mine, but there were several, Spanklo being one of them, I'd wanted to try to move to the practice squad. "We're working on a trade with Dallas for Bigger."

I wasn't supposed to tell them that, either.

"Yeah. Don't say anything until words get out, but I expect it by Wednesday."

"No shit?" Davis's eyes sparked with excitement.

"Keep your fingers crossed and your mouths shut," I told them with a wink.

"On it." Davis mimed locking his lips with a key.

I'd given Ruby enough time to anticipate whatever was about to happen.

I could guarantee it wasn't nearly as exciting as what she was hoping for. Driving her mad was becoming my second favorite game.

I said my goodbyes to the players and excused myself inside. Fortunately, there were only a few kids running around, all the adults outside, and unlike my house that was completely open, Jassen's was more closed off. I was able to find the hallway I assumed led to the bathroom. Probably should have known where that was first, without having to go through the kitchen where female voices echoed.

I knocked on the first closed door, and slowly, almost like she was hesitating, Ruby peeked out through the barely open slit. I palmed the door and pushed it in, closing it behind me before anyone could see she was already in there.

"Hey," she whispered, and her voice was shaking.

The blush that had risen on her cheeks now traveled to her chest, the peaks of her breasts visible outside the top of her bikini.

I didn't waste any time. We didn't have it.

I reached out and pinched her nipple. Ruby gasped, and I kept my eyes on her. "Did you wear this to tease me today?"

Red and white. Like our home jersey colors. I didn't even know if she knew the significance until her nose wrinkled. Even with the pressure on her nipple, she still smiled.

"It only seemed fair since you tortured me all weekend."

Yes. I blinked and glanced down at her bottoms. I could have asked her to take them off and she would have. But those bows were tantalizing. I let go of her nipple and with two quick tugs, undid the bows.

The offensive fabric fluttered to the floor and then it was only me, Ruby, her sex on display, and her chest heaving with desire.

"Are you wet for me now?"

I had *never* asked Vanessa that question. But damn, watching Ruby struggle to answer me honestly was a turn-on in itself. I settled my hand at her hip and brushed my thumb over the soft flesh above her shaved mound.

Her inner thighs glistened, telling me all I needed to know, and every part of me demanded I drop to my knees for a taste. But someone could hear, and I was not touting us in a bathroom in her brother's house.

"Yes," Ruby finally rasped.

"Good." I leaned in, tightened my hold on her hip, and kissed her.

Without waiting, I dove my tongue into her mouth and cupped the back of her head with my other hand. My dick throbbed to be released from the confines of my trunks, and my stomach clenched with the unbearable need to sink inside of her. God, I couldn't *wait* to know exactly how she felt. The sounds she made when she didn't muffle her orgasms.

Soon. It'd happen soon, but for now, teasing her brought me enough pleasure.

I kissed her harshly. It wasn't rough. It wasn't smooth. I

poured all my frustration into that kiss while I slipped my hand between our bodies and ran two fingers over her clit. It was swollen, soaked with her own juices, and as soon as I touched her, she made an animalistic sound deep in her throat.

I played with her because I couldn't *not*. Because I loved the slickness that coated my fingers. As her body began to tremble. As her hands dug into my arms hard enough they could leave marks, and right as those cries and that pulsing began—

I stopped.

Took everything I had in me to yank my hand from her sex and end the kiss.

Her eyes were still closed, lips swollen, and cheeks flushed. I waited until her lashes fluttered and she gaped at me.

"No..." she whispered. "You wouldn't..."

"I will." I put those two fingers coated with her into my mouth and made a humming sound as I tasted her. "And I did."

"You cannot let me go back out there like this."

God, she was cute when she was full of all that pent-up sexual need.

"I'll take care of it later." I leaned forward and kissed her.

To continue the torture, I shoved down my shorts, yanked out my hard length, and quickly finished myself off.

"You're a bastard," Ruby panted. But she watched. She didn't move to touch herself and she hadn't even grabbed her bottoms and retied them.

"I think you like it," I groaned, right as my own climax hit. I came in my hand, all over my fingers and I had to be the sickest bastard in the world because when a drop fell to the floor, landed right on her bottoms, I chuckled.

She stood there, frozen, as if she couldn't believe what I'd done as I washed and dried my hands and once I was done, I bent to my feet and slid her bottoms up to her hips.

After they were retied, I pressed my lips to her belly button and gazed up at her. Her cheeks were no longer flushed, but there was irritation on her features.

I stood and kissed the hinge of her jaw. "I promise I'll make you feel better later."

"I think I hate you," she whispered back.

I laughed. "I think I liked that, too."

I smirked at her, opened the bathroom door, and ducked out before anyone could see us.

Or before she could chuck the glass bottle of hand soap at the back of my head.

CHAPTER 19

RUBY

THAT FREAKING, no good, rotten man! I was going to murder him. He left me gaping at him in the bathroom, standing there like an idiot, and all his promises of making sure he took care of me later could be right down his stinking, sexy throat.

Ugh. It took forever to calm down to leave the bathroom. Not only was my hair a mess, but my cheeks were flushed, and I had to clean myself off from the damage he did to me.

Logan Caldwell was *not* a nice guy. He was the devil disguised in sexy abs, buff biceps, and swim trunks that hugged his ass and showed off those damn calves.

I stomped a foot onto the rug, fisted my hands, and bit back all the curses I wanted to rain down on him like a torrential downpour. There was no way I was going back to his house tonight.

No freaking way. He spent all weekend playing with me, especially when he didn't say anything to me at all and then he thought he could saunter up to me in front of all those people, make demands, and leave me like this?

Screw that.

Screw him.

This had been all my idea to begin with, and it was time

Logan sweated a little bit. No man would have the upper hand on me again, least of all a six-foot-two, sexy man with a dominant streak I couldn't help but follow.

I flung open the bathroom door, jaw aching from grinding my lips together, and almost ran smack into Molly.

"Oh!" I pressed my hand to my chest. "Sorry, you startled me."

"You okay in here?" Her head twisted and she looked toward the kitchen.

"Yeah, great. Why?"

"Because you've been in here for a while."

"Oh. Well, you know…" Easy breezy, beautiful. I sucked at lying and being put on the spot. "Yeah, just, you know." I cringed and my hand dropped to my stomach. "Stomach issues."

Molly laughed and I finally stepped out of the bathroom, turning so she could go in. "I understand that for sure."

"Right, so, I'm gonna just… go back to the party." Hopefully, by the time I reached it, I wasn't acting like an idiot.

I shoved my thumb over my shoulder and stepped away. I didn't head straight outside. I went to the kitchen instead, where many of the players' wives or girlfriends or whatevers had decided to cool off in the air conditioning. Couldn't blame them there. If they weren't around, I'd be back to shoving my head into the freezer.

All because of Logan. He might have held the upper hand in our little game all weekend, but I was taking back the top spot next time I decided to deign him with my presence.

I munched on carrots and cucumbers, soaking them both in dip.

I talked to Maggie some more. I held her baby while Maggie got herself a plate of food and I brought her water when she sat in the living room to nurse her. Maggie was sweet. Jassen had filled me in over the weekend on most of the women my age who would be there, especially Maggie. Mostly because she hadn't made the national news earlier this year due to escaping some cult or something, but she was also becoming a hugely popular, rising country star. She'd had her debut on a stage back in the winter, had spent the spring in recording studios, and Jassen didn't have to tell me she had two million viewers on TikTok where she posted herself singing her new songs or having fun with covers because I already followed her.

She was also the nicest person I might have ever met, and as soon as we were introduced treated me like she'd known me for years, so of all the women I met at the party earlier, she was the one I drifted to the most.

I left her to the privacy of feeding her baby and went back to the kitchen to keep the growing mess easy for a later cleanup, when Molly came out of the restroom and shooed me back outside.

"Go." She waved me off like an obnoxious neighborhood cat on her doorstep. "Get out there. Go meet people. I've got this."

I chomped down a carrot stick. "You're getting awfully grouchy, Molls."

She scowled at me and pointed to the backyard. "You're hiding out in here for some reason I can't understand and my house isn't yours to take care of. Go."

"All right, all right." I raised my hands in defeat but couldn't resist one last parting shot because she had no idea what she was throwing me into. "You'd be prettier if you smiled more."

"Ruby!"

"Bye! Toodles!" I ran out the back and flashed Maggie a wink even though she was giving me a look that said I could die at any moment.

Oh how wrong she was.

Molly wasn't going to kill me.

It was Logan forcing me *not* to have orgasms that was going to kill me.

But he'd pay for that.

I'd make sure of it.

———

I dawdled leaving Molly and Jassen's house. The kids ate burgers and hot dogs, and the men ate most of the food. The women had kept the backyard mostly picked up from errant trash and swim towels and pool toys all afternoon, so as the trail of men and women and kids in tow started leaving, there really wasn't much left to do to help.

Molly had already banned me from the kitchen and I wasn't about to get into a fight with a pregnant woman, no matter how insane she acted before. I didn't even have to pack my bag to head back to Logan's. I'd had that done by nine o'clock in the morning.

Of course, ten hours ago I was excited to get back to his place where we could have privacy.

Now, I was in revenge mode.

Logan and Amelia weren't the last to leave, but they were definitely near the end of the group. I was risking life and limb from Molly by emptying several of the remaining salads and dips and sides into to-go containers so I could snack on them throughout the week. There was no way they'd be able to go through all that food, anyway.

Amelia ran to me, hair still soaking from the pool, tangled in her ponytail, and tugged on my hand. "Miss Ruby?"

"Yes, sweetie. Did you have fun today?"

"I made friends." Her brows scrunched together. "I think. They seemed nice."

I made a mental note to figure out who she played the best with. Maybe I could set up some playdates for her.

"Well, that's good." I laughed softly. "You and your dad going home?"

"Yep! Are you coming with?"

No way in hell was I riding in a car with them.

"I'll be there later. But you'll probably be sleeping, so you have fun, okay?"

Logan stepped up behind her. "Will you be there soon? Or are you helping clean up?"

"Molly will shank if I try to help. I'm gathering some leftovers for snacks this week, so I'll probably be a while." I'd been focused on pressing lids onto containers and glanced at him. "Or I might come over in the morning. You don't have to be at work until nine, right?"

His jaw ticked, and a wariness darkened his eyes. "Amelia, go make sure we didn't leave anything out back, okay? But stay out of the pool."

"Okay! Bye, Miss Ruby!"

I grinned, watching her go, and then went back to studiously ignoring Logan. He made it difficult, considering his mere presence had me wanting to lean in, see if the chlorine had washed away his oaky scent.

"You're pissed," he muttered.

"I'm not pissed." I grabbed another set of tongs and started filling a bag with carrots. "I'm busy."

And oh, the way his body was vibrating. He sighed, gave the area a quick glance, but the lingering guests were still outside talking with Jassen and Molly. For now, we were alone. "I wasn't trying to hurt you earlier. I thought this was fun, but if I overstepped..."

Oh shit. That was where the wariness came from.

I could have pity on him. He said this was all new to him. Hell, maybe he wasn't understanding what was happening as much as I wasn't. I *loved* him taking control. It was the denial I was struggling with, even when I loved it. See? I was a mess.

"I liked it," I said to him quietly. "I liked it a lot. It also... confuses me."

"We can slow things down."

I shook my head. "I don't want that. I just…" Hell, what did I want? "I want to get even with you for all the torture you put me through this weekend."

His brows rose high on his forehead and then his lips curled at the corner. "You can certainly try."

The throb was back. I set down the tongs and braced my hands on the counter. It was a flip of a switch and he was making my pulse race and my nipples pebble.

"Yeah?"

"But I promise you one thing—" He glanced back at the door. Cole and his son Jasper were heading inside, so he turned back to me and lowered his head. "You can try to play this game. You can try to beat me, but if you come back to my house tonight, I'll prove to you how much more fun this will all be for you when you're willing to lose."

"Daddy! I got our stuff!" Amelia's shout was a bucket of ice and we both stepped back.

My hands shook as I grabbed a fresh bag for more veggies.

Logan's warm breath skated across my jaw. "If you delay this too long tonight, it'll be even worse for you tomorrow."

My knees wobbled and I blew out a breath. He was infuriating! I was standing at the counter, far too long, while he went and scooped up the pool bag he'd brought for Amelia, took her hand, and shook Jassen's goodbye.

Damn the man.

He'd made me weak and wet for him all over again, and he appeared entirely unshaken.

———

His outside lights were on, but the inside of his house was dark when I finally pulled into his driveway. I stayed at my brother's long enough to help bathe Brittany while he took a shower with Luke. Molly insisted she was capable of cleaning, but halfway through, she started yawning and her face turned green, so I sent her upstairs to go to sleep.

After I finished the task, I kissed my niece and nephew, said goodbye to my brother, and I wasn't quite certain if I'd stayed long enough to torture Logan a little bit, or if I was hoping he'd torture me.

By the time I pulled into his driveway, my hands were sweating on the steering wheel and my thighs were pressed together. I'd changed out of my swimsuit and rinsed off, then redressed in comfortable, loose, black lounge pants and a simple tank top.

Forgoing the bra and underwear was a bad decision. If there wasn't a wet spot on my pants, showing my arousal, my hardened nipples would give me away as soon as I stepped through the door.

But if I stalled too long, Logan would worry. Or make me pay for it. The second one had me considering staying in my car until he knew I was stalling coming inside. He'd have seen me pull up. His phone gave him a notification of all incoming vehicles for security purposes, and I had no doubt he was keeping an eye on his phone for my return.

That had me curling my lips, taking a deep breath, and exiting my car. A few seconds later, my weekend bag in my hand, and I was stepping into Logan's house where the only light was the soft, muted glow of the light above the stove.

Weird. But maybe he'd headed to bed early?

It was after nine, so it wasn't too late.

I made sure to lock the door and dropped my bag by the staircase, kicking off my shoes into the mudroom. If Logan was sleeping, I wanted to be quiet. He'd had a hard day and I knew the upcoming week heading in to his first game was going to be stressful.

Stepping into the kitchen, I went straight to the wine fridge.

I'd wanted a drink all day, especially after the bathroom incident, but hadn't wanted to risk drinking too much to drive.

With a glass filled, I checked the screen on my phone. It lit up enough that when I turned toward the living room, a shadowed figure appeared in the chair.

"Jesus." I gasped. "You scared the shit out of me."

The shadow moved, and a lamp flicked on. Logan was sitting in a chair, back to his backyard, legs spread, wearing nothing but a pair of cut-off sweat shorts and a scowl.

He held a tumbler loosely in one hand, and the glass rattled like a gunshot through the living room. After a sip, he set it back down.

I was still standing in the living room, gaping at him, and he appeared, like usual, wholly unbothered by my presence.

"Come sit," he finally said, and I moved.

And he had to be joking. There was no way I'd stayed still until he *told* me what to do. This was getting out of control. I took a seat in the middle of the couch because *I* wanted to enjoy a glass of wine before bed and curled my feet under me.

"Amelia go down okay?"

"Out before I finished the first book. All that playing exhausted her." His stoic expression was doing crazy things to my stomach. To my core. If he was mad at me, he wasn't showing it. If he wanted me to strip naked and rock his world, he didn't seem in too large of a rush.

It was the unknowing that was driving me crazy.

I sipped my wine. He took a drink of his drink, whiskey it looked like.

"How was your weekend?" he asked. The gentle, deep rumble of his voice washed over me like a warm blanket. Soothing me. Warming me.

God. This was dangerous.

"It was good." I shuffled my feet beneath me for no other reason than he was making me antsy. "Yours?"

For the first time since I left on Friday, a genuine smile broke loose. Small, but there. "Amelia and I went shopping. You'll see it tomorrow, but we bought a kayak and some stand-up paddleboards. Spent every morning on the lake. Don't be surprised if Amelia begs you to take her out."

"That sounds wonderful."

"I thought of you the entire time." And he didn't sound like he liked that much.

"Oh?"

"Wondered if you'd want to be out there with us. Wondered if there was any way I'd be able to fuck you in the kayak."

Probably an impossibility, but my mind was spinning with possibilities. "You don't sound happy about it."

"I wasn't happy you left all weekend, no. You left me to take care of myself all weekend."

"And you denied me."

"You didn't have to listen."

Shit. He was right. "I wanted to please you," I admitted, so softly, it surprised me.

Another grin broke loose, this one darker, no less pleased. "Good girl. I liked that you did."

"Shit," I rasped as a pulse started in my core. I *was* liking this. The *sir* and the bossing and the *good girl* made my nipples feel like they were being pinched. Hard.

"If I asked you to come sit on my lap while you have that wine, would you?"

I was already moving my feet. He knew the answer. Had to have.

I scrambled to my feet and felt my sex pulse with need with every small step it took me to reach him. When I did, he spread his legs, helped me down onto his lap so my thighs were draped over his, and my shoulder rested against his chest. His hand cupped the back of my head and he curled his fingers in, grabbing my hair and tugging my head back.

Sparks of pleasure erupted down my spine with his firm, commanding hold and I couldn't hide them from him as he pressed kisses to my throat, my shoulder, back to my jaw. My body shivered under the brief touches of lips against me.

He stopped, brought his whiskey to his lips, and sipped.

"What do you want to do now?" I asked.

"Drink your wine and let me play."

CHAPTER 20

LOGAN

"WHAT ABOUT AMELIA?"

It wasn't the first time I had my hands on Ruby where she looked uncertain, but this was the first time she seemed truly worried. She was so expressive, every nervous glance, every hesitant decision she made danced across her face.

"I put her baby monitor on. She makes so much as a peep in her sleep, and I'll hear it."

"Oh. Okay then."

"Okay what?" I wanted to hear it. My chest ached to hear the words fall from her pink lips I'd devoured hours ago.

"Okay... you can play with me, sir."

She blushed and sipped her wine. I leaned in close and whispered in her ear, "You are such a good girl."

A full-body tremble rolled through her and I hid my pleased grin. I wasn't about to get her off. Not clothed, and not in my living room. But I'd spent all weekend desperate for the feel of her skin beneath my hands. I wanted to memorize the softness, find the places that drove her wild. And later, when I was ready and she was on the verge of strangling me, I was going to take her to my room.

"This okay?" I asked, and I dragged my finger down the

length of her arm. Goose bumps followed the path and she licked her lips.

"I've liked everything you do to me."

She leaned in and pressed her lips to the hinge of my jaw. I closed my eyes and breathed in the ocean and beach. Apparently, she'd decided to have her own playtime because the more I brushed my fingers along her arm, beneath the hem of her tank top, and along the waistband of her pants, she followed my teasing with her own kisses and brief flicks of her tongue at my collarbone.

"You're supposed to be drinking your wine. You'll get your playtime."

To prove I meant it, I pulled back, lifted her hand, barely remembering to hold on to her glass, and raised it to her mouth.

"Maybe I don't want the wine anymore."

"Maybe you should take your time and enjoy it." The wine. Me. My touches.

She hmphed but stopped her kisses and rested her head on my shoulder. Closing her eyes, she sipped her wine. I took advantage and lifted the hem of her shirt, exposing her breasts.

"Jesus, Logan," she rasped, but her eyes were still closed. She was surprised, not worried.

I was the one who should have been. Vanessa and I never had sex when or where Amelia could walk in, and there I was, bending down to taste my nanny's nipples in the goddamn exposed living room.

I still couldn't find it in me to care.

Her free hand lifted, her fingernails scraped gently against my scalp, and harsh little whimpers fell from her throat. I paid attention to both, tugging, nipping, and sucking on them until her hips were rocking before I moved my hand down her stomach and cupped her heated core.

"Need something here?" I pushed my fingers against her covered opening.

"Please."

Fingers dug into my scalp, making me wince.

I pushed harder until she brought her wineglass to her mouth and drank. "I already know you're not wearing a bra, but are you wearing underwear?"

She shook her head and took another drink.

"That excited to see me?" Her pants were thin enough I could feel how excited she was, how wet she was getting. And damn if that wasn't the hottest thing ever. "Did you need me so bad inside of you that you couldn't be bothered with getting fully dressed?"

She moaned as I pressed my fingers inside of her, used the soft seam of her pants to abrade her clit. "I figured you'd make me take them off anyway."

I had. I absolutely had intended to watch her do that for me again. It made me carnal. Sent me straight to my baser instincts, but her offering herself to me? Choosing to be bossed around and liking it?

Hell yeah, it made me hard.

"Finish that up," I murmured against the racing pulse of her throat. "I need your thighs wrapped around my face and your breasts bouncing on my dick."

She cursed, swallowed the rest of her wine, and set it down on the table.

I wrapped my arms around her and pushed to standing. Her hip jabbed against my hard dick and I fought back a groan as I carried her across the house to my bedroom. It was the only room I'd left a light on, and both of us blinked from the harsh lighting. But I wanted to see her, every single inch, while I took everything I wanted from her and gave her everything she needed.

As soon as we crossed the threshold into my room, I set Ruby on her feet. With one hand holding on to her arm so she kept her balance, I slid down the lights so they weren't so blinding.

"I need to go get my phone. I want you naked on the bed when I get back."

I'd miss the strip show, but the benefits that followed would be worth it.

"Logan?" Her voice carried a tremor, and she chewed on the bottom of her lip.

"What is it?"

"Can I have a kiss first?"

Was that it? "Absolutely." I cupped her cheeks without hesitation and slipped my tongue slowly into her mouth as she opened for me. She melted against me, soft little mewls that shot straight to my chest. I didn't rush the kiss this time. I didn't take her roughly and I didn't command everything.

I let her know with a kiss that I wanted this, wanted her, and I'd want all the same even if she didn't always like being bossed around.

"You okay?" I pulled back and pressed my forehead to hers.

She answered with a smile, stepped back, and slipped off her pants.

Like earlier, all I saw was her bare mound and her smile. "I'm okay."

She was better than okay.

She was magnificent, and she was all mine.

At least until Christmas.

Shit.

———

I jogged out of my room and did a quick check of the house, making sure all the doors were locked before I grabbed my phone and hurried back to the bedroom.

"Better than I imagined." My breath stalled and then left me in a whoosh.

Ruby had listened. I wasn't surprised, but it was a beautiful sight to see. She was on my bed, clothes left in a pile on the side of the bed. Naked. Propped up on my pillows, her arms were splayed out to the sides, one leg crooked with her foot planted to the sheets. Her other leg was straight out, and it was then I noticed she'd taken the time to remove my duvet.

I followed the path of her straight leg, past her breasts and that slim throat to her tender but needy grin.

"Are you going to stay there all night and watch me or join me?"

I stepped forward and tore off my shirt. "Who says we can't do both?"

Her lips parted in surprise, but I'd teased her enough. I was past the point of taking this slow, sweet, and easy. We'd blown past that last week when she slipped out of her underwear in my office. Before I joined her, I went to the nightstand on my side of the bed and tore out a strip of condoms from the box I'd bought and opened over the weekend. I tossed three to the bed off to her side and her eyes widened with interest.

"All three?" she asked, and her voice was already thready.

"A guy can dream," I teased her before climbing into the bed at the foot of it.

I kissed her shin, the calf of her bent leg. I kissed a path up to her thighs, her hips, circled her nipples with my tongue. Soft moans escaped her parted lips and her head pushed back to the pillows, eyes glazed with lust and barely open. I wanted her eyes open, watching me, but I'd bossed her around enough and she'd listened so well.

She deserved her reward.

I sat up on my knees, grabbed her hips, and with one quick yank, I had her flat on the bed. Her laugh pierced the intensity hovering in the air and I bent over her, silencing her with a kiss. "You're still going to have to try to be quiet, okay?" I whispered the question with my lips on hers and down, along her jaw.

"I can do that."

We'd see about that. My mission was to make it as difficult as possible for her. I retraced the path my mouth took on the way up and crawled down her body. Sliding my hands from her hips, I trailed them down to her knees and spread her legs wide.

Soaked. She was so damn wet for me. A groan escaped my mouth before I leaned forward. I licked her from front to back, all the way back to an area I was certain no man had gone on before and her surprised gasp proved it.

"Logan," she whispered, uncertainty in her tone.

I grinned up at her. "I'm just playing. Trust me."

She swallowed, shoved one of her hands into my thick hair, and nodded.

I wasn't a big ass man, not when it came to anal, but I suspected she'd never had much playtime down there, which could enhance everything else I was about to do to her. I kissed her thighs until she relaxed, slid a finger deep inside of her, and when her nerves were gone, I dove back in. I added a second finger before I added my tongue to her clit. I drank in her scent, the taste of her until she was writhing in pleasure, biting down on her lip to stay quiet, and rolling her hips against my face.

She didn't sit there and take what I gave her. She fought for her own pleasure and seeing her so into it, so close, made my dick pound against my shorts, demanding to escape, begging for its own release.

Her thighs trembled and her pussy clamped around my fingers, my tongue when I slid it inside, and right as she began to come, right as that peak hit and she cried out before biting down on her lip, as her entire body trembled through the force of her orgasm, I slipped my fingers back to her puckered hole and pressed them against it. I wouldn't enter, not without better preparation, but the pressure was enough to have her throwing her head back. Her hips arched off the bed and her back bowed. I kept eating, kept pressing against that forbidden pleasure center until she was chanting curse words over and over until her fingers were digging into my scalp, and until her body finally went boneless on the bed.

I kissed her again, and her body jolted from the sensitivity before I finally eased off.

Her arm fell to her side, and I shook off the lingering pain from her nails on me.

"You okay?" I ran my hand up her abdomen, between her breasts. I curled my hand around her shoulder and brought it back down to her thigh, her knee. I avoided her breasts, her pussy, helping her calm down.

"That was... a lot," she finally whispered. Her breath was ragged, her blue eyes hazy, and her lips curled into a sleepy smile as she licked them.

"Can you take more?"

I wasn't nearly done with her. I'd only begun, but I'd kept her on edge all weekend and teased her earlier. If it was too much, I'd wait.

"Please." Her hands reached for me, but she was so limp from her orgasm they fell right back onto the bed. "More."

I bent over her and kissed her. It was languid, smooth. She hummed against my mouth and when I settled my still covered dick against her core, her hips rolled against me. She sought friction, and I pulled back. With one hand braced by her head, I used the other to shove down my shorts.

As soon as I was naked, I returned, sliding through her slit, gathering her wetness.

Heaven. Her body was heaven, a body that was meant to be worshipped, and when she pushed her hand between us and wrapped it around me, pumping slowly, firmly, I bit her lip. "Careful, Ruby. I'm barely holding back here."

"I needed to feel you after seeing you so many times."

I laughed against her mouth and reached over and grabbed a condom. Once it was torn open, I leaned back.

She watched with rapt fascination as I rolled it down my

length and then held myself at her center. As soon as I began to push inside of her, her chin lifted, eyes fluttering closed. "Ohhh... that is..."

"Fucking perfect," I grunted and pulled back out. I took my time, sliding in and out, giving her body time to adjust, but hell, it was like her body was made for me. Her walls rubbed against my dick so deliciously, I was already clenching my jaw to keep from coming.

Once I was fully seated inside of her, I leaned forward, braced my elbow by her shoulder, and wrapped one of her legs around my hip. The move tilted her, opened her up further. She reached out and clung to my hips on a pleasured groan that vibrated straight down to my balls.

God. She was incredible. So damn young, but so confident. Knew exactly how she liked it.

I started moving slowly, kissing her deeply, and I drank down every single one of her cries and sounds when I hit the end of her deep inside.

"Logan." She squeezed me tight, tearing a grunt from me. "Quit playing and *move*."

Her voice was desperate, impatiently needy.

I kissed her again and smiled against her mouth. "My pleasure."

I quit playing. Quit teasing. I pushed off my elbow, rolled back to my knees, and grabbed her hips, then pulled her against me. Her legs curled around my hips as her cries became more feral, deeper. Her breasts bounced, nipples hard points. My mouth watered to taste them, but I held back. Instead, I gripped the backs of her thighs with both my hands and pushed them up to her calves. Straightening her legs, I held them in a V as I pounded into her.

"Oh God." She grabbed a pillow and bit down on it. I pounded into her, drank in every whimper, every cry, and my own groans mingled with hers.

"Logan!" She shattered. Her entire body quaked from the power of my thrusts, the position. I kept going as her pussy clamped down on my dick, her walls pulsing around me. I rode the wave of her orgasm, biting back my own until hers started to slow.

I slammed into her once, two more times before I draped her legs over my shoulders, bent over her, and kissed her while I groaned, releasing inside of her.

Her arms went around my back, hugging me to her as I came, and for the first time I could remember, I hated the condom. Hated I couldn't fill her up with me.

"Holy shit," I gritted, pulling back to kiss her cheek. Her jaw. Slowly, her legs slipped from my shoulder to my sides, and she kept a firm hold on me.

"Holy shit is right," she whispered. "That was... well, you're amazing."

I chuckled against her soft flesh and groaned as I pulled out of her.

Amazing indeed.

Everything about Ruby Moore was.

Which meant this game we were playing just got a whole lot riskier.

CHAPTER 21

RUBY

THE SHOWER WATER WAS RUNNING, and I was stripping out of my swimsuit when Logan sauntered into my private bathroom, that look on his face telling me exactly what he was craving.

For the last week, we'd controlled ourselves during the day and around Amelia. There were glances, winks, but absolutely no risking any touches or kisses. But as soon as Logan was assured she was sleeping, our nights were carnal.

He had me on my knees, blowing him while he worked in his office. He had me bent over his desk, biting down on his favorite pen while he took me from behind. He had me spread open, playing with myself in a chair facing him while he took a late-night phone call in his office. And by the time he whisked me away to his bedroom, on the nights we made it there, he made me fight down screams so loud that had I been able to unleash them, would have shaken the foundations of his home.

This was, however, the first time he'd come to me in the middle of the day.

I stepped back as he closed the door behind him and locked it.

"Where's Amelia?"

I'd left them outside in the pool, where I'd lounged on a chair, chasing the last of the hot summer sun on my skin.

Logan didn't answer. He set his phone on the counter, opened an app, and soon, loud rock music blared through the tiny speaker.

Like every time he behaved this way, my knees went weak and my stomach warmed. I grew wet at the sight of him, especially when his dark as night eyes trailed every inch of my skin, stalling on my breasts.

"Get in the shower," he grunted and began taking off his shirt. "This will be fast and hard, and you have to be silent. But I need to have you one more time before I leave for the hotel."

Just the thought of a night without him had me moving. I scampered into the shower and stood facing him. I had the glorious view of seeing his ass in my bathroom mirror as he stood before me, kicking out of his swim trunks.

His body was a work of art and made my mouth water. Every inch of him was not only pure muscled perfection, but I'd had my lips on every inch of his body when he allowed me time to play. I'd memorized every muscle, every birthmark, every place on him that made him laugh and every place that had his hands digging into my hair with pleasure.

I stepped back as he entered the shower, my mouth watering, my core already clenching.

He reached out with both hands and fondled my breasts, while keeping his eyes on mine. He twisted, pulled, and as a sound escaped my throat, he pinched harder.

"I said silent," he warned and increased the pain.

I pressed my lips together and swallowed.

"Can you do that?"

He'd torture me for answering, but I couldn't help it. Every time Logan got his hands on me, I relished the pain. The pleasure. The commands.

"Yes, sir," I whispered and clamped my lips together again as he twisted. Oh... it hurt. But it also sent a direct shock to my core I loved so much.

His eyes flared with approval, despite the glare, and he released my nipples, only to settle his hands at my shoulder. "Kneel. Suck me hard and make it quick."

Fuck. God. His words. The darkness in them.

I dropped to my knees and took only a second to admire his thickness. The veins on his dick. The length of him. He was glorious and perfect and large everywhere, and before he could admonish me again, I wrapped one hand around the base of him and took him in my mouth.

I didn't play. He rarely gave me time. With one hand at his thigh, to brace myself, I slid my hand from his shaft to his balls and took him deeper.

He'd only allow me the illusion of control for so long, and while he did, I gazed up at him.

He stared down at me, eyes already lost in pleasure, lips soft. One of his hands came to the back of my head and I took him deeper until I gagged, and he allowed me to move back. I swirled my tongue around his thick head, tightening my cheeks as I took him into my mouth.

That hand on the back of my head tightened, and I already knew what was coming before he said it. I stopped playing with his balls and rested my hand on his hip. "Open, all the way. Breathe through that nose and let me fuck you."

My throat loosened on what was becoming instinct, and before I could prepare, he slammed his dick to the back of my throat, past the gag reflex that made tears pour from my eyes, and down my throat.

It was painful. It was incredible. He hadn't taught me how to deep throat him so much as he *did* it and expected me to adjust. For all the softness he had outside the bedroom, outside sex, as soon as Logan got me alone, he was all rudeness and roughness.

And I loved every single second.

"Fuck, I love the way you take me." His words were gentle. His hips thrusting hard and fast against my face were not. His balls slapped my chin, and I dug my fingers into his hips to steady myself.

It was messy. Loud. I took every thrust and treasured every pain-filled grunt he made until he clasped his other hand at my head and held me still. He slammed his dick into my throat and came. His dick pulsed, and my jaw ached. Tears fell down my cheeks and spit dripped off my chin.

"You're so fucking beautiful like this," he murmured, pulling himself out of me. He wiped my tears from my cheeks and helped me to my feet. "Turn around and brace your hands on the wall."

On shaking legs, I listened, bending over the bench in my shower that Logan had come to love so much. He slipped beneath me, took a seat, and once he was settled, he helped me climb up. My feet were outside his thighs, my hands on the wall behind him. I had to trust him not to drop me, had to plant my feet on wet tile.

His fingers dug in so hard they'd leave marks on my ass I'd have to hide in swimsuits, but all that thinking and planning vanished when he yanked my sex to him and he *ate*.

I loved the way Logan went down on me. Like the rest of him, he wasn't gentle. He wasn't soft. He ate me like it was his singular focus in life, like he had to have me *now*. He ravished me with his tongue, quick, painful nips of his teeth at my clit.

He sucked, moaned, the vibrations driving me wild. And with the position, squatting over him, I had to drop a hand from the wall and grip his shoulder as my body trembled.

God, he was good at this. He could make me come faster than I made myself, which had to be some sort of heavenly gift God bestowed on him. I came, grinding my teeth and probably bruising his shoulder, and still, I was silent.

He ate me through aftershocks, played with my clit to drive

me wild after, and then he was gently pulling me down to his lap where I draped my arms over his shoulder and pushed his wet hair off his face.

He glistened from my own wetness, and I leaned forward and licked his lips to taste myself.

"Fuck, I love it when you do that," he whispered, hands at my lower back.

After he was rough, then Logan turned gentle. He took care of me, made sure I was okay. He brought me down from my high he forced until I was limp and liquid in his arms.

"That was a surprise," I whispered and climbed off him.

"And a risk." He stood, and his now soft dick swung thick between his legs. He grabbed my body wash, gave himself a quick rubdown, and then kissed me. "And I can't stay. I really do have to get to the hotel."

The Steel's first game was tomorrow, his first regular season game as the head coach. All players and coaches stayed the night at a hotel the night before, but I knew that Logan would carry the burden of a loss on his shoulders even if he did everything right. It would also be my first night home alone with Amelia and while she and I were getting along and she was her usual friendly self with me, I had special plans for her so she didn't think about not having her mom or dad around.

"I know." I grabbed my shampoo and started scrubbing my hair. Logan lingered, eyes dropping to my breasts and further below. "You need to get moving."

"I know. But now I want to fuck you again." To prove it, he grasped his hardening dick.

The man had little to zero refractory period. Insane. Some nights, I was sure he could go much longer than I could.

I smiled, knowing I did that to him.

He smirked, then brushed his lips over my wet cheek. "You're bringing Amelia to the game tomorrow?"

I rolled my eyes. We'd been over this all week. "Yes, I'm

bringing her to the game. We'll be there early so she can spend time on the field with you if she wants and if you have the time. We'll sit in the seats you have for us, and we'll cheer super loud. And if you're a really good boy, we'll come down and see you after."

He scowled. Stepped out of the shower and dried himself off with a towel.

"I hope you know I'm going to spend the night in the hotel, alone, my hand on this dick you made hard again, and think of all the ways to make you sorry for that sass."

I grinned. I couldn't *wait*. "Yes, sir."

He cursed, said something I couldn't hear in a low grumble, and tossed my towel to the floor before he dressed. "Sweet dreams, Ruby. I'll see you tomorrow."

———

"Can I ask you something?" Amelia and I had ordered pizza for dinner and were happily eating beneath the large blanket fort I made in the living room. Complete with air mattresses and all the pillows I gathered from every bed in the house except for Logan's. We were enclosed in a dark cocoon, only able to see the TV mounted on the wall.

"Of course. You can ask me anything."

She peeled off a pepperoni and plopped it into her mouth. "You like my daddy?"

I liked everything about her daddy. I liked him so much I hadn't stopped thinking about him since he left, counting down the hours until he was back in his home and Amelia was sleeping tomorrow night.

I didn't think that was what she was asking. "Sure, I like your dad. He's a nice man."

"And you're friends, right?"

"We are..."

She tilted her head. The French braids I put in her hair after I gave her a bath after Logan left draped down in front of her shoulders. I pushed one back before the tips could land in her pizza. She picked every topping on her pizza before she ate the crust and sauce last.

"Like Mommy and Renaldo are friends?"

I hid a smile as she said Renaldo, making the L in his name more like a W. I hadn't seen him yet, but I imagined him as very Italian. When Amelia said his name, it made me think of the old picture books, *Where's Waldo?*

Oh. She meant that type of friend.

"Ummm... I think your dad and I are a different type of friend." In the way we had to hide all the sex we were having and act strictly professional when we were around each other. At least, until the sunset, when he let his dark side out.

"Like how? Because I like my mom and Renaldo. He makes her laugh, and he takes her places. Daddy makes you laugh, right? And he brought you with us to the park, so he takes you places, too."

Bless her four-year-old little heart.

"Well, then I suppose in that way our friendships are similar, but your mommy and Renaldo go on dates and hold hands and spend time alone. So that makes their friendship different."

She was quiet and pushed her lips out. She didn't look at me when she said, "They were married and now they're not."

It was the first time she'd so much as broached that topic since they had their family call over a week ago. Logan had ordered her an iPad that weekend and she now talked to Vanessa twice a day through it.

"No, they're not. But there are lots of mommies and daddies who aren't married, and we go on to have friendships with other people. That's okay. They still love you bunches."

This was probably not the conversation I should have been having with her. If there was a way to distract her, I would have.

The last time I tried to explain anything to her, Logan flipped out.

I hoped that wouldn't happen now, but there had to be a way to get out of it.

"Why are you asking, sweetie?"

She shrugged, peeling off the last chunk of cheese. "Mommy looks happy, and Daddy doesn't all the time. I thought if you were friends with him like Renaldo, he'll be happier."

Oh. *Oh.* I set down my paper plate and scooted closer. I gave her little knee a quick pat to get her attention and once I had it, I brushed my finger along her temple, brushing away wisps or short baby hairs. "I think your daddy is happy because he has you with him and that makes him smile and laugh lots. But his job is hard, and so he's worried sometimes. I think once his team wins, then he'll be very happy. Do you know how we can help him do that?"

Her eyes rounded, large pools of blue I now knew she got from her mom. "We can cheer super loud tomorrow?"

"Exactly." I held out my hand for a high five. She returned it. Sufficiently distracted, I went back to the pizza. "So what movie do we watch first?"

"Duh. *Frozen.*"

Obviously. "You got it."

I pulled up the movie on Logan's TV, cleaned up the pizza mess when she was done eating, and then I made popcorn, surprising her with boxes of candy. We pigged out on junk food and Disney movies until her eyes were drooping and she couldn't find her yawns.

It wasn't until after I had her in bed, asleep, the living room cleaned up and was back in my own room getting ready for bed when I checked my phone.

Thinking of you…

It was a text from Logan, with an image attached. I climbed

beneath my sheets before opening it and my mouth watered at the sight.

It was him. *HARD*. With a drop of precum on the slit of his tip with his hand fisting his shaft. He'd paused to take this, mid jerking off, over an hour ago.

I slipped my hand beneath the sheets, down to my thighs. Remembering what he'd told me last weekend, to not get myself off without him, I paused.

He hadn't said anything about it before he left.

But...

I sent him a quick text.

Can I do the same? Sir?

I waited. Stared at my screen. It was well past ten and was early for him to be sleeping, but he had a big day tomorrow. He could be meeting with the coaches or already sleeping. Time stopped as I waited for three gray dots to appear, and with every second I waited, I was tempted to forget I even asked. He couldn't *stop* me. He'd probably never know.

Finally, when I was feathering my fingers over my center, my underwear a barrier, the gray dots appeared.

Only because you were a good girl and asked nicely.

Thank goodness. It took me minutes. I shoved down my underwear and spread my legs. I was already so dripping wet and swollen it took me a few brushes over my clit before I pushed them inside. I found that sweet spot and with my heel on my clit and my fingers inside of me, I came quietly.

And not nearly as strong or enjoyable as when Logan did it.

Damn it. He really was ruining me for self-pleasure.

This time, though, I didn't mind.

There'd be a day I had to get over it, to move on, but I had months of fun before that happened. I might as well enjoy it.

I climbed out of the bed and washed my hands, then

splashed cold water on my cheeks to cool down. I was back in bed when another text came.

Enjoy yourself?

I couldn't let him know he had the upper hand. Or how much I missed him. How much I craved him.

Immensely. It was so good. Good night.

It'd make him mad. It'd make him grumpy to think I could take care of myself. I had no doubt he wanted me to tell him it was better with him. Our games wouldn't allow me the satisfaction.

I turned my phone to *do not disturb* so I wouldn't get notifications from him.

Take that, *sir*.

LOGAN

I LOVED THIS GAME. I loved everything about it. I loved the smell of both turf and grass, the lingering scent of freshly painted sidelines. I loved the smell of sweat, the clang of a hard tackle. I loved the roar of the crowd, the comraderies of the players.

There wasn't a damn thing I enjoyed more than football, except for maybe recently, being buried in Ruby's sweet, warm cunt.

Her last text of the night had irritated me. Knowing she pleased herself without me, even if she'd done it thinking of me, had thought to ask me first, made me jealous. I didn't want anyone in charge of her orgasms, even herself, until our time together ended. I went to bed cranky because of it. And the fact I knew she'd silenced her notifications to be sassy. Crazy how well she knew me.

I was over it in the morning, pushed it to the side while we had a quick morning meeting with the team and then a walk-through at the stadium before the gates opened. We warmed up, then went back to the lockers. Guys who needed the attention spent time in the physical therapy room, getting massages and being taped up. Other guys headed to the bikes to keep their muscles loose and warm.

Others sat their behinds down on the couches and played video games. A few kicked a soccer ball around to stay loose, too.

I sequestered myself in the coach's office with the rest of my team. We drove ourselves crazy, going over our list. Was there anything else to do? Any changes to be made? We had two hours until game time and the only thing that could have distracted me from getting this first win, setting the expectations for our team and the fans, and letting the entire league know without doubt I was the best coach to lead this time, was the awareness that at any moment, Ruby and Amelia were going to be out there, cheering my team on.

"We need to stop this." Allen Jacobi shoved his iPad out of the way and dropped his head into his hands. "We're driving ourselves crazy."

"I agree," Tom Hansom, the defense coach, said. He closed the cover on his iPad with a resounding snap.

"I know. I know we do. We're ready." I tugged off my ball cap, scrubbed a hand through my hair, and resettled the hat on my head. "Right?"

I scanned the table. For all of their moaning a bit ago, all the coaches glanced at each other. They nodded, but they were slow, hesitant nods that didn't give me the confidence I was hoping for.

The call was mine to make.

They were right. We were ready. I doubted I'd ever feel one hundred percent ready for a game. I never had when I played or when I ran the offense in California. Doubts came with the job. Small tweaks could always lead us closer to perfection.

Constantly doubting myself would make me hesitant when it came time to call the plays.

"You're right," I told them all and met each of them in the eyes. "We're ready. The team is ready. Cole is healthy, our entire defense stepped it up last week. Special team has been explosive, and Moore hasn't been kicked in a game since November last season. There's nothing we can do to be more ready for this game."

Small smirks followed by grins broke free on all of them. "Hell yeah, Coach."

Damn, I loved being a coach. I shoved back from the table. "I'm going to grab lunch and hope like hell I don't throw up on the sidelines."

Jacobi chuckled. Hanson rolled his eyes. "We're ready. We have the best team in the league even with trades and rookies, and the guys know what they're doing. Bonus, Los Angeles is projected to have one of the worst defenses, so that's helpful."

Right. I'd been ignoring my first game as head coach was against my previous team. It should have given me more confidence. I knew their plays, their offense. Unless the new OC had come in and changed everything up, we were more than prepared for this game.

Hanson's reminder only made me jittery at facing my old head coach as an equal. We hadn't spoken much since I left, and he wasn't thrilled or encouraging of me to leave.

It was more I had to prove.

I glanced back at my iPad... maybe we could...

"No." Jacobi slapped his hand over my tablet and slid it away. "Don't doubt yourself now."

I glared at him. "Fine."

"Go eat."

My scowl deepened. A grin broke out on his face. "Go, Logan, before you have an aneurysm before the kickoff happens."

"Fine." I laughed, threw my hands up in defeat. The team was ready. I was ready. And Ruby and Amelia were waiting.

———

I ate. I checked in on the players in the physical therapy room. I double-checked the laminated card that held all of our plays and my game plan before tucking it back into my pocket. With nothing left to do except worry and second-guess myself for the umpteenth time, I headed toward the field. I breathed in the excitement from the fans who were arriving. The marketing trailers and the team's promotions on the screens. The lights of the field had me adjusting my hat against the glare, and I stepped out of the tunnel onto the corner of the field.

This was it. A lifetime goal I'd had for myself ever since I knew I wouldn't continue playing football. I was there, leading a team. Soon to be surrounded by almost seventy thousand fans, many critics included. My pulse raced and my hands burned with nerves, but it wasn't only nerves.

It was the excitement. The thrill. I stepped farther out onto the field and turned in a slow circle. Los Angeles was just leaving the field and there was a small group of my own players down by our closest goalpost. Jassen, Knox, and others kneeled on one knee. Their elbows planted on the other. Their foreheads rested on their fists while the group gave one final prayer.

I took in the sight. Memorized it. The coolness of the stadium that would soon be overheating from adrenaline, and I stopped, staring into the stands.

Amelia and Ruby were allowed in the coaches' and managers' suite. They were always welcome there, and it was usually where the wives watched the game. However, Ruby had asked for regular seats. She'd reminded me there wouldn't be kids in the suite with her, most likely, and she wasn't a wife.

I bought them two seats. Five rows up from where I stood in the corner where I'd be able to see both at the railing when I entered and left the field.

The seats were empty, but that wasn't surprising.

I was about to leave when Amelia's quiet shriek came from the tunnel.

"Daddy!"

There they were.

A grin broke out on my face, and I squatted down right before Amelia slammed her body into mine. "You made it."

Ruby fixed a black and red bow at the end of Amelia's braids. "She refused to be late."

Her grin was soft, mixed with nerves and excitement. I immediately thought back to last night.

Immensely.

She knew it would irritate me. The nerves on her face now had nothing to do with the game like mine, but my upcoming retribution.

"Sleep well last night?"

Ruby's cheeks burned and she glanced away.

"We made a fort! And ate candy and popcorn and watched movies!" Amelia shouted and I set her on the ground.

"That sounds like so much fun. *Immense* fun." I tugged on her braid, glancing at Ruby.

She was staring anywhere she could look. A cement wall had never appeared so stimulating, but it must have been to her. Even while her cheeks burned as red as our jerseys.

"Can I see the field now? Please?" Amelia jumped up and down, her black and white pleated skirt bouncing along with her.

"Absolutely." I grabbed her hand and headed toward the field. Ruby was still in the tunnel. "Coming?"

Her nose wrinkled, and she stayed a couple steps behind. "Not likely anytime soon," she muttered as she followed us out.

I hit the field laughing, Amelia asking me why and Ruby following behind.

A thousand new wicked ideas spun in my mind thanks to that lovely comment.

———

We were winning. Sweat dripped down my back from the heat and adrenaline. I was doing this. Sure, it was with less than two minutes left in the second quarter, but our team wasn't just winning, we were annihilating Los Angeles.

"Yes!" I threw my fist in the air as Cole sailed another pass to Yeets. He was tackled on the forty-two-yard line, but it was two more yards than we needed for the first down. With another four plays ahead for us, I barked out the play into Cole's helmet.

The crowd was infectious. There weren't nearly enough Los Angeles fans in the stands to come close to drowning out the roar of the Steels, and our fans were loving every second of this game. I couldn't blame them, either. Cole was on fire. So far, he'd had only one incomplete pass and his ankle didn't seem to be bothering him at all. He fired off passes to Yeets and handed off the ball to Davis with perfect timing. Dawson had both run and caught the ball.

Everything I'd worried about pregame and during preseason was nonexistent as I coached the team through our first half, already winning twenty-one to nothing.

A blowout, and we were marching down the field with high odds we'd score again. JJ, our other wide receiver, leapt into the air on another long pass from Cole. He was taken down at the twenty and our team rushed to the line of scrimmage.

I shouted into my earpiece. "Run it. Take it slow. We've got time, but the running backs need their touches."

Cole nodded, glancing at me. I waved him off. He knew what to do.

Second down, we had another first down at the eight. First down we were at six. Second down the third. The clock was ticking down. Thirty seconds. One pass and we were scoring and then lining up for a kickoff, giving LA time to move the ball. The way they were playing meant the odds were slim they'd score, but they could pull off a field goal.

I wanted to go into the half up so damn far the guys remembered this first half all season.

"Go. Go, go, go!" I was screaming into my microphone, shouting plays at Cole.

With all the ease and confidence he carried himself with, he handed off the ball to Butler. Butler bulldozed him through the first line of defense and leapt over a back who dove for his ankles.

"Touchdown!" I screamed, throwing both of my arms in the air.

We were killing it!

Allen slammed his palm onto my shoulder. "Told you we were ready!"

Our offense jogged off the field, everyone smiling, everyone celebrating. There wasn't a calm player on the sidelines or an ass in the chair in the stadium.

Jassen took to the field, and as much as I tried to ignore her all game and pretend she wasn't there, I turned and watched as both Ruby and Amelia stood near the railing. Their red shirts lost in a sea of red and black, but I could find her anywhere.

She chewed on that bottom lip while Jassen lined up the kick, and when he ran toward the ball, covered her eyes.

As soon as the stadium shook with their cheers, she dropped her hand, checking the scoreboard. Her hands cupped her mouth as she screamed, cheered, and jumped for her brother, and pointed him out to Amelia.

Her gaze swung to the sidelines.

Our eyes met.

She picked up Amelia and shoved her finger in my direction and I couldn't see what she said, but Amelia's little hand rose in the air and waved at me.

My chest swelled three sizes.

They were here. My daughter was cheering for me. Proud of her daddy. And Ruby? She might have been proud of Jassen too, but damn... I hoped she was proud of me, too.

I lifted my hand in their direction, acknowledging them, and then I slapped Cole's helmet as he ran by. "That's how it's done!" I shouted.

He grinned and tugged on his chin straps. "Good job, Coach. You're killing it."

Again, that heat hit my chest. I turned back to the field as our special teams lined up for the kick.

Eighteen seconds later, we were running off the field toward the tunnel. I was stopped by the media, gave a quick, ten-second review of the game from my perspective, but in truth, I had no idea what she asked me.

I thanked her for her time, then headed toward the tunnel. Hands were dropped through the railings for high fives, but I ignored them all except the ones that mattered.

"Daddy!" Amelia was crouched as low as she could, her little arm dangling.

I had to jump to reach her and barely grazed her fingers. "Love you, sweetie."

I winked at Ruby and disappeared into the tunnel. I had a game to finish, a team to keep focused, and later, I had some very different plans for Ruby.

It was, after all, my birthday. Not that she had any way of knowing that.

———

We won the game. Forty-one to three and only then because I ended up pulling out Cole, Hall, and Butler. They were pissed, understandably, but we were ahead by thirty-five to nothing when I pulled them. The risk of their injury was greater than the reward of having them out there at that point.

Our defense held LA to a field goal. Jassen kicked two of them to give us another six points. At the end of the game, my old coach barely had the manners to shake my hand and begrudgingly mutter, "good game" before walking off the field.

I didn't give a shit about his attitude. I celebrated with the team in the locker room. Praised them all for the way they played. They did so well, I canceled their Monday workouts, told them to sleep in, and be at the field in the afternoon for films and light conditioning.

By the time I made it out of the locker rooms and into the tunnel, I assumed Ruby would have taken Amelia home. Instead, they were there, Amelia sitting with a coloring book on her lap, and Ruby on her phone, leaning against the wall.

The scene threw me back to my earlier playing days and even first year coaching. When Vanessa would wait for me. Throw her arms around me and kiss me like no one was around. Those days were long gone, and I hadn't realized how much I'd missed that support upon leaving until I had it then.

Ruby's eyes shone with happiness and she pushed off the wall.

"How'd I do?" I asked, and Amelia's head jerked up.

"Daddy!" She tossed her book, scrambled to her feet, and ran to me. She'd spent the fourth quarter in the family room, and I only knew that because Ruby had texted me when she did it. She knew I wouldn't see the text, but I liked that she checked in to let me know. "You were great! And you won!"

"The team won. I only helped."

Behind her, Ruby rolled her eyes. "So modest. Congratulations."

God, I wanted to hug her. Kiss her. I wanted to slam her body against that wall and ravage her. I couldn't for a dozen known reasons, but none of it stopped me from wishing it could happen.

"Should we head out?" I had Amelia's hand in mine and Ruby packed up her coloring book and crayons into a bag she'd brought for Amelia.

"Actually," Ruby said, "I think I'll let you two celebrate alone. I'll be back later."

"Why?" I barked it out and Ruby jerked, tucking her hair behind her ear.

"Um." She shrugged and looked away. "I just... I have some things to do?"

Did she now... She was lying. At minimum hiding something.

"I was looking forward to celebrating together." I said it as a whisper, letting her see my disappointment. I kept it quiet enough so Amelia couldn't hear.

She flinched. "I know, but I'll be back later tonight."

I couldn't force her. I wouldn't force her to want to spend time with Amelia and me. But I wanted it, more than I'd ever expected to want another woman. I wanted Ruby with me, celebrating both my win and my birthday.

"All right." I sighed. Grinning down at Amelia, I took her hand. "Just you and me, squirt!"

"I want McDonald's for dinner."

McDonald's. I'd just won my first game as the head coach for an NFL team and I was going to be suckered into eating McDonald's for dinner.

What a glorious life.

Next to us, Ruby giggled. "She's been asking for it all day and was upset she couldn't get it here."

"Whatever my girl wants..."

I let that hang and gave Ruby a wink.

Fine. No birthday dinner with her or family time. That was probably the safest thing anyway. I was starting to think about her too much. Want her too much.

This was only sex. Hottest sex of my life, but sex all the same. I needed to remember that.

Ruby was leaving us, and it was best, at least for Amelia's sake, if we didn't get more attached than necessary.

Right. For Amelia's sake.

Ruby wasn't the only crappy liar.

CHAPTER 23

RUBY

I HURT HIS FEELINGS. I saw it in his frown and the way he grew silent as Logan walked me to the car on the same ramp where he'd parked his. Benefits of working for the Coach? Hella good parking on game days.

But I had a surprise for him. Earlier, Amelia had been on a FaceTime call with her mom, and at the last moment, Vanessa reminded her it was Logan's birthday. There was no time to do anything or buy him anything before we left, but that hadn't stopped Amelia from being near tears on the way to the stadium.

I made her a deal. She kept it a secret that we knew, and tomorrow, once we had time to go shopping, we'd throw him a great big party and surprise him. The surprise convinced her.

So not only did I have a bunch of shopping to do with her tomorrow, I'd also lied. Because I was going to get my own gifts and give Logan his very own surprise tonight. Lucky for me, I knew exactly what he'd like.

His thirty-seventh birthday. God, I was too young for him. Fourteen years now separated us. It was no wonder he was so good in bed. He'd had so much more time to practice. To perfect the art of pleasuring a woman. It'd made me uncertain earlier, as I thought about it all, but then I remembered whatever we were doing was new to him too. He'd admitted it more than once. I brought out this new side of him.

Me. His twenty-three-year-old nanny.

I shook off the doubts as I pulled into the sketchy, poorly lit parking lot. It was empty on a Sunday, and I could only hope it stayed that way. As soon as I stepped inside, I regretted it. Sexy toys were *everywhere*. All shapes. All things. I'd come with a plan and ignored the twelve-inch dildos as big as my forearm and all the anal toys. The lingerie wasn't nearly as sexy or classy enough for where I was headed next, and after perusing the aisles, ignoring videos and masks and gags, I finally found what I was looking for.

Handcuffs. Straps. It was a risk. A huge one. But the more Logan bossed me around, the more he took control, I had to believe he'd enjoy this. Having me tied up for his use? Seemed the exact kind of thing that would drive him wild.

I paid, blushing the entire way. The female worker behind the counter was professional and if she saw my nerves or my embarrassment, she said nothing. My items were packed in a discreet black bag and I tossed them into my glove compartment as soon as I got into my car.

Two more stops for presents and a quick bite to eat later, and I was pulling into Logan's house.

The lights were dark. It was later than I'd planned, but I'd try to time it so Amelia would either be asleep, or he'd be putting her to bed.

Her light was off, but the soft glow of a lamp shining through her closed blinds told me I timed it perfectly.

I hurried inside, set one of the presents on the kitchen counter, and dumped the rest in Logan's bedroom on a chair in his sitting room.

He was still upstairs, or somewhere, when I returned to the kitchen, so I took a moment in the half-bath to settle myself. I fixed my hair, used the restroom, and rinsed my mouth with mouthwash I'd taken to keeping under the sink.

Back in the kitchen, I poured myself a glass of wine and Logan a whiskey. I imagined he'd want a drink after the day he had.

So I was ready, ready as I would ever be, by the time his footsteps thudded on the wood stairs.

———

His eyes widened as he turned the corner to the kitchen and saw me.

"Hey. Good game today."

A cautious smile broke out on his face. "Thank you. What are you doing?"

"I got you something. Here." I handed him the glass I poured for him.

He smirked. "Thank you. How thoughtful."

I snorted. "That's not it." I turned and grabbed the cake still in the store-bought container and spun back to him. "Happy birthday, Logan."

His jaw dropped, the glass of whiskey freezing in his hand halfway to his mouth. Slowly, his brows rose. "You knew?"

"I found out. Yeah." I'd explain about Vanessa later.

"And you bought me a birthday cake?" His surprise wiped away to pleasure.

"Sort of?"

He chuckled and moved toward me, eyes lighting up. "I'm not sure what sort of means when it comes to birthday cake."

"Well, a birthday cake usually says *happy birthday* on it. And has sprinkles and candles. They couldn't do that on such short notice, so... it's for you, for your birthday, but not really a *birthday* cake."

"I didn't realize cakes were so complicated."

He was teasing me. I had no problems with this kind of game. *Fun* Logan didn't make a frequent appearance. I stepped away from him and pulled the cake closer to me. "It's also more of a brownie."

"Are you going to let me take the top off so I can see it or are you going to hold it all night?"

"I haven't decided. I *really* like brownies. I might keep it."

A full laugh thrust from him. I smiled so wide it hurt my cheeks.

I was still smiling when he wiped away the humor softening his features and turned serious. He sipped his drink, set it gently down, and splayed his palms on the counter. This was the Logan I knew so well. The Logan who made my knees wobble and my stomach flip.

"I will tackle you for that dessert, Ruby."

"Such violence." I tutted three times and shook my head at him. "I believe that would not get you the rest of your presents." I filled the last word with all the innuendo I could muster.

"Show me. Please?"

Oh, he was getting desperate. I relished this part of him. "The rest of your presents? Those will come, but only if you're a good boy."

His eyes turned to that hard iron and his nostrils flared. He either liked that or hated his own words being turned around on him. Let him think on what else was coming for a little while.

I lifted the lid and inhaled. "It smells so good, and oh..."

"Ruby..." My name was a growl that sparked excitement in my veins. I felt that rumble in my nipples.

"Fine." I gave in. I popped off the lid and set it on the counter so he could see it.

"Dang... That is no ordinary brownie." Logan and Amelia had a soft spot for sweets. They devoured more ice cream in a week than I could in a year. I knew he'd like this.

There was a thick, creamy chocolate sauce covering the

brownie along with two scoops of ice cream. A mountainous mound of whipped cream sat on top along with two cherries.

"It's a molten lava extreme brownie cake with a chocolate filling, too."

My mouth watered for it. For the man staring at the cake and then up at me. He took two steps to me and divested the plate from my hands before setting it on the island.

Logan was inches away from me, focused on me, and I still had my hands in the air like he hadn't swiped it from me. I pouted, looking at the cake. It really did look delicious. How serious was he about that tackling stuff?

"Thank you, Ruby. It's been a while since anyone's been so thoughtful to me."

His voice had turned so soft, so genuine. If fun Logan was rare, soft Logan was an anomaly.

"You're welcome."

"And since I'm a nice guy, I'll share it with you."

"Even better."

We dove into the cake with two forks, not bothering to plate it.

I sipped my wine. The chocolate cake was great and all, but I had other surprises waiting for him I couldn't forget about.

But Amelia hadn't been down long enough and there was no way, depending on Logan's reaction, we could risk being interrupted.

"Were you happy with how the team played today?"

His eyes popped wide. Surprised. When was the last time anyone asked him that? Took care of him?

A while, based on how he'd said his marriage slowly eroded.

"Yeah," he finally said and slid the side of his fork through more chocolatey goodness. "I was happy today. Thanks for asking."

"I ask because I care."

About him. His happiness. His daughter.

I was starting to care about Logan far more than having sex with him. It was dangerous, and I couldn't find it in me to stop.

He watched me for several moments, gaze searing into me while he brought the fork to his mouth. "I do, too. You know."

"Yeah?" That dumb hopeful lift in my voice couldn't be squashed before it appeared.

"Yeah, Ruby. I care about you."

As far as admissions went, it wasn't much. The weight of it felt heavier than it should have.

I set down my fork and refilled my wine. Two glasses would leave my nerves at bay for later. "Need another drink?"

He shook his head. "I'm good. Think I'll need my wits for whatever other surprises you have."

At least one of us would have them.

———

His dark eyes glittered with amusement. As soon as I told Logan his gifts were in his bedroom, he finished his drink and jogged there.

"Stop!" I settled a hand on his chest. He'd changed after the game and was wearing a black polo shirt and khaki pants. The shirt had the red Steels logo stitched at the chest. My fingers brushed over it as Logan looked down at me, one brow quirked.

"You're locking me out of my own room?"

"For one minute. Maybe two. I want to set the presents out." Take a second to gather my nerves. This was happening, and I wanted him to like the idea.

I'd already been on edge thinking about what was coming, what could happen, what he could do to me.

"All right." He glanced at his Apple Watch and set a timer. "Two minutes, no more."

I rolled my eyes and laughed. "Patience, sir. Now stay here."

I was grinning when I entered his room and flicked on the

bedroom light. I adjusted it from brightness to a gentle glow. Romantic, sensual, but bright enough he could clearly see what I set out for him.

I'd let him have the pleasure of choosing what he wanted to do.

The lingerie set I bought was two pieces. A tight, black lace corset with a deep V beneath my chest. It tied at the back and after I tried it on at the store, I'd loosened the straps enough so I'd be able to redo it myself later. The panties, though? They were the kicker. And he wouldn't see until he was *right there*. My sex exposed through the crotchless lace.

"Oh God," I groaned and balled my hands into fists to chase away my nerves. Horses might as well have been galloping across my chest.

"One minute!" Logan called out.

I set out the lingerie, hiding the surprise, and then unwrapped the other items from the back. Everything was black, a stark difference from the white duvet cover. The metal of the handcuffs gleamed in the light, looking more severe than they had in the store.

And the other bindings? Well... my pulse raced and I fingered the soft leather of them before I rubbed my hands together and grabbed the garbage. I tossed it in the bathroom trash and hurried to his door.

Once there, I opened it slowly, barely enough he could see me. His bed was out of view, but he still craned his neck to see over me.

"Okay. Before you come see, there are rules."

His gaze snapped down to mine. "You're setting the rules now? It's *my* birthday."

Oh my. I gripped the doorknob tighter to stay standing.

"Rules. I bought some, um... things," I finally choked out.

Brows arched. "Did you..."

"And, well, we don't have to use them. So if you don't like it, no worries, but I thought... well, with how you like to boss me, you might like other things."

"Ruby?" He hadn't moved an inch and yet my name on his lips, his dark, familiar, rough voice was a caress over my heated skin.

"Yeah?"

"Move out of the way."

I stumbled backward, staying at the door as he walked into the room. I couldn't get near him. Couldn't bear to see if I'd overstepped. If he *hated* it.

He went to the lingerie first, smirking at me over his shoulder. With one hand, he reached out and drew his finger down the center of the lacy corset. He might as well have been trailing that finger around the swells of my breasts for as much as I ached, watching his eyes narrow into slits as he took in the rest.

He smirked at the handcuffs.

And once he held one of the leather cuffs to the other bindings in his hands, my body shivered.

His lips pushed out, gaze narrowed. His chest heaved and oh God. He did. He *hated* the idea of all of this. Fear raced through me as he stood so still, all but that finger tracing the leather. Like he didn't know how to let me down.

"I want your ass over here and on your knees in three seconds or you're going to see a side of me you haven't met."

Maybe I was wrong.

I tripped over my feet, over the edge of his rug in my hurry to get to him and by the time I fell to my knees, my heart was a giant ball in my throat.

His hand came down, brushed through my hair, and cupped the back of my neck.

"You want to try this?"

I swallowed, but my mouth was dry. "I thought you would like it."

"But do you want it?" He gripped my neck, forcing me to tilt my chin at him. His expression was still unrecognizable. So tense.

"Yes, sir."

He nodded, dropping his hand from my hair. He went back to fondling the bindings. There were two sets that would go beneath the mattress. The cuffs would bind my ankles and my wrists. I pictured myself, spread eagle on his bed in all that black lace against his white sheets and almost wept with neediness.

My lingerie set appeared in my vision. "Go put this on. Take your time. It'll take me a minute to get everything ready."

He was choosing the bindings. Not the cuffs. I'd wondered if he'd start with the simpler choice, but I should have known.

When it came to Logan and me, nothing was simple.

Why start now?

He curled his hand on my biceps and guided me to my feet. I hugged the lingerie to my chest as his thumb pressed beneath my chin. "Thank you, Ruby. I *love* my gifts."

"We haven't used them yet."

"Trust me." He leaned down and brushed his lips over mine. "We are going to *love* them."

LOGAN

I WOULDN'T LET her go. Not after Christmas. Not when Vanessa returned. I didn't give two little shits where she wanted to go to school. We'd make that work. But no woman, no woman I'd ever met in my life, was as incredible, as loving and kind and gracious, and also *kinky* as Ruby Moore.

She was a vision, spread eagle on my bed. As soon as I had her tied up, I couldn't stop. I'd already brought her close to an orgasm by twisting, pulling, and sucking on her nipples. They were shoved high on her chest. The cups of her corset tugged beneath them. She could barely move due to her limbs being stretched so far and as I slid down the bed, my fingers trailing down the center of her stomach, her rasps and panted breath were an angelic harmony. *God*, I didn't want to let her go.

I kissed her legs. I teased her, trailing my tongue along the waistband of her panties. They'd have to come off. I went to tear them, when she whispered my name.

"What?"

Her eyes were filled with lust and desire. My own had to be mirroring the same look. "Look closely." She dipped her chin down toward where my fingers were brushing back and forth over the lace.

"Oh... I like this."

Crotchless. I tugged at the edges of her panties, and her entire soaking wet pussy was exposed. Her inner thighs glistened and... "Hell yes. You are perfection," I groaned against her clit before I licked her. I could live in the crux of Ruby's thighs for a lifetime. She was delicious. So damn sweet. I was hungry for her, desperate for her every time I was in the same room with her. Tonight was no different.

I shoved my tongue inside of her, ate her like she was the most delicious dessert, and when I focused on her clit, I pressed two fingers inside of her. Her body thrashed in the bindings, the jingle of them adding to the intensity.

She'd *wanted* me to tie her up, to do these wicked things to her. Hell if I'd ever been this hard. I soaked my fingers with her, bit down on her clit, and then dragged those fingers out of her cunt and to the back. I'd played here before, nothing too serious, but she was ready. *God, I hoped she was ready.*

I kept licking her, flicking her clit. The noises she made and the tightness of her abs told me she was close and as I pressed a finger against her puckered hole, I focused my eyes on her. She peered down at me, whining my name and her need, and as I slipped that first finger inside her ass, the most guttural, incredibly sexy moan filled the room.

"Logan..."

"You're okay. Relax." I kept up the distraction with my tongue, waiting until she settled, until the pressure eased around my finger and then pushed it farther in.

"Oh God. Fuck. That feels..."

Her voice trailed off. Her shaking body said enough. With my mouth at her sex, I continued tasting her. Teasing her. I shoved my finger the rest of the way inside of her and her back bowed off the bed. Noises escaped her I'd never heard before.

"So fucking perfect, Ruby. Come for me." She was close. Thighs trembling, her sex pulsing.

She came like a rocket and so hard, so fast and so loudly she didn't have time to smother her cries. I drank her in as she came wildly, and I thanked the heavens I'd had enough sense to buy a house with my room on the completely opposite side from Amelia's.

Her body thrashed, and I kept going. She jerked from the sensitivity of her first orgasm as she rolled into another and as she came again, I moved my finger inside of her faster. Harder.

And as soon as she came down, spent, breathless, her chest heaved. Those gorgeous nipples were hard and tight points in the air, and I climbed up her body and sucked one into my mouth as I grabbed the condom, then sheathed myself.

"You doing okay?" I asked, kissing her chest, the swell of her breasts.

"I'm dead." She laughed, and I leaned over her, brushing the hair off her forehead. "You're killing me."

"I hope not. I'm not done with you."

"Fuck," she rasped and turned her head. I slammed my mouth to hers and gripped my length. I gave her no time to prepare before I slammed inside of her.

I took her hard. Fast. I took her with all the impatient build-up I'd felt since I saw those bindings on my bed. An offering to me.

The most treasured offering I'd ever been given.

She met every powerful thrust with the same desperate need, which only made holding off my own climax harder.

I was close, and she was exhausted, but I still wanted one more from her. With one hand, I reached beneath her ass, tilted her, and lifted as much as possible while I kept kissing her.

Kept my mouth pressed to hers, our tongues dueling while I pounded into her until she cried into my mouth. I slammed inside of her one more time and came. The walls of her pussy clamped around me, milked every drop I had, and when were done, I pulled out and rolled off her.

Her arms had to be tired, her legs sore from the stretch. As much as I wanted to lie there with her, continue playing with her body, she needed the rest.

———

"This was the best birthday gift I've ever gotten." Not because it was things. Because she gave me *her*. She not only liked this crazed new side of me, she encouraged it. Sometimes I thought she got off on it more than I did.

Tonight, she definitely got off way more times than I did.

Her corset was shoved beneath her breasts, her underwear still on. Thank God for crotchless panties... those were a gift on their own.

A thousand wicked ideas spawned as soon as I saw them. Sitting next to Ruby at dinner, shoving up her skirt or dress and slipping my fingers inside of her. We could be at a table with a dozen people at a fundraiser, a black-tie affair. We could be at home, with Amelia distracted. There would never be a time she'd deny me that access. I couldn't think of a single scenario when I wouldn't want it from her.

Shit. I needed to stop thinking of a future with her. Jassen would hate me when he found out what we were doing. I'd lose the team's respect. I'd lose *her*. Jassen was all she had. There was no way she'd choose me over her brother.

"You okay?" She peered up at me, and I did my best to erase the doubts and the worries. I went back to unbuckling her wrists, rubbing circulation back into them.

"Perfect." I kissed the inside of her wrist. "Any chance you could give me one more birthday present?"

"What's that?"

"Stay with me. Tonight. You wake up before Amelia anyway, so it shouldn't be a problem."

"Logan..."

"It's my birthday." The manipulation made my stomach churn, but hell... would we ever have a night where we could share the same bed? Where I could wrap my arms around her and we could watch a show, fall asleep in each other's arms?

"You don't have to convince me. As long as you're sure."

"I'm sure." I kissed her nose.

"Then let me run upstairs and brush my teeth, wash my face. I'll be back in ten?"

"I'll lock up the house."

———

Less than ten minutes later, she was curled in my bed, the taste of mint on her lips and wearing her standard oversized shirt and shorts.

"Just in case," she'd said, tugging at the hem of her shirt when she stepped back into my room.

I kissed her temple and held her tight to me. "Thank you, again, for tonight. It was incredible."

"It was," she hummed, "and maybe I shouldn't have skipped past all those anal toys in the store earlier."

She said it with a laugh.

"You like that." I could tell she had, but she seemed nervous to admit it.

"I think I like everything you've done to me, Logan."

"Then maybe someday I'll make my own trip."

She hummed again, getting sleepy, and my mind was racing with ideas. Other things we could try. Now that she'd awakened some sort of animalistic beast, I wasn't sure he could be caged. I didn't want him to be.

Her body was limp in my arms, and her breathing slowed. I assumed she was falling asleep, until she whispered, "I lived with this guy in Portland."

I flinched from the surprise. That she was opening up.

"Yeah?" I moved my hand at her stomach, to the curve of her hip, down her thigh, and back up.

"He was a dick. Well, he ended up being a supreme dick, but until I learned that, I'd thought he was perfect."

Her voice was thick with emotion. My chest tightened. As much as I didn't want to hear about other men she'd been with, her brother's concerns and her own brief mentions had me interested. "What happened?"

She laughed, but it was a sad sound. She reached up, clasped my hand on her hip with her own, and tangled our fingers together.

"He moved in with me in my junior year of college. I thought he was the one. He was so perfect, so kind. He traveled a lot, but when he was there, he was the perfect boyfriend."

I stayed silent even though I was already envisioning beating the guy who hurt her. That wouldn't help.

"He was married with kids."

"What?"

"I didn't know. I swear, I didn't know. But Paulie, God, he was such a scammer. Jassen and Molly met him and they adored him. He was only a few years older... not old, but older."

"Like me." Shit.

"No." She chuckled then. "He was only twenty-six. You're way older."

"And better," I teased her to keep the mood light, but inside, I wasn't sure I wanted to hear any more.

"Definitely better," she agreed, then yawned. "Anyway, Paulie was married. And he apparently didn't even travel for work. He traveled up to Seattle to see his wife and kids. I was so stupid, so naïve. Even when things started to not feel right, I stayed with him. He made me believe he loved me, that he was working hard to help pay for my grad school, and God, I was an idiot."

"Believing in people doesn't make you an idiot."

"No, it makes me exactly like my mom. My stupid mom who always chose the worst men."

Ouch. That hurt. She wasn't talking about me, but she was, because if she made stupid choices with men, then what in the hell was I? We already knew this couldn't go anywhere.

"Ruby..."

I trailed off. What was I supposed to say?

She rolled onto her back, out of my hold, and shoved her hands into my hair. I was already up on an elbow, leaning over her.

"I kicked him out as soon as I found out. I got suspicious, decided to do a background report on him. Found his marriage certificate, found his wife on Facebook. The day before I found her, she posted pictures, of her and her kids celebrating one of their birthdays."

Tears ran down her cheeks and she swiped them away. The pain in my chest wouldn't ease. For her pain, for what I feared she was implying with me. With us. She needed to end this. Stop making such shitty decisions with men. Find someone who could truly be there for her in all the ways.

She needed someone who wouldn't keep her a secret.

Fucking hell.

"He stole all my money." She choked on another cry. "That's why I won't take any from Jassen. He knows we broke up, but he doesn't know all of it, and he doesn't know that all the money he'd already given me to help, Paulie cleared out of my accounts the day I broke up with him. He wasn't even upset, said he was only with me because of Jassen. I was stupid and rarely checked my accounts, but when he moved in, I gave him my sign-ins so he could take care of the rent and stuff, pay the bills for me, that kind of thing. He'd been slowly siphoning all of my savings out in the year he lived with me and the day he left, he took it all."

"Fuck. I'm so sorry."

"I'm such an idiot." She sobbed then and moved to roll away with me. "So dumb."

I reached for her before she could get far and pulled her to my chest. She was tense, ready to flee, and her cries tore at my soul deep inside of me. I wasn't sure my chest hurt this much when Vanessa cried when she told me she wasn't making the move out here with me.

That'd been almost inevitable.

This was pure pain.

"You're not an idiot and you're not stupid, Ruby. You were young and you trusted someone who played a part to get you to trust them. You can't fault yourself for that. That's Paulie's fault, not yours."

She cried then, hugging her pillow. I waited for the moment she realized, the moment she ended things.

The moment she said something like, "And here I am, doing it all again."

It never came. Her cries quieted and her breathing slowed.

I clung to Ruby long after she fell asleep, knowing it might be the only night I got to hold her, and I wasn't nearly ready to let her go.

I WAS AN IDIOT. An absolute moron. As soon as I woke up, wrapped in Logan's arm with his gentle breathing behind me, I couldn't believe the things I'd admitted before I fell asleep. I blamed his comforting hold when he wrapped his arms around me, the fact he wanted me with him. I blamed the orgasms and the intensity of the night for scrambling my brain, loosening my lips before I could stop them.

I had never planned on telling Logan any of that. Jassen sure as hell was never going to learn how dumb his sister had been. And how would Logan look at me now? Now that he knew I made dumb choices when it came to my life and who to trust.

How could he trust me to take care of his own daughter when I'd made such a fool of my own life?

How could he want to be with me ever again, knowing I'd spent years sleeping with a married man with children and had been too naïve to pick up on the clues earlier.

God, they were all so clear now. The phone calls he'd ignore, the texting he'd do. The way he'd hide his phone, always keeping it in his pocket. Two years I ignored it. Ignored the fact that outside of the clothes he needed "for work," he barely filled the drawers in our dresser.

Stupid. So damn stupid.

And I was making the same choices all over again. This was no longer sex with Logan. This wasn't some heartless, sexual exploration.

I was falling for this man. His daughter. I was starting to love every single moment I spent with him, and the more Amelia opened up to me, the less she became some girl I nannied for, but a girl who was claiming my heart.

There was no way for this to end well, and like before, with red flags paving the way to misery, I was being way too dumb in not walking away, in not ending things before they got worse.

I could, though, give us some space.

Careful not to wake Logan, I slipped out of his hold and the bed. My ankle knocked one of the bindings that had fallen down when he released me from them and I paused. Glanced over my shoulder.

Logan hadn't moved a muscle and there wasn't a hitch in his breath.

I climbed out of the bed, took the second, then two, to drink him in while he slept. The sheets were shoved beneath his chest, showing me those muscular pecs but hiding the abs I adored so much. He was softer in his sleep, his full lips parted. God, he was gorgeous.

Perfect.

I slipped out of the room without looking back and took the time closing the door so it wouldn't click too loud. It was four in the morning, based on the clock on the kitchen wall, and while there was no way in hell I was falling back to sleep, I also wasn't going to be in the kitchen when he woke and realized I was gone.

I scurried to my room, grabbed my phone, and pulled up a book. Logan and I needed to talk, but hell if I knew how, or wanted, to be the one to start that conversation.

At some point, I ended up falling asleep. I woke to sunshine bright in my windows and leapt out of my bed with a start.

Amelia. She had to be awake. She had to need me for something. I hurried out of my bed, washed my face, and brushed my teeth. With any luck, I wouldn't have to see Logan but for a moment before he left for work and I could put off the inevitable.

I was rushing back to my room when my gaze caught on a flash of yellow outside.

I stopped, backtracked to the window, and shoved open the curtains.

They were there. Amelia and Logan were out in the backyard. She was sitting cross-legged on one of the paddleboards and he was standing on it. They must have just gotten started because he had his paddle in one hand, vertical, with the other end on the floating dock for balance.

They pushed off, and even from my window, the way his back muscles rippled with every movement he made had me wishing I could be out there with them. Joining them on a daddy-daughter morning ride. Listening to Amelia's excitement over turtles and ducks and her nonstop chatter about all the fish she wanted to catch but didn't want to touch.

My heart squeezed and then sank to my gut.

If there was any way I could fix this, I would. And that assuming Logan wanted anything more than I was already giving him.

Which I still didn't even know. Despite his admission that he *cared* about me, I wasn't sure it was enough. Not for what would come next.

―――

I was on the back patio, drinking my coffee and planning out Amelia's week with old-school notebook and pen when they returned. I'd already managed to fill out the grocery list, planned a few easy meals I could make, and added it to the app. There was another list I had going, for my own personal products. Amelia would be excited about a trip to Target with me, for sure.

Logan and Amelia pulled up on the paddleboard. I'd tried to ignore them, but who was I kidding. I watched every moment of their trek around the lake, even when I could only make them out as a blurred shape in the distance. It was the entire reason I was outside, anyway.

That, and as soon as Logan wanted to talk, the air inside would suffocate me.

Amelia ran up the backyard first, her arms flailing in the air and her long hair a tangled mess. So someone had been in a hurry to get outside as well.

"Miss Ruby, Miss Ruby! Did you see us? Daddy took me out today because he doesn't have to go to work, and…"

He wasn't working? He always worked Mondays. I stopped listening to everything Amelia said after. My quiet "Ohs" and "That's nice" must have been sufficient because she was still happily chattering away about whatever she was talking about when Logan reached us.

"Amelia."

"Yes, Daddy?"

He held out his arm. "Can I have your life jacket?"

"Oh." She glanced down and undid her buckles. With a quick flip, she tossed it on the patio. "I need to potty!"

She ran inside, and I chuckled. It couldn't be helped. Pretty sure throwing it on the patio wasn't at all what Logan meant.

He glared at me as he bent to scoop it up and kept that glare on me while he draped her jacket over the back of the couch. Crossing his arms over his chest, he finally spoke, and when he did, spikes of ice traveled down my spine.

"Sleep well? Up awfully early, weren't you?"

Shame hit at the same time as irritation. Logically, there was no reason to be upset. "I woke up and thought it'd be safer to be in my room."

"Before five?"

He'd woken up then? He usually didn't rally until six thirty.

"Better safe than sorry."

He leaned forward, lips thin and teeth bared in a way that should have had me scared. But my stupid, traitorous libido perked up and sent a rush of warmth through me. God, I was *sick*.

"I woke up wanting to make love to you. Wanted to start my day with my dick deep inside you. Wanted to have to cover your mouth from your cries and have your cunt for breakfast. And I woke up, and you were *gone*."

My core clenched. I would have *loved* that.

Before I could speak, before I was able to form any meaningful words with all those ideas racing through my mind, he continued.

Leaning forward, he curled his large, strong hands around the back of the couch. "And if Amelia weren't here right now, I'd be punishing you for that. Don't *ever* leave my bed again, especially when there's obviously shit to talk about, but don't treat me like what we have is some dirty, meaningless playtime when you know damn well it's not. Not anymore."

He shoved off the couch and stormed into the house. I jumped from the slam of the sliding door closing.

I stared at the spot where he'd stood long after he was gone. My body was a live wire. Strung tight. But it wasn't only arousal racing through me, and it wasn't fear. Hope? Maybe?

Why else would he be so mad?

And did he...? Did he say *make love to me?*

———

By the time I found the courage to go back inside, Amelia was sitting on her chair at the kitchen table, eating a bowl of Cheerios. Seemed healthy, but not with the amount of sugar she dumped on it. She was also pouting when I refilled my coffee and took the spot across from her.

"What's wrong?"

She stabbed her cereal with a spoon. "Daddy's home today."

Well, yeah, I kind of wanted to stab something because of that too. For entirely different reasons. "I would think that'd make you happy."

She gaped at me, cereal forgotten. "The *party!*" She whisper-yelled the words, so upset while trying to be so quiet. Fortunately, Logan wasn't anywhere around.

He was probably fuming in his office or getting a workout in. "Is he here all day?"

She shrugged, scooped a bite of cereal onto her spoon, and scowled at it.

"It's okay. We can still go to the store and get stuff."

"But it was going to be a surprise."

"We'll figure it out. You're sure he didn't say anything about going in today?"

"I don't know. Sometimes he talks and I don't listen."

This girl. I chuckled. I was seriously starting to love her. "Happens to the best of us."

Despite how angry Logan was with me, Amelia had been thrilled yesterday at the idea of throwing a party for him. I'd completely forgotten about it, but I wasn't going to let her down. It was her dad and his birthday. He deserved to be celebrated.

"Let me go talk to him and see if I can figure it out. If he's not going in, we can always send him to the store so we can decorate, okay?"

"All right." She shoved a mouthful of sugary, soaked Cheerios into her mouth.

It wasn't hard to find Logan. As soon as I reached the mouth of the hallway that led to his office, the clang of weights echoed from farther down the hall.

Blaring music came soon after. It was so loud, so when I

opened the door to his workout room, he didn't notice my entrance. Heavy rock music bounced off the walls, making my head vibrate from the bass.

And that wasn't all that was buzzing. Logan was shirtless, sweat dripping down his spine as he stood with his back to me and deadlifted a weight bar. It fell to the ground and he looked up, must have caught sight of me in the mirror to his left because he turned to face me.

His features were steel, his eyes furious. But his heaving chest and all that sweat, those muscles, had me licking my lips.

He scowled at me, stomped to the stereo system, and slapped a button. The music silenced and all I heard was his heavy breathing and the sound of my own pulse thundering.

Why did the man have to be so beautiful? And so freaking sexy when he was angry?

"Are you going to work today?"

"After lunch. Gave the guys the morning off. Why?" He shoved his hands to his hips. "Want to have that talk *now*?"

Oh hell no. With the way he was acting, I wanted to rewind the clock and never enter this room. Hell, maybe reverse it to last night and not stay in his bed. Not feel comfortable and safe. Not open my stupid mouth.

"Not particularly," I told him.

His lips curled in displeasure, and he grabbed a towel off a weight bench, scrubbing it over his face. He wiped away the fury along with the sweat and when he tossed it back to the bench, his voice was softer.

"I'm not mad at you."

"You're not?" He could have fooled me. Still seemed pretty angry.

"Fine." He rolled his eyes. "Maybe I'm a little mad, but only because I was disappointed you were gone and I liked having you in my arms last night. I'm mad at the situation, but not you."

My lips, my whole throat burned to ask the questions. Start the conversation. *What situation?*

Now wasn't the time. Not right then. "I need to take Amelia to the store this morning. Anything you need?"

He huffed and gave a little shake of his head. His disappointment hit me hard and fast.

"Come here, Ruby."

Not really the time to play the game, not at all. But he'd sounded nice, almost like it was a question and not his usual demands.

"I think I'm safer here," I told him. And definitely less sweaty.

"Trust me, you're not safe anywhere when I'm near you." It should have been a threat. Instead, that stupid, stupid part inside of me he seemed to have full control over, woke up and smiled, stretching with glee. He still wanted me. Despite my idiocy.

I took a step toward him. He took the rest toward me and then his hands were at my cheeks, his thumb brushing the soft flesh beneath my skin. He knew exactly what he was doing, and I wanted to kiss off that cocky grin his lips curled into.

"We'll talk later. Figure it out. Okay?"

"All right." It came out as a wheeze. And then Logan's lips were on mine, soft, seeking. I kissed him back because I had to, because I craved him. And as his mouth opened and I followed and that first brush of his tongue hit mine, sparks erupted down my spine, straight to my toes.

I hummed against his mouth, and he pulled back. He ended the kiss quickly, much too fast for my liking, and then whispered against my mouth, "Don't ever sneak out of my bed like that again unless it's an emergency."

"All right," I agreed. I couldn't not.

He still wanted me in his bed. That had to be good. Right?

I turned to leave and wished I hadn't when he said, "And

don't for one second think you can get yourself off today while thinking about me."

My knees wobbled. He knew exactly what his kisses did to me and he'd *meant* to do it. Game on. I glanced at him over my shoulder. "And if I do it *not* thinking about you?"

A feral sound tore from his throat that had my stomach quivering. "You *ever* think of another man while your fingers are on my pussy and there'll be consequences."

I melted. Right there. His words hit me like a bomb, and I exploded right to the floor. Damn him. Damn him for being so bossy and sexy and so damn *perfect* for me.

I fled from his workout room, his wicked chuckle following in my wake.

I was in trouble all right. In more ways than one.

HAVING practice at all today had been a mistake on my part. The guys listened and the film meeting went well, thanks to other coaches clearly seeing I was distracted and taking over. I was the problem. I hadn't been able to stop thinking of what Ruby told me the night before and I still couldn't stop wanting her so badly. The shit I told her that morning was dangerous. I'd shown my hand far too easily, but wasn't that good? If she needed to know I was in this for far more than how we started, she had it.

I could figure the rest out.

By the time I was on my way home, for the first night since Amelia arrived, I was dreading her being in the house. Ruby and I needed to talk, and it wouldn't happen for hours, and after the way the morning went, waiting those hours was going to be pure hell.

The house was oddly dark and even more strangely quiet when I walked in.

Ruby's car was in the driveway, so I knew they were home, but the lights in the living room were all off, along with the kitchen. Ever since Amelia came to me, my home was always lit up. Every light in the house was on when I returned, plus the sound of Amelia or Ruby at minimum in the kitchen or outside.

Tonight, it was pitch-black, and I flipped on the light in the entryway as I took off my shoes, dropped my bag to the floor, and removed my keys and wallet from my pocket. Maybe they were having another movie night in the movie room. Maybe they were...

"SURPRISE!"

I jolted at the screams, at the lights as they turned on and my house lit up. Amelia rushed to me, holding a large balloon in her hand. "Surprise, Daddy! Happy birfday!!!!"

My hand was on my chest, heart racing. It took a moment to realize what she said, that the balloon she was shoving into my hand had Happy Birthday scrawled on it.

"Oh goodness. You scared me!" My heart was still racing.

"Come on! We're having a party for you!" She tugged my hand and yanked me toward the kitchen. As soon as I reached it, my eyes widened, and my jaw fell.

Ruby was at the island, beneath two gold balloons that made the number thirty-seven. Beneath them was a banner that read "over the hill." She'd pay for that one.

"Happy birthday." She smiled as she said the words.

"Happy birthday, Coach." Jassen was there. It took a second to register.

How in the hell did he beat me to my own house so fast? "Hey."

And why was he at my party?

"Amelia and I went shopping today for your surprise party and she insisted that only two people weren't enough. She wanted Luke to come, but then she said you also needed your own friend."

And since I didn't have any friends... Jassen would do.

Ruby explained it, and for a moment, worry tightened her features. Right, because this wasn't going to be awkward at all.

"Thanks for coming." I reached across the bar to shake his hand and nodded toward Molly. "You too, Molly. Thank you. And your kids."

"Happy birthday!" Luke shouted. He and Amelia were jumping up and down in the eating area, balloons in their hands they were trying to bat away from the other. Their giggles helped. Because this was awkward as *fuck*.

"Need a drink?" Jassen asked and brought a beer to his mouth.

The man rarely drank. I'd been drinking way too much since moving to Tennessee, but hell. It was my party. And this situation called for it. "Yeah, man. Thanks."

He helped himself to my fridge like it was his house and not mine. Once I had my opened beer, I turned to Ruby and Molly. "So, a surprise party?"

"Amelia wanted to do something yesterday, but we didn't have time before the game, so I convinced her today would be better. More of a surprise that way."

Her cheeks turned pink as she explained. Realization struck. She'd made up that excuse so she could have her own party for me last night.

"It's certainly a surprise. Thanks to you guys for coming last minute."

Molly grinned and bounced Brittney on her hip. "We'd do anything for Ruby."

Of course they would. Probably, that included murdering anyone who hurt her. Or used her. Like me.

I swallowed a drink to wash away the burn in my throat. "Does this party include dinner?"

"Yep." Ruby grinned and went to the fridge. She pulled out a platter of hot dogs and brats. "Amelia said it was your favorite thing to eat and insisted you'd want to cook because you like to grill. I tried to convince her otherwise, but..."

I knew exactly how insistent Amelia could be. "How

thoughtful of her. Better than the McDonald's we had last night, I guess."

Ruby chuckled and Jassen laughed. "Isn't being an NFL coach glamorous?"

"So glamorous," I admitted.

———

Jassen joined me outside while I grilled. The kids were chasing each other around the patio, and we had one eye on them, one eye on the grill. At least Brittney had stayed inside with Molly. I didn't have to worry about her falling into the pool.

I was trying to avoid the conversation I really wanted to have with him. No sense in ruining the night before we ate.

"So, how in the hell did you get here so fast?"

Jassen laughed. "I snuck out early."

"Awesome. Thanks for letting me know." I was teasing him. Hell, the fact that Ruby had invited him because Amelia wanted to be around Luke was enough reason for me. It gave her a friend, and I wasn't complaining about that.

"Ruby called me while I was on my way in. I talked to Leer and explained. He said he'd cover for me. I'm guessing you didn't know that I never came back from the bathroom?"

I hadn't noticed shit all day. "Obviously not. Thanks, though. Know you guys have enough going on and the party last week was more than enough."

"Like Molly said. We'd do anything for Ruby."

"Thank you for making my party not about me at all."

Jassen laughed. "Sure thing. You can take it."

I could take a fair amount of ribbing indeed. And torture, which I'd only recently learned.

Not the safest thing to be thinking about with his sister twenty feet away, though.

Lucky for me, Jassen changed the subject. "Think we'll look as good this weekend against Ohio as we did last week?"

Football. Blessed football talk. I could do this all day.

"Ohio's defense is much stronger, so that'll make it difficult. But I think we have the struggles from preseason behind us. What do you think?"

"Definitely. I was worried there for a bit, not about you," he assured me, but that wasn't necessary. I knew he'd at least always respected me. "But the team. I think we have something special going on, something we can only keep building especially after last year."

"Yeah." I flipped the brats and hot dogs. "This is a special group of guys when you're all working together."

He went on to talk about the guys. Gave some more insight to the players on a personal level. Things I hadn't been aware of. The fact that Cole's wife, Eden, and he had a long, difficult history. I never would have guessed that. He talked about other players, their commitment to the team. I appreciated his perspective. As a kicker, he was often isolated from the team at practice, doing his own thing. Probably part of why I didn't realize he left today.

By the time dinner was cooked and we told Luke and Amelia to go wash their hands, I realized more than the fact I was starving.

I was thankful for this. Spending time with Jassen. He was a good guy, and he could become a friend.

Only if I stopped lying to him. I could lose his respect and never regain it if Ruby and I kept doing what we were doing and he found out a different way.

Amelia and Luke's constant chatter took over dinner. Brittney babbled right along with them, saying the few words she knew.

The distraction eased the tension broiling inside of me. I hadn't talked about this with Ruby. Hadn't had the time, and even if I had, I wasn't sure I would have asked for her permission. She was too likely to tell me not to say anything.

She'd willingly put me in charge since that very first day in my office, and I wasn't letting go of that control now.

The waiting, though, was hell. I gritted my teeth through a loud and highly off-key rendition of Happy Birthday. Amelia and Luke blew out my candles before I could make a wish.

We laughed through it all, and more than that, I was comfortable. For the first time in a long time, I didn't only have a woman I was growing to care a great deal for, but her family was fantastic. Kind. Welcoming. I could see Christmases, four kids tearing through presents in the blink of an eye. Hell, I could see more than that. I was *only* thirty-seven. I could have more kids. I'd never wanted Amelia to be an only child anyway. It'd been my own selfishness that prevented us from having more. But Ruby?

God. Damn. Way to put the cart before the horse. She was only twenty-three. She had school to finish. Dreams to chase.

Hell... maybe I was reading the last twenty-four hours all wrong.

As soon as the cake and ice cream were eaten, and the women went on clean-up duty out of habit, I suggested Amelia and Luke go watch a movie in the movie room. As soon as they were out of the room, I turned to the remaining adults and Brittney.

"I have something I need to say."

The room went so silent a pin could have dropped. I glanced at Ruby. Her face had paled.

Whether my tone of voice or my stance, she opened her mouth, reading me perfectly. "Logan—"

"What's going on?" Jassen's gaze bounced between the two of us.

Molly stared at her feet. Did she *know*? Oh no. Had she seen us? Or worse… *heard*?

"Logan." Ruby snapped my name like a whip. She was so worried, the dish she held in her hand was shaking.

I turned back to Jassen. Risks be damned, I was doing it. Even if it all blew up in my face. "I need you to know something, and you're probably not going to like it, but I'm telling you because I respect the hell out of you and the kind of man you are."

His face turned to stone and his arms crossed over his chest. I'd *never* seen him look so serious.

Ruby was walking around the island, eyes wide. As if she could stop me.

"I'm seeing your sister."

"You're what?" His brows shot high on his forehead and he gaped at me. Blinked. Moved to look at Ruby. His gaze bounced back to me. "You're her *boss*."

Obviously. "I care about her."

"It's been three weeks!"

I knew all that too. "I still care about her."

He could spew all the reasons why this was wrong, all the things I'd already considered, but only one thing made this good.

"You…" he sputtered, still gaping, still wide-eyed and blinking. He reminded me of a fish out of water. "You're *fucking* him?"

"Watch it," I growled. "I'll talk about this all you want but don't talk to Ruby like that."

"It's okay, Logan." She set her hand on my arm and her voice was soft. Not angry. Sad maybe, but when I yanked my glare off Jassen and resettled on her, she was smiling up at me. "I will kick you in the shins for this later."

I'd take the pain.

"It just happened," she said to her brother. "I don't know

what will happen, and I definitely wasn't planning on telling you tonight, but—"

"I won't lie to you," I told him. "Especially after tonight. You dropped everything you had to be here for me because Ruby asked you to because you love her. I don't... hell, I don't know what will happen. I don't have a crystal ball, and I *am* asking you not to tell anyone on the team quite yet, but I do care about her. And you."

Molly, for her part, was smiling, or trying to fight one. Yeah. She had to have seen us in her house. Fortunately, she wasn't throwing me under the bus for it.

Jassen would probably blow a gasket. Bleach his entire bathroom.

"You're fourteen years younger than him," he told Ruby. Like we hadn't already done the math. "And Paulie..."

"Don't." Ruby's soft smile wiped clean. "Don't bring him into this."

"But you *loved* him, and you only broke up a few months ago. How can you be ready for... And you." He glared at me. "Your ink on your divorce is barely dry."

"But I *am* divorced, and she's not with Paulie."

"He was good to you," Jassen stated, and if Ruby's coloring turned any darker like her name, she was going to be the one blowing a gasket. "I liked him."

"Everyone did," Ruby seethed. "Especially his wife and kids."

Holy shit. This was spiraling out of control quickly.

"You moved in with a married man? Holy shit, Ruby! What the hell is wrong with you!?"

"I didn't know!"

"Okay. Okay." Thank God for Molly. She appeared in the blink of an eye, out of nowhere, with Brittney no longer on her hip. Her hands were out, palms facing her husband and sister. It was a good thing she got in the middle too because I was two seconds from doing something to Jassen that would make Ruby hate me. "Let's take a breath."

"I can't believe you would move in with a married man." Jassen's voice had turned raspy. "How does that even happen?"

"How does a married man date me and you think he's so awesome?"

Ruby had a point there. I knew how hard this was for her. Knew she didn't want Jassen to know. The fact she wasn't backing down or falling apart was a testament to her strength. I reached out and settled my hand on her back. If she needed me, I was there for her.

Jassen's glare cut to me as soon as he saw me move.

I didn't let him speak. "Take a breath, Jassen. And listen to Molly."

He stepped back, whirled around, and put his back to us. "Okay," he finally said and faced us again. "I..." He shook his head. "I need to get out of here."

"Jassen." Ruby stepped forward.

"No." He shoved his hand up, palm out. "Give me the night. Let... Jesus, Rubes... Paulie was married?"

It was then the anger left him, filled with disgust, but this time at least it wasn't directed at his sister.

She caught it like I did, and her chin wobbled. Voice shook. "I didn't know. Until the end, I never knew. He traveled and..." she hiccupped.

I pulled her closer to me. Jassen glared at me, jaw popping out, and refocused on Ruby.

"That was why I kicked him out."

There was more to it. More that would make Jassen hate him.

"You've only been living in this house a few weeks."

"And I can't tell you it'll last, but like I said before, I care about your sister. And you. After what Ruby's already been through, it didn't feel right to keep it a secret."

She'd already been one. Hidden and lied to and kept in the dark. I wouldn't do that to her.

She shuddered next to me and covered her mouth with a sob.

"It's okay," Molly whispered, and I think it was to all of us, but mostly Ruby. "Let me go get Luke. Jassen will calm down and you two can talk, okay?"

She settled her hand on Ruby's cheek, thumb swiping away some of Ruby's tears. "We still love you. This is all a surprise."

But the way she looked at me, it wasn't that much of a surprise at all. I should have felt bad. Hell, I never should have touched Ruby inside their house, but what was done was done.

We couldn't take that back. And as long as Jassen didn't find that out, we were good.

"I do love you," he said, tone gruff. "But I don't like this."

"I know," she said.

His gaze cut to me.

"All I'm asking is you don't tell anyone on the team until we're ready." After all, he was right. It'd only been three weeks. This could blow up in our faces at any moment.

"I won't, but we will be talking."

I dipped my chin. Once he calmed down, I had no doubt we would, and I'd listen to what he had to say. I respected him that much.

Molly returned with Luke. Amelia followed, pouting. "We forgot to give you your presents, Daddy."

"Let's say goodbye to our friends first, then you can give me the presents."

"Why are you crying?" She went straight to Ruby.

Ruby sniffed and swiped at her cheeks.

"You sad on my daddy's birthday?" Oh, the sweet innocence of childhood.

Ruby bent down and smiled. "I'm okay, and I'm not sad. I'm excited for your dad to see what you bought him. Can you go get them?"

"Yes!" She ran off and at the last moment turned around. "Bye, Luke!"

She shot off like a rocket. Molly hugged Ruby and whispered something in her ear that made her smile. I'd ask her about that later.

Jassen kissed her cheek.

No goodbye for me. Not surprising.

Soon, they were gone, and while Amelia was still gone, I kissed Ruby's temple. "You okay?"

She glared up at me and growled, "A warning would have been nice."

"Yeah. My bad."

"Daddy!"

I'd apologize to her later.

I had presents to open.

The perfect distraction.

CHAPTER 27

RUBY

I KEPT my mouth shut while Amelia gave Logan his presents. We spent the afternoon making him a card. When Amelia insisted she needed red glitter for his present earlier, I'd hesitated. Everyone hated glitter.

After the drama he created earlier, I'd hid my smile beneath my hand when he opened the card and glitter fell all over him. He deserved it.

I was still mad, even if a part of me was grateful he'd taken control earlier. My secret with Paulie was out, at least most of it. Jassen didn't need to know the rest of my stupidity, but at least now I knew he'd never talk to Paulie again.

And he'd calm down. Eventually. He loved me too much to stay mad at me forever.

I waited until Amelia was in bed and until Logan went to his room to change. I was out on the back patio when he returned, waters for both of us.

He took the same spot he'd done that first night and it was hard to believe that was only weeks ago.

My brother was right. I'd moved way too fast with this guy, but I wasn't sure I was ready to slow down or stop either. Maybe what we had was sexual chemistry and lust, and it would eventually burn to ash. I was prepared for that.

"That wasn't cool, what you did earlier."

He twisted the top off his bottled water. "I know."

And yet there was no apology. I waited, gave him a minute.

Logan leaned back against the couch and threw an arm out over the edge. "I hadn't meant to say anything, but when I was outside with him earlier, I realized I liked him and respected him. I didn't feel right lying to him."

He'd already said that.

"It was still mine to tell."

"Would you have?"

My lip curled. It wasn't an admonishment as much as a question, but guilt still slithered around my chest and squeezed tight. Would I have had the guts to do it?

"Eventually," I muttered and drank my water to wash away the half-truth. Sure, *eventually*.

"What did Molly whisper to you?"

Logan had to have known already, or at least assumed. She'd been way too calm during the entire earlier encounter and her whisper to me confirmed why.

"I saw him leave the bathroom. Never saw you enter. When I knocked, I expected the bathroom to be empty. I put two and two together, but I'll also take this secret to the grave. And honestly, damn girl. Good choice."

It'd taken everything in me not to laugh while Jassen stood behind her, seething with anger and mad at me.

"She figured it out at the party," I told him.

"I assumed. Is that what she whispered?"

"Basically."

"Ruby."

"What?" I faced him, and his iron eyes were soft. Sweet. In fact, he looked entirely relaxed in a way I wouldn't be until Jassen and I talked again.

"Come here." He wiggled his fingers, and I went, reluctant, but if there was anything that would help, it would have to be being in Logan's arms.

As soon as I sat next to him, my head fell to his shoulder and his arm at the back of the couch wrapped around me. "I'm sorry for making Jassen mad at you, but if we're going to do this, there will be hurdles to jump. I thought it'd be better and easier for you if you had some support in the long run."

He kissed the top of my head, and I settled further against him, gave him my weight, and closed my eyes. "I'll forgive you for all of it once Jassen's speaking to me again."

"Molly will talk him around. And he has to realize you're an adult, too, you know. This really isn't any of his business as long as it doesn't affect my coaching or his position with the team. And he's too good for that to be a concern."

"Probably."

We drifted into silence, me in what was becoming my favorite place.

All too soon, I was waking up on floating clouds, an aching sensation between my thighs, and the tease of soft hair at my inner thighs.

"Oh God," I groaned, and my eyes fluttered open.

I was in Logan's bed. Again. And all I saw was the shadow of his face between my thighs, the soft but firm flicker of his tongue against my clit.

"Morning." He nipped at my clit, grinning up at me before he dropped his head.

"Shit. What time..."

"Talk later."

I couldn't talk anyway. He recommenced doing delicious things to me, adding fingers, two firmly inside where he found that exact spot that drove me wild. I grabbed the pillow to muffle my cries and when he slid his fingers from me, pressed one against my ass, I tensed like always at the first hint of intrusion.

But damn. "God that feels so damn good," I grunted, whining as his finger pressed into my ass. I could have never imagined *liking* this so much, but every time Logan went back there, sounds I never knew were human fell from my throat. Nerves lit up I never knew existed.

It was scary. Pain with pleasure, and sometimes was too overwhelming.

But damn did I like it.

I came on a cry, while his tongue kept lapping at me and his finger kept moving. I came until he pulled out of both and settled between my thighs.

He tore the pillow away, tossed it off the bed, and as he kissed me, he whispered, "I've been wearing condoms. But are you on the pill?"

"Religiously," I whispered against his mouth. "Every day, same time for years."

I would never risk being my mother. Getting pregnant with a man who wouldn't stick around.

The tip of his cock brushed against my sensitive sex and I yelped. "Oh. You want..."

"Can I?" He brushed my hair off my forehead, then buried his face in the crook of my neck. "Goddamn. Every time I'm close to you, I think of the ocean and sunshine. You smell so damn good, Ruby. If you're not okay, I can grab a—"

"No." I stopped him and then laughed.

"What's funny?"

"You say I remind you of the ocean and sunshine, but you always smell like fall and campfires to me." Like home and comfort and lazy days curled up on the couch.

I didn't tell him all of that.

"No condom," I whispered as he smiled down at me, that soft, sexy smile that could make my knees wobble even while lying down. "I want to feel you."

I'd never done that. Not with my high school boyfriends and

never with Paulie. He'd never even asked, which now made sense, but for the first time, I wanted it to be Logan who would be bare inside of me.

I trusted him, and despite last night's frustration, he proved he was an altogether different kind of man. A good one, worthy of the trust I gave him.

His head pressed against me, and then there was that first stretch as I accommodated to him. He still had his face in the crook of my neck, and he groaned a low sound as he pushed inside. This was different. Better. Without the condom, I could feel *everything*.

And it was incredible.

"Holy shit, you are so damn warm and wet for me. It drives me crazy." He moved then. A firm, hard thrust in that made me bite down on my bottom lip and a slow, torturous pull out until he was moving. Slowly. Grunting against my neck and kissing my heated flesh. He sucked, and I moved away.

"No marks," I rasped as I clung to his hair. His shoulders.

He pushed off then, grabbed my hips, and it was the first sign this wasn't going to be slow and romantic.

Logan's features were tight, and he grabbed the back of my thighs and shoved them toward me. He had me bent in half, and the move made him go deeper. Feel tighter.

"Oh God. I'm going to..."

"Don't come yet," he rasped. "Hold your knees and keep still."

Shit. Like hell I could do that. My palms were sweaty as I did what I was told, though, and Logan yanked my hips up to his thighs as he sat back on his heels.

"Oh damn. Shit." Fuck, that felt good, even if I was bent in half and at an angle, but oh my God.

"Logan," I whined.

It was coming. Powerful. So overwhelming it was almost terrifying and he kept pounding, staring down at where he slammed inside of me. He released his hold on one of my hips and his fingers went to my clit.

"Shit. I can't... I can't stop..."

"Not yet," he groaned, tossing me a glare. "Hold it, Ruby."

Oh God. The pain. The tremble in my thighs and the insane sensations happening inside of me were too much. That hand moved off my clit, pressed to my lower belly, and I screamed, completely forgot reason and where we were, and I clamped down on him to hold it off, but then his pounding increased, hitting that sweet, agonizing spot inside of me, and he finally grunted. "Come."

And shit. I did. I came like a rocket, throwing my head back into the couch and my entire body writhing with blissed out pleasure that made sparks light up behind my eyelids and sent explosions throughout my limbs. I came, kept coming, while Logan slammed inside of me one more time. He bent forward, braced himself on the bed next to my head, and I turned to bite down on his wrist to silence my screams.

He came then. The swell of his cock filled me and then he pulsed deep inside of me. And holy shit, he was a freaking miracle worker in bed.

My orgasms rolled, one into two, and he played with my clit before throwing me into another all while he stayed sheathed inside of me.

"Too much," I finally rasped. "Too damn much."

He huffed a laugh, slowly slid out of me, and then curled me into his chest.

"I had no idea I could orgasm like that," I admitted, my heart still racing.

He nipped at my ear, and I could feel the smile curling his lips at my cheek. "So what you're saying is, 'Damn, Logan. You're the best I've ever had, a literal god in bed.'"

He was teasing.

I absolutely wasn't when I answered, "Yes, sir."

———

"My daddy is the best coach, isn't he?" Amelia was dancing in circles in the team's family room.

Sherrie, Logan's mom, took her hand and spun her in a larger circle. "I think your daddy is the *bestest* guy in the whole world."

"Me too!" Amelia sang.

Doug, Logan's dad, laughed at both of them.

Logan's mom and dad were in town, and while I'd tried to excuse myself for the weekend so he could have his family time, Logan hadn't wanted to hear it.

For the last month, the only nights I hadn't slept in his bed with him were when he was at the hotel on nights before home games and on the three weekends he'd had away games.

I still made sure I was up and out of his room before Amelia woke, but lately, it'd been getting harder to feel okay with all of that.

I pushed my thoughts to the side. My worries. The Steels were currently undefeated six games into the season, and I was officially a football fan in a way I never had been before. I brought Amelia to the home games, where we now mostly watched in the coaches' suite. And during the away games, she and I were glued to the television.

Every single time the camera panned to Logan and I caught sight of him on the television, scowling or cheering on his team, my stomach warmed. And the nights when he returned? I couldn't get enough of him. He couldn't get enough of me, and those bindings were used frequently, along with a few extra purchases he'd made in the last several weeks.

Molly came to my side. She didn't come to all the games since she was pregnant and had to wrangle the two kids, but she'd been there today, for me, so I didn't have to sit alone with Logan's parents. "How are things going?"

"Good," I said, but I couldn't keep the worry out of my tone.

Jassen still wasn't thrilled I was dating, or rather, sleeping with his coach since we still hadn't had an actual date. He wasn't mad, or at least he didn't take it out on me, but he wasn't pleased, and he made that known. He hadn't told anyone, though, but our secret was getting harder to keep.

I'd now met and loved several players' and coaches' wives. We now acted like a family at home, eating dinners together. There was no more running off, sneaking away for him to have alone time with Amelia. And yet, he hadn't broached the topic of telling anyone. Not even discussing it with the coaches or management to see if there was a problem. The season started and Logan went into tunnel vision. It was the same issue he told me about with his ex-wife. I didn't blame him at first. Expected it. But the more I spent around the coaches' wives asking me if there was a man in my life, hiding it was harder. Making me lonelier. I was now lying to people I cared about, and that was the only reason why Logan told Jassen in the first place.

Yet every time I tried to broach the topic with him, he told me, "Later. We'll talk about it later."

The door to the family room opened, and Dawson Butler stormed in. The man was intimidating. Not only because of his large muscular size and his untamed long dark hair. The man moved like a lion and only had smiles for his girlfriend, Hailey.

Like she'd been expecting him, she turned to him and smiled. That smile vanished as he prowled to her, and the entire room went silent. A tension filled the air, and as I gave a quick glance around, everyone had noticed.

We were all staring at Dawson and the way he'd commanded every single person's attention with his presence and aura alone.

He stopped in front of her. The rest of the room had circled around, giving them space. He still held his familiar, permanent scowl and Hailey looked up at him.

"What's wrong?" she asked.

Nothing happened. He didn't so much as twitch and when

Hailey whispered his name again, filled with concern, he dropped to his knee.

And *oh. My. Goodness.*

The man hit his knee in front of her like she knocked him on his ass.

Without preamble, without kindness, and almost like he was annoyed, he said, "You didn't want to elope, and it was hell talking you into moving in with me, but I've waited as long as I can, Hailey Parillo. I want our life together, a home with babies and friends and family. I want it all with you, and I swear to you if you don't agree to marry me today, I'm going to lose my damn mind."

Hailey laughed and started to cry.

He reached into his pocket and held open a box. "Marry me, Hailey. Let me love you forever with you being my wife and not just my girlfriend and give me all the dreams I started having the day I met you and the chance to create and conquer more dreams together."

It was the rudest, most honest proposal I'd ever seen and tears burned my eyes.

She had someone who didn't give a single shit what anyone thought. Of him. Of their relationship. He didn't care if the entire team saw him act like a fool.

I was grinning as the room erupted in cheers as he finally convinced Hailey to say yes, but there was pain burning in my eyes.

As if Molly understood, she reached out and squeezed my hand.

Our situations were different, but was it so wrong to want that? So wrong to not want to be hidden any longer?

The door opened and Logan walked in. He was wearing his Steel baseball hat, the same black three-quarter zip shirt he always wore to his game. His gaze stopped as he took in Hailey and Dawson, the cheers ringing through the room and the happy faces. Understanding dawned and he clapped along with the rest of his team.

But when he reached me, met my gaze, he had to see the pain in them.

His smile fell. He took a step toward me and stopped. His eyes widened and scanned the room.

He was frozen. Stuck there.

There was nothing he could do, and we both knew it.

But I was starting to wonder, even if he could, if he was ready to take that step anyway.

CHAPTER 28

LOGAN

I HURT her and it was the last thing I'd wanted to do and certainly not what I ever intended to do. And it sucked because she stood across from me, an entire room of family and friends celebrating Dawson and Hailey as he kissed her like they were the only two people left on this planet, looking at me like I'd slapped her.

Shit.

I was the one who pushed the honesty. I was the one who stood up to her brother a month ago. He was still pissed at me, rarely talked to me at all anymore. He certainly didn't hit the field and ask me how my sister was doing, and I knew from talking to Ruby, curled in my arms almost every night, both of us spent and sated, she was hurting from that as well.

But as for the rest? I hadn't done a damn thing. We'd agreed to wait, but how long was enough when she was sharing my room?

She was still a secret. Still sneaking out of my bed before there was the chance Amelia would wake up. And even though I convinced her to stay the weekend while my parents were in town, she'd gone back to her room.

We hadn't discussed it, and I was almost relieved when she made that choice.

I didn't want my parents to know I was sleeping with my nanny before they had the chance to meet. Before they could fall in love with her like Amelia had done in less than ten days. Like I was afraid I was well on my way to doing in less than a couple of months. If Ruby could get me thinking of a future, of dreams of a larger family and more children, and sharing a life with her, my parents would easily be head over heels for her by the time they left Tuesday night.

And when she slipped into the back passenger seat of the Yukon I was letting my parents drive while they were in town and told them I'd meet them back at the house, the fact she didn't look in my direction once terrified me.

By the time I got home and had my Audi in the spot next to the SUV, I was prepared to do anything. Hire a skywriter. Send a mass communication email to the rest of the coaches and players. I hadn't so much as checked my contract for the details of the morality clause I knew was there, but I'd do anything to ensure that pained look never again appeared on Ruby.

Amelia's pounding little feet reverberated against the kitchen floor before her tiny body slammed into mine. She was dressed in a swimsuit, lime-green Crocs in sport mode on her feet.

"Daddy! Daddy! Grampa's taking me fishing!"

"He is? That's great. Are you going to catch us dinner?"

So far, we'd caught a handful of crappies no larger than the size of my fist. I'd convinced Amelia to continue returning them to the lake so they could grow big and strong.

"Do you think they're ready?" She sighed, eyes wide with excitement.

"Probably not, kiddo. You ready?"

My dad was at the kitchen counter, two towels thrown over his shoulder. I wasn't at all surprised they were heading out fishing again. They'd spent almost the entire weekend together on the water.

"You good to go out with her again?"

My dad scowled at me. "What? You saying I'm too old?"

He turned sixty in January. The man wasn't close to being old, but it had been a long day and he'd been up with the sun to fish. "I would never. Where's Mom?"

If they were going to be gone, I could go hunt down Ruby. I should probably figure out what to say to her first, but I needed to see her. Make sure she was okay.

"She's already outside, waiting for us. Said she'd float on the paddleboard or watch from the dock."

"Have you guys talked about what to do for dinner?"

The bonus to having my parents in town was I didn't have to cook. Mom swept in and took over my kitchen like it was hers. I'd long since given up fighting it. What idiot would do that?

He pointed to a Crock-Pot sitting on my counter. I'd never seen it in my life. "Went out this morning after you left and bought that and a roast. Surprised you couldn't smell it from the garage. Said it'll be ready in less than two hours now."

My favorite meal. He was right. Mom made a killer roast with carrots and potatoes. I had yet to make the gravy as good as she did. I usually scented it out.

We'd be eating late. I didn't care. I would wait until midnight for Mom's roast.

It also gave me time to find Ruby and smooth things over.

"Right. I'm going to grab a shower and relax then while you adventurers go explore the lake."

"It's just fishing, Daddy." Amelia rolled her eyes and turned to my dad. "Race you, Grampa!"

She took off.

He shook his head. "Now that is something I am too old to still do."

He followed Amelia out the sliding back door and as soon as it clicked, I headed up the stairs.

My shower could wait.

Ruby could not.

———

I knocked on her door softly, my hands balled into fists and all the words I wanted to say to her sticking to my throat.

It took a moment. Two. It took long enough she'd either been in the bathroom or had debated whether or not to open it. As she opened the door, blocking it at her shoulder, it was definitely the latter option.

"Can we talk?"

Her eyes were red, as if she'd been crying, and the pain of hurting her earlier returned tenfold. She rested the side of her head against the doorframe.

"Can I come in?"

"I'm packing."

Packing? "You're leaving? Why?"

But oh, I knew why. Me. She was leaving because for all my bluster a month ago, I was treating her the same she'd been before, and she deserved better. So much better than that. So much better than me. The season started and I grew tunnel vision like I'd always done before. I was self-aware to know that.

I would *not* fail at this again. And that wasn't my pride. That was because I was not letting this woman get away from me.

"I think you should enjoy the time with your parents. While you have it. That's all."

"Bullshit." I slapped the palm of my hand to the door and pushed firmly. Not hard enough to hurt her shoulder, but it was enough that she had to step back.

I stormed into her room and a vice gripped my chest at her suitcase. It was stuffed full, almost overflowing. She wasn't taking the time to fold anything, but she must have ripped it off her hangers and thrown it in there. Shoes were in a pile next to it.

It was way more than she needed for three days.

Every argument, every word I wanted to say to her, fell straight to my gut and I faced her, flinching at the wretched expression she wore. Her blue eyes were no longer the ocean, but a storm.

"This doesn't look like a weekend at your brother's."

"I thought, maybe, your parents could stay longer and I could go see Gina for a while."

"No."

"No?"

"Absolutely fucking not. You are not leaving me and you are not running across the country to go lick wounds that I can heal right here."

She choked on a laugh, though there was nothing funny about this. My hands slammed to my hips so I didn't reach out and grab her. Shake sense into her.

"How are you going to do that, Logan? Take me out on a date in public for once?"

"Yes." I was seething. Furious. She wasn't even trying to talk to me about this. "If I have to, if that's what you need, then yes. Always yes."

"Far be it from me to make you *have* to do something."

"That's not what I meant. But, Ruby, I get it. This hasn't been easy and I know I haven't been able to show you off in public."

"Or to your parents."

Now wait a damn minute. "You were the one who insisted on coming back to sleep up here."

"You didn't stop me. For all your blustering with Jassen and not keeping secrets from a man you respect, you certainly haven't seemed to have any problem in doing it to your own parents."

"We didn't have time to talk about it!"

"We had a month!"

She stomped her feet, then stormed to her suitcase. Full of anger and a decent-sized amount of indignation, she started throwing her shoes into the suitcase. Which was so full, the shoes just fell right off. She screamed her frustration, grabbed another shoe, and spun back around to face me.

The shoe in her hand, she held it like a baseball, ready to whip it at my face. I braced for impact as she threw it to the floor.

"Just go! Leave me alone right now, Logan. I don't want to talk about this."

"No way. *Talk* to me, Ruby, because up until a couple hours ago you hadn't seemed upset about any of this, and I know this is my fault, but I didn't know it was eating at you. You said you'd give me time."

"And you said you wanted to wait until you knew this was going to last, and how long is that going to take?"

"What?" I jerked back, but screw this. Distance never did anyone any good. "Ruby..." I went to her then. Curled my hands around her shoulders.

For the first time ever, she flinched at my touch.

I held on tighter so she couldn't run away.

"I haven't meant to hurt you, and I'm sorry. Please, stay the weekend. I'll talk to my parents. I'll explain—"

My phone went off with Vanessa's ringtone. I tried to ignore it, but Ruby stepped out of my hold and went back to packing.

"Take the call. It's probably important."

"You're important." There was a hitch in her movements. A moment where I thought she'd calm down and give me a damn moment, or a conversation to talk this through.

"And it's the middle of the night wherever she is. Take the call."

The ringer stopped. Good. This was... it started again and I sighed.

"Don't go. Please don't leave until we can talk," I told her, pulling out my phone. Because she was right.

Vanessa wouldn't call me unless it was important.

"Hey, Vanessa." I answered her FaceTime call and immediately saw tears falling down her cheeks. Her cries filled the room loud enough that Ruby stopped her packing.

"What is it? What's wrong?"

And why was she calling me?

She cried into the phone. "Oh, Logan. I broke up with Renaldo and I think I made a huge mistake."

"What?"

"I need to talk. You have time, right? Your game is done?"

It'd been two years since she'd even asked about my game. "Yeah. Hold on a minute, though, okay?"

She nodded through her tears, and I glanced at Ruby.

She too had tears in her eyes.

Awesome. I was killing life with the women in it. "I'll be back," I mouthed to Ruby.

She glanced at the phone, face paling, and shrugged.

As soon as I was downstairs in my office with the door closed, I unmuted the screen. "What happened? But also, remember I don't want to hear anything about you and Renaldo."

"It was dumb of me to come. Dumb of me to leave. I knew it. But after you left, I was so upset, and Renaldo swept in and made me feel so good, but he's a jerk, Logan. An absolute jerk and he doesn't even want me to be with Amelia at all when I come back. He said today he didn't like kids. Never wanted them. Asked if I *had* to keep her, and I can't keep being so far away from her, and..."

She kept going. My head kept spinning.

Upstairs, the woman I was falling in love with was packing to leave.

And the woman who left me, who I'd once loved with my

whole heart, was... What? Why did I need to know *any* of this? Unless...

"Vanessa. Hey, calm down. Take a breath." She was still rattling off about missing Amelia and coming back, still crying. I could hardly understand her.

"Vanessa," I called her name again with more bite to it.

She paused then, sniffed, and grabbed a tissue to blow her nose.

"What? You think it would be good, right? To have me close to Amelia again? That would be best for her, right?"

"Of course." I sighed. She wasn't doing this. She couldn't be. We'd already had the miscommunication once, but this sounded different. She didn't at all sound like she was talking about coming back to LA or the States. "Of course it would be best for Amelia if you were here, Vanessa, but..."

I looked up. The door to my office was opened and Ruby stood in the doorway. No suitcase in sight, but her purse was over her shoulder, and she had a small overnight bag in her hand.

"I just came to say goodbye," she said, and she was gone. Tears streaming down her cheeks as she ran away.

"Vanessa..."

"So, it's good. Right? If I come back and maybe instead of California, I come there?"

"No." Shit. I had to catch Ruby, had to talk to her. I knew exactly what she heard. How that sounded. But damn it. She had it so wrong.

So very, very wrong.

"You can't come stay with me, Vanessa. That would give Amelia the wrong idea."

"But—"

"No buts, Vanessa. We're through, and besides the fact we're already divorced, I've met someone who means a lot to me. I'm not moving backward."

Her hazel, large, round eyes widened. Tears shone in them, but she gaped at me. Blinked. Blinked again.

And then the largest laugh I'd ever heard fell from Vanessa. "I didn't mean move *in* with you, Logan. Gross, no. I don't want you *back*. I thought I could stay for a bit while I found my own place to live! I miss Amelia like crazy and it wasn't for me to leave her so long! I meant how would you feel if I moved closer!"

She was still laughing and crying. She choked over her cries and then started laughing so hard blood rushed to my face.

"Vanessa... You have no idea what you've just done."

And how badly I'd seriously fucked up.

"Who's the girl?" she asked, now smiling and laughing and wiping tears away.

At least one of us was laughing.

I didn't hesitate. Vanessa first. My parents second. Soon, I'd let the entire world know who I was dating if they asked.

"Ruby," I told her. "The nanny."

I OVERREACTED. I knew as soon as I flung my bag and suitcase into my car and peeled down Logan's driveway. I knew before then, when I was shoving everything I'd brought to his house into my suitcase that I was being immature.

Of course I needed to say that to him. Of course I needed to apologize and we would talk this out. I hadn't given him any warning. Hell, I hadn't even realized I was so upset about our arrangement until his parents came and he didn't mention saying anything to them. I hadn't realized I was feeling like a hidden secret all over again until Dawson dropped to his knee in front of his entire team and Logan couldn't even come stand near me and hold my hand.

It'd all happened so fast, and my emotions ran away with me.

Of course I was being a fool. I'd fully intended to go apologize, tell him I was just going to go stay with Jassen while his parents were there, and we'd figure it out once they left.

Until Vanessa was crying about needing him, wanting to be with Amelia, and he told her it'd be the best thing for Amelia if she was.

He'd *loved* her at one point. He never hid that from me. He also never hid the mistakes he made with her. The mistakes he was making with me. But if it came down to some girl who took care of his daughter and the woman he'd spent a decade loving?

I had no expectations of where I fell on that totem pole.

I burst into Jassen and Molly's house with not so much as a text warning them I was coming and threw my small bag on the floor.

Jassen was standing behind his living room couch, football game on the television, and froze at my abrupt arrival.

"What in the hell did he do? I'm going to kill him."

"Don't." I swiped drying tears off my cheeks and went to my brother. "He didn't do anything. It was all my fault."

He wrapped his arms around me and hugged me. He threatened Logan's life more than once, and soon, I was being turned in Molly's arms.

"I'm so sorry."

"I was an idiot," I cried. "A huge stupid dumb idiot. Again."

They held me while I cried, and then Jassen returned, glass of wine in his hand he held out for me and a scowl etched so deep into his features I wasn't sure the lines would ever go away.

"Drink. Take a second and tell us what happened."

Molly guided me to the couch and returned a few seconds later with a box of tissues. I took one, waited until I could breathe without a sob hitching my throat, and I peered up at both of them.

Molly's expression was softer, patient, like always. Jassen's was so scary I ignored him. "I fucked up. Started a fight when we didn't need to be having one and we couldn't even talk about it with his parents there. And then Vanessa called him, and I'm pretty sure she wants him back. And he said it'd be best for Amelia if she did."

"What?" Molly's jaw dropped in shock.

Jassen's nostrils flared, eyes burning hot enough to set me on fire. "That fucking dick."

He stomped off and the next thing we heard was the garage door opening.

I jumped off the couch to chase after him, but Molly stopped me. "Let him. He hasn't liked this because he thought Logan was taking advantage of you and he's been holding it in for far too long. His game is starting to suffer from it, so let him go. He needs to get this off his chest, have it out with the man he respects but hasn't done a great job of loving his little sister."

"But—"

"He'll be back and it'll be fine. Trust me." She kissed my cheek, bent down, and picked up my glass from the coffee table. "Drink up and tell me everything."

———

I passed out before Jassen returned home. I told Molly everything. Well, not *everything*. Sweet Molly didn't need to know about how much I enjoyed being told to get on my knees or tied up. I didn't need to give the woman a heart attack. I told her all the rest. How everything started. How I'd told him I didn't want anything with feelings and how the *just sex* had been my own idea. I told him how it went from that party at their house to me basically living in his room with him.

And then I told her the part that scared me the most.

In the last month, I hadn't once thought of what I would do after Christmas. I hadn't once thought about the day I would have to leave and head to grad school. I hadn't once *missed* school or had a single urge to return. And I had not given a single moment's thought to the day when I would have to say goodbye to Logan or Amelia. It wasn't even because I was too terrified of that day coming and hurting too much. It was because I couldn't fathom there being a day when I didn't see them, when they weren't in my life.

Molly listened through all of it. When I started yawning, she walked me to the guestroom and brought in my bag even though she was pregnant and I was more than capable of taking care of myself.

"Let me," she'd insisted.

And I let her. Because hell, when was the last time anyone had ever, truly, taken care of me?

———

I woke to sunshine, a splitting headache, and cold sheets next to me. Groaning, I rolled over and buried my face into the pillow next to me. I'd made a huge mistake yesterday. Or maybe the best decision for me.

As I flipped through the haze of yesterday, I tried to remember everything I'd said to Molly, all the advice she gave me.

Jassen.

I flung up and instantly regretted it. I pressed the heel of my palm to my temple and scrambled out of bed. "Shit," I grunted as the room swayed and wobbled, and pain pierced through my skull.

"Never drinking again," I muttered.

It was a lie, but I didn't dwell. Jassen had still been gone, late last night when Molly helped me to my room and tossed me the pajamas I was currently wearing.

What in the hell happened when he went to Logan's last night?

And did everyone survive?

As much in a hurry as I was to find my brother, even though it was possible he was already at the field for practice, I took a few minutes to wipe away yesterday's makeup and mascara, brush my teeth, and slather my dehydrated face with some mois-turizer.

Feeling slightly more normal, I hurried down the stairs and

the hall and pulled to a sudden stop when my brother was sitting at the kitchen counter.

He was turned on the stool, hands to my sister-in-law's quickly growing belly. She was saying something I couldn't hear, that sweet smile on her face and he was laughing, looking up at her.

I would have felt bad for interrupting or given them their sweet private moment.

Except for the fact that my freaking brother who stormed out of there not even ten hours earlier was sitting at his counter, relaxed, happy enough to be laughing, and without a single scratch or black eye in sight.

"What'd you do?" I demanded and hurried to the counter on the opposite side of the island.

Jassen turned that irritating smile in my direction, still happy.

"Go home, Ruby."

"Excuse me?" I jolted.

Jassen's smile vanished and he stood. He slid an arm around Molly's waist, and she went to him, leaning against him and also... smiling.

What in the ever-loving hell?

"I said, go home. Now."

I blinked. "But. This is my home." Except it wasn't. So really... "I don't have a home."

"Yes, you do." Molly kissed my brother's cheek and turned back to me. "So go home, Ruby. It'll be okay."

They were crazy. They'd lost their minds. Jassen I could understand. Logan probably punched him so hard he had a concussion, but Molly didn't make sense.

"Did you two slip and fall or something this morning? Smack your heads? Break something vital inside your brains?"

"No." Jassen crossed his arms over his chest. "And I have instructions that if you don't willingly leave as soon as I tell you to get out of here, I've been told to throw you into my truck and take you there myself."

"Why? Why would he want that? Especially with Vanessa and—"

"Ruby?"

"What?" I snapped at my brother. He wasn't making sense.

He planted his hands on the counter and glared at me. "Get the fuck outta my house, and go. The. Fuck. *Home*."

It penetrated then. I blinked, rapidly this time. It was too early to cry. Too early for any of this.

"Home?" I asked on a warbly breath. "You mean..."

"You'll never know unless you go talk to him," Molly said.

"And he didn't kill you." I pointed at my brother. "You're sure? And you didn't hurt him?"

"Logan will explain everything. But only if you—"

"Go home," I finished this time and a smile broke out on my face.

Molly's mirrored it.

"I think I get it. Fine, I'll go," I told them.

I ran up the stairs and gathered my things. Faster than I would have thought possible, I was back in my car, breaking speed limits and testing my old Corolla's limits in my hurry to get to Logan's.

To... my home?

What was *happening*?

There was only one way to find out, but for the first time since I freaked over nothing except my own shitty communication skills, I wasn't worried. My chest wasn't tight, and I wasn't afraid of what Logan was going to say to me.

I was going *home*, and that said enough.

———

The Yukon was missing from the garage when I pulled up to Logan's driveway. He'd been letting his parents use it, so I assumed they weren't there. Hopefully, we could have privacy for the talk we had to have and I didn't need witnesses to my apology.

I'd reacted so poorly the day before. So very immature. But if Jassen was right, it would be okay. My heart was racing. My head was still pounding. Hope and excitement were bubbling in my chest, almost overflowing, and still, I stayed in my car, hands gripping the steering wheel.

If Jassen was wrong, though...

Inhaling slowly, I managed to turn off my car and unpeel my sweaty palms from the steering wheel. My hands were shaking so badly, it took several attempts to open the door, and my legs were jelly as I closed the door and walked up to the side entrance.

The house was quiet when I entered, and I stepped farther inside. There wasn't a single sound. Not the hum of the air conditioner, no appliances running. There was only the natural sunlight coming in through the windows, a tension growing so tight in my chest it was possible my heart would be squeezed to death, and then, there he was.

Logan.

He was standing in the middle of his living room. He had on linen shorts. A tight, sky-blue T-shirt. His hair was that wavy mess that told me he'd scrubbed his hands through it relentlessly and that one wayward curl I loved so much fell over his forehead. And he stood like he was preparing for battle. Feet planted on the living room rug. Arms crossed over his chest.

His stance and demeanor did nothing to settle the raging storm inside of me.

"Hi," I whispered. "I'm so—"

"Kneel."

I'd moved toward him, but at the barked command, one word he *had* to know what it'd do to me, I stopped. Blinked.

"What?"

He nodded to an area in front of him. A pillow sat there.

"You heard me."

Oh God. I had not, in any of the scenarios that raced through my mind on the way here, at all considered this was how this would go.

"Logan..."

"I have things to say and you're going to listen, but you're going to be doing it on your knees like a good girl and not the sassy little brat you were yesterday."

I opened my mouth to argue about the brat part, to apologize, but Logan stayed in his spot, glaring at me in a way that *dared* me to argue with him or disobey.

And dammit. I didn't want to do either.

"Yes, sir," I whispered, and my voice was already raspy. Dry. Desperate.

I slipped out of my sandals and hurried to the pillow. My knees hit it with a soft thud, and as soon as I was there, on my knees in front of him, tears I thought had dried up last night resurfaced.

"You're okay," he murmured and tilted my chin with his thumb. "Stop that," he said, and it was so soft, I laughed. He wiped tears off my cheeks.

I nodded, swallowed down the rest of the tears, and cleared my throat.

"It occurred to me that when we started this, I was always in charge. And you've always been such a good girl when it comes to letting me lead everything. But I failed at that, Ruby, and I didn't communicate everything I was thinking, what I wanted from you."

I shook my head. This wasn't his fault. I opened my mouth to tell him, but he pressed a finger to my lips.

Looking down at me, the dark storm in his eyes melted. "You take my direction in the bedroom, but it didn't occur to me you might need it outside of the bedroom as well. So here's what's going to happen. You ready?"

I nodded.

He arched a brow.

"Yes, sir," I whispered.

He grinned. It was wicked and fierce, and my body ignited with desire for him.

"Good. First of all, what you heard when I was talking to Vanessa yesterday wasn't what you thought. And frankly, I'd misunderstood her as well. I'll explain it all later, but I want you to know, right now, even if she showed up at my door and begged me to take her back, I wouldn't. And I made that very clear to her."

"You did?"

"I also told her I was with you."

"You did?" I squeaked.

He pressed his finger to my lips again to silence me, but this time, he was smiling. "Shh. Let me talk."

I rolled my lips together and nodded, but my cheeks were starting to burn and that pulse in my core was a throbbing mess. God, I *loved* being like this for him. And I'd screwed it up so badly.

"Second, my parents also know. You were right, yesterday, too. When you said you'd sleep in your room while they were here, I assumed that was what you wanted, but I never took the time to tell you that was *not* what I wanted. We both screwed up. I wanted to tell my parents about you, but I thought you didn't want them to know. The rules of our game changed a month ago, Ruby, and I don't think either of us has done a good job communicating that."

He was so right. I'd been the one to float the idea of just sex.

Keeping it casual. Sex with him was hot. And I never gave him any indication I was thinking anything different.

"I'm still sorry I left yesterday, though," I whispered quickly, in case he tried to shush me again.

"I know you are. And I'm not mad at you for that, but you do have two options now to choose from to make it up to me."

My nipples tingled, and my heart raced with anticipation.

"Okay."

He stepped back and settled his hands on his hips. My gaze rose, followed the movements, and in front of me, front and center, behind the shorts he wore, he couldn't hide how turned on this was making him either.

My mouth watered to lean in right then, tear down his zipper with my teeth, and take him. He wanted it. I knew he did. He loved me on his knees in front of him, taking him deep in my throat.

Instead, he threw me for another loop when he held out his hand. "Option one." I settled my hand in his and as he guided me to my feet, he continued, "I can take you to my bedroom, and I can bathe your body with kisses and make love to you. I can whisper all the reasons why I'm falling in love with you and why you're not leaving this house and then after, we can figure out what our future looks like together, especially with your schooling."

"Falling in love with me?" Tears were starting again, and my words trembled as they fell from my throat.

He cupped my cheek with his other hand and brushed his thumb along the corner of my mouth. "You heard me," he whispered.

He leaned in, gently pressed his lips to mine, and pulled back.

"Or you can choose option two."

Nothing could sound better than the first option, but still my mouth went dry at the look in his eyes, and I was dumb enough to ask. "What's option two?"

"Go to my room and find out. The choice is yours and I'll be there in five minutes."

"Logan—"

"Go." He kissed me. Hard. Logan slammed his mouth to mine and stole my breath and thank God he was still holding on to my hand because he would have knocked me to my ass with the power of that kiss had I not had a hold on him.

"Time's starting now. Don't keep me waiting."

I grinned up at him, and as his brow rose, I turned and fled toward his room.

Option one would be sweet, soft. He'd make me feel so good, and I absolutely wanted to hear him tell me all the things he loved about me so I could return the favor and tell him all the things I loved about him. I thought about it for a moment. How *good* he made me feel when he went slow. The mornings when it was quiet and he slid inside of me before I was fully awake and he took his time. Our bodies pressed together in the sunlight.

But option two?

I deserved it.

I knew it as soon as I hurried to his room. Two items were set on his bed, and they couldn't have been starker against his white duvet. Handcuffs and a toy I had never purchased and had skipped over the day I bought the handcuffs.

Oh yes. Logan might have given me option one and would have done it for me if I needed it, but this... this was what he wanted. This was where we connected.

I stripped out of my clothes, folded them on the chair in his sitting room, and took a seat at the edge of the bed. Naked. Seconds passed. A ticking clock on his wall a countdown to when he'd walk in.

Five minutes was an eternity and I was already dripping wet, heart racing with anticipation. I ignored the fear of that *toy* and what it meant, where it'd *go*, and knew he chose to wait so long to begin my torture because I deserved this.

The wait killed me.

He absolutely *knew* I'd choose this, but I could still surprise him.

I scooted back on the bed, spread my legs, and planted my feet at the edge of the bed before leaning back. I picked up the handcuffs and held them in my hand.

An offering to him.

A thousand heartbeats later, his door opened. Click closed behind him. I kept my gaze on the ceiling. He stepped toward the end of the bed, and I glanced at him. His gaze was in between my legs, and he was now without a shirt.

"I've missed this," he said and reached out. He brushed his fingers along my seam and groaned at the wetness there. Without delay, he shoved two fingers inside of me and I yelped from the surprise, the hint of pain before he began working them slowly. "You want this?"

He added his thumb, and I bit down on my lip to keep from screaming already.

"Please."

He worked me into a frenzy with his fingers and thumb. He circled my clit, found the sweet spot deep inside of me. The handcuffs in my hand rattled as I fought to stay still, to take this, because I knew what was coming and for me, it would be a wicked ride until he finally let me finish.

The sounds of my own wetness increased, and Logan's gaze stayed focused on my eyes. He didn't once look down, but his jaw tightened as he used me roughly for his own satisfaction and right as my breath hitched, the telltale sign he knew I was close, he stopped.

"Shit," I rasped. I'd known it was going to happen and it still frustrated me.

"You didn't think I was going to let you come yet, did you?"

"No, sir," I wheezed. I tried to press my legs together, but he stopped me and grabbed my hips. With one quick tug and flip, I was on my stomach, toes on the carpeted rug, and my hands were being dragged behind my back.

"I love this ass of yours," he whispered and brought one of his hands to my backside. He palmed it and squeezed even as he clicked the handcuffs around each wrist. "Let me know if it gets too much, and I'll stop, okay?"

"I trust you."

He brushed his lips over my shoulders and down my spine. "And that's reason number two."

Oh. I got it then.

"And this," he whispered, and his hand was no longer at my backside but running through my slit, gathering my own wetness before he dragged it back and up. "You letting me play and have you here is reason three."

His finger pressed against the tightened puckered hole and he worked me slowly. My eyes rolled back into my head and I groaned from the pleasure, from the surprise.

"There you go," he crooned, now in my ear. "You're so damn sexy. So fucking hot for me all the time, that might just be reason number four."

I whined, a low keening sound as he shoved his finger inside of me. And *goddamn* he was *so freaking good at this*.

He nipped my ear and chuckled darkly. "These are in no particular order, too, you know."

"Of course," I rasped and then groaned as I felt the pressure of a second finger. He peeled his chest off my back and then there was a soft click.

"Might be cold," he warned me and drizzled a liquid all over my ass, his fingers now lodged inside of me. "You okay?"

I was on fire. My core was dripping. Throbbing with the need to be filled. Every time he shoved a finger inside of me, I pushed forward, nipples abraded against the soft fabric of his duvet, and yet he kept going. Kept working me, whispering how good of a girl I was, and then his fingers were gone and something harder was there.

He curled one hand around my shoulder. "Tell me if it hurts. I'll go slow."

"Please. Do it. Anything. Everything." I was already mindless with pleasure and need, and I swore, if he so much as flicked my clit, I'd scream the heavens down.

He chuckled, brushed his hand up and down one of my cuffed arms, and slid the plug inside.

"Oh God," I moaned, shoved my face to the bed, and bit down as he kept pushing. He pulled it out slowly, then pushed it in. He tortured me slowly, until there was a larger sting of pain and then relief.

"Fuck, I have never seen a sexier sight than you, Ruby. Cuffed. Plugged. I am going to fill you up and take you hard and fast, and I swear to you, you will love every minute."

"Yes. Please," I whined. "Logan."

"Reason five," he stated out of nowhere, and there was a sting on my ass as he smacked it. "Is not only that I think you're sexy like this, but I love that we have this. I've never felt more like a man than when you give yourself to me like this. So thank you."

He kissed my shoulder, and I turned my head so he could kiss my cheek. My jaw. He nipped at my ear again and then kept kissing me softly.

"I love this," I whispered. "Love everything about the way you touch me."

"Good. I'll go slow. Tell me if it hurts too much, okay?"

"Yes, sir."

"God, you're fucking perfect for me."

I preened beneath him. Cuffed and plugged, and my toes barely touching the floor, I couldn't move, but *oh* those words coming from him. And then he was there, one hand on my hip, the tip of his thick head pushed against my opening.

"Holy shit," I chanted, over and over again, as he held me still at the hip and slid his dick inside of me. He was tight. So damn tight and with the plug inside of me, he was even tighter. I was full. Stuffed so full of him I'd never forget this. Never. "Fuck, I love this, Logan. Love... Love..."

He slammed inside of me. Hard. I didn't need the slow. I kept chanting yes and I loved it as he seated himself deep inside of me. He bent down, and *fuck* that plug. Every time his dick brushed against that wall and shifted the plug, sparks of painful pleasure sent shockwaves through my body.

"Finish that," he grunted and pulled out. "Tell me what you really love, and I'll make you come so hard, Ruby."

I couldn't. I could barely remember my own name I was so lost in him and the things he was making me feel and all the sensations of his chest against my cuffed arms, the power of his thrusts and the damn plug that made my body burn with a pleasure I didn't know possible.

"Say it, Ruby."

"I love... I... I love you!" I screamed, unable to hold back as the orgasm shattered me. It came out of nowhere and everywhere all at once. It set my body on fire and I kept chanting it as he pounded into me.

He pushed off me, grabbed my hips with both his hands, and thrust once. Twice. Three more times until his own animalistic groan broke through and he slammed deep inside of me. His dick pulsed as he came, and his lips were at my neck.

Realization struck as I slowly came down, as he brought me back to reality with his gentle peppered kisses against my heated flesh.

"Logan..."

"Reason six," he whispered, "of why I've fallen in love with you is not because you give me your body to use like this, but because you're sweet and kind, and you make me laugh and you love my daughter and because when you're not with me, I can't wait for the minute I can see you again. I love everything about you, Ruby. Your heart and your body."

"That's a really long reason," I whispered. He was still lodged inside of me, and I was still plugged, and I was barely conscious as his laugh rumbled against me and he slowly pulled out.

"I can think of a thousand more if you need them."

I didn't need a single reason from him.

"Hold still," he said, and his voice was quiet. His hands first went to the handcuffs. He released them and rubbed my wrists before his palms went to my ass. He flicked at the plug, and it jolted inside of me. "Someday, when I have you all to myself for an entire day, I'm going to make you wear this plug and nothing else."

"Oh God." I buried my head back into his bed as a tremor rolled through me.

Logan's response was a dark, evil chuckle. "I knew you'd like that."

He removed the plug, then led me to the bathroom where he took the time to help me shower before showering himself. He washed every part of my body methodically, barely teasing me, and didn't let me touch him before he dried us off.

It was after we were dried off and he'd gone to grab my bags from the car and we were sitting on his bed, covers a wrinkled mess, when he kissed my cheek.

"My parents took Amelia to the zoo, so they won't be back until dinner."

Reality returned. I couldn't help but ask.

"What's really going on with Vanessa?"

"She broke up with Renaldo and she's coming back to the States."

"Here?"

"I talked her out of it. She thinks she might move nearby because she hates being away from Amelia, but I convinced her to go back to LA. She doesn't need to make any major decisions yet, so I told her to go home and give it time."

"It would be good for Amelia to have both her parents close." That was what he'd been talking about, and I felt like a fool. "I really am sorry for yesterday and for not trying to talk to you sooner. I didn't realize anything was really bothering me until Dawson proposed in that room and all I thought was, 'Logan can't even hold my hand,' and that sucked. And then I got inside my head, and everything spiraled..."

He kissed me. Slipped his tongue into my mouth and curled his hand around the back of my neck. "I know, and I have a few calls to make later, but we don't have anything to be concerned about. I've talked to the team. I made calls to the captains last night when Jassen was here. None of them give a shit who I'm dating, even if it's Jassen's sister. There's no clause in my contract that says anything. At this point, the only gossip between us might be our age difference and the fact you're still technically Amelia's nanny, but we can deal with that. Right?"

"I can deal with anything if it means I get to be with you."

He grinned, a panty-melting, body-heating grin that could have turned me into a puddle of want and desperation for him right there.

I meant it, too.

I'd do anything to be with Logan. And I'd definitely work on my own communication skills.

"I promise you I won't run again either when there's something we need to talk about. I'm sorry I did that."

The storm returned to his iron eyes and his brows arched. "I don't know. I kind of like the way I get to punish you for it."

Of course he did.

THIS MIGHT GO DOWN as the strangest, but best Christmas I could ever imagine having. A year ago, if someone had told me I'd be celebrating Christmas with my ex-wife, my girlfriend, my daughter, *and* my parents at the Westhaven Country Club at a wedding reception for Dawson Butler and his new wife, Hailey, I would have demanded my money back from that fortune teller.

Yet, that was exactly what was happening. Ruby was at my side, glass of champagne in hand, sleek and sexy black dress highlighting every single one of her curves and making her olive skin even more beautiful in the muted chandelier light.

When Dawson's wedding and reception invitation came in the mail, I'd originally put Ruby and Amelia and myself down for attending both. But then I talked to him and tried to back out of the wedding. News of my parents and Vanessa coming into town changed the plans. It was Hailey who called Ruby the next day and said, "It's a party and it's Christmas. Bring whoever wants to come."

Vanessa was staying at a hotel, still living in California, but she'd found a virtual assistant job at a social media marketing agency that allowed her to work remotely, so she traveled to see Amelia frequently. She also recently talked to both Ruby and me about moving to Nashville. When she returned from Italy, she went back to California and after a week there, still hated being so far from Amelia. So, she'd been here several times, renting an Airbnb to see Amelia on the weekends whenever her schedule allowed it. At first, Ruby was hesitant.

I could understand. But we'd come a long way in the last couple of months, and she'd finally admitted that due to all of Paulie's lies, it'd taken her a while to believe I wouldn't race back to Vanessa.

That wasn't going to happen, and now Ruby, Amelia, and Vanessa sometimes spent days together, out shopping, getting pedicures. Less than a year ago, I was hoping my wife and family would move to Nashville with me when I got the coaching job out here, and now my girlfriend and that ex-wife were friends.

It was strange, but we all agreed it was best for Amelia and above any hard feelings, any hurt, and any pain between Vanessa and me, we would always put our daughter's needs first.

That morning, we'd all trekked over to Jassen's house, and opened Christmas presents before we had to get ready for the wedding. It was the most chaotic morning of my life and one I would never forget. My parents took both Jassen and Ruby in like they'd always been in their lives, and they fell in love with Molly too. It was one large mess of a twisted family scenario and somehow, we made it all work.

"I love this," Ruby said next to me. "Your dad is the best."

We were standing off to the side of the dance floor, watching him twirl Amelia and then Vanessa around the dance floor. My mom was spinning Luke in circles like he was her own grandchild.

"I think you're the best."

She laughed and grinned up at me. "I never had this. A family that was weird but normal, and I never had a dad, you know? Out of everything you've ever given me, this is the best gift from you."

She slayed me. There wasn't a single day since I met Ruby when I hadn't craved to know every single depth of her and yet the more I learned, the more I searched. And there were some times, like right then, when she would lay out all her vulnerabilities so sweetly, it only made me love her more.

I wrapped my arm around her waist and guided her to the dance floor. Once I had her in my arms, I brought my thumb to her chin and kissed her. "You are my greatest gift. The best thing life ever brought me besides Amelia. I hope there's never a day that goes by where I don't let you know that."

She tucked her head into my chest and let me lead her in a dance.

She was in my arms, *mine*, and the best between us was yet to come. And ever since she walked into my life, I'd spent every day being thankful for all I had.

My team was still undefeated, coming up with one regular season game left in the season. We were looking to not only be divisional champions again, but had our eyes on claiming another Super Bowl. I had my daughter under my roof almost every night, parents who had always supported me.

And best of all, I had Ruby. Who gave me everything she had, both with her heart and her body, and for as long as she loved me, I would always make sure she knew that whatever game we'd started, whatever risks we took, she would always end the night in my arms, as the main love of my life.

Forever.

I didn't have a ring. And some would think I was crazy. Everything about Ruby and me was crazy, though, from the moment we met.

So I took another risk and brushed my mouth over her ear. "Marry me, Ruby. Marry me and make me the happiest man in the entire world."

She peered up at me with tears in her eyes and a smile stretching her face. "Are you serious? You're doing this *now*?"

"I'll buy you whatever ring you want later but agree to marry me."

Tears fell from her eyes and her smile shook. "You're crazy. Of course I'll marry you. I'd marry you today if I could."

I kissed her, and God, I loved being able to do that freely. Jassen still bitched and moaned about it whenever he saw, but as her brother, that was his right.

My team didn't care. The coaches had raised their brows in surprise, and Ruby had said the first few games she spent in the coaches' suite with Amelia after I let them know was awkward. But slowly, everyone accepted us. As for Ruby, she decided not to go back to grad school. I still asked her if she was sure, but she assured me she didn't mind. Instead, she started volunteering at two of the local art museums and was working on getting a children's art museum program set up where young elementary students could have a hands-on art experience to grow their interest from an early age.

I loved it.

I loved everything about her and her art and the fact she was still pursuing her passions while wanting to be with the family we were creating.

Thanks to Ruby, I loved everything about my life and was no longer the singular-focused asshole I'd once been.

I was a man in love with his woman, and I would fight to the death to keep her happy and in love with me until the day I died.

———

Thank you for reading and enjoying the Nashville Steel Series! 2024 book news is coming soon! To make sure you're the first to hear what's coming up next, sign up for my newsletter: **https://bit.ly/3nC4exd**.

THANK YOU

HUGE thank you to Nina and all the incredible women at Valentine PR for throwing your full enthusiasm and support behind me and these books. I love with working with you.

Thank you so much to my editing team for all your amazing hard work and refining the hot mess drafts I send you.

Shannon, you're the best. Always. Forever. Your talent is astounding and I'm thankful I can call you a friend.

To my Sweeties! I love you ladies and your excitement for my books!

To all the bloggers who devote their time and passion into reading books, book tours, release events, leaving reviews, promoting and pimping – you are all rockstars! Thank you for all the love over the years.

My family— I love you all to the moon and back. I don't know what I would do without you in my corner, cheering me on every step of the way. Your support is everything to me and I love you all with all of my heart.

To the SteelP! May we forever reign.

And last but definitely not least – to you, the reader. I'm blown away with every release how much you adore my books.

You have made my dream a reality and I hope I can cheer you on with yours. Please don't forget to leave reviews on Goodreads or whichever retailer you've purchased this copy from. It helps us so much!

ABOUT THE AUTHOR

Stacey Lynn likes her coffee with a dash of sugar, her heroes with a side of bossy, and her wine a deep shade of red.

The author of over fifty romance novels, many of which have been best-selling titles, she loves being able to turn her vivid imagination into a career that brings entertainment and joy to her readers. Focused on sports romance and emotional, small-town romance, she also loves stretching herself in different genres.

Born in Texas and raised in the Midwest, she now makes her home in North Carolina and loves all things Southern. Together with her ultimate tall, dark, and handsome hero, she has four children. Her life is a loving, chaotic mess, and she wouldn't have it any other way.

Subscribe to her newsletter so you can stay up to date on all her new releases. www.staceylynnbooks.com

OTHER BOOKS BY STACEY LYNN

Nashville Steel ~ football romance

Sneak Attack

Time Out

Tight Spot

Risky Game

Las Vegas Vipers ~hockey romance

Final Shot (free on all retailers)

Game Changer

Dream Maker

Rule Breaker

Shot Taker

Goal Chaser

Secret Keeper

Ice Kings Series ~hockey romance

Playing With Fire (free on all retailers)

Playing To Win

Scoring Off The Ice

Hooked One Her

Hard Checked

Fighting Dirty

The Rough Riders Series ~football romance

Dirty Player

Filthy Player

Wicked Player

Cocky Player

Love and Lies Duet ~angsty slow burn, romance

All the Ugly Things

All the Beautiful Things

Love and Honor Duet ~angsty, romantic suspense

Twisted Hearts

Unraveled Love

Love In The Heartland ~small town romance

Captivated By You

This Time Around

Long Road Home

Before We Fell

Crazy Love Series ~small town romance

Fake Wife

Knocked Up

28 Dates

Weekend Fling

The Fireside Series ~small town romance

His to Love

His to Protect

His to Cherish

His to Seduce

Tangled Love Series ~erotic romance

Entice

Embrace

Enflame

The Luminous Series ~BDSM romance

Dominate Me

Crave Me

Long For Me

Just One Series ~rockstar romance

Just One Song

Just One Week

Just One Regret

Just One Moment

The Nordic Lords Series ~MC romance

Point of Return

Point of Redemption

Point of Freedom

Point of Surrender

Standalones

Remembering Us

Don't Lie To Me – billionaire romance

Try Me – A Don't Lie To Me Novella

www.ingramcontent.com/pod-product-compliance
Lightning Source LLC
Chambersburg PA
CBHW061221310726
48971CB00007B/1893